for the rest of us

for
13 FESTIVE HOLIDAY STORIES
the
TO CELEBRATE ALL SEASONS
rest
EDITED BY DAHLIA ADLER
of us

Quill Tree Books
An Imprint of HarperCollinsPublishers

HarperCollins Children's Books, a division of HarperCollins Publishers, 195 Broadway, New York, NY 10007

HarperCollins Publishers, Macken House, 39/40 Mayor Street Upper, Dublin 1, D01 C9W8, Ireland

Quill Tree Books is an imprint of HarperCollins Publishers.

Library of Congress Control Number: 2025932716
ISBN 978-0-06-335178-3

Typography by Jenna Stempel-Lobell

25 26 27 28 29 LBC 5 4 3 2 1

FIRST EDITION

For Micah, the very biggest fan of the holidays

Contents

Editor's Note

Holiday stories are hardly a new concept in young adult literature, but as an Orthodox Jewish reader, I always knew I wasn't going to be cracking open those pages to find characters singing "Dayenu" at the Passover seder or shaking their noisemakers while wearing Purim costumes and listening to Megillat Esther. When I *did* finally start to see more varied holiday scenes making their way into books by some of my favorite authors—Juneteenth celebrations and feasting on mooncakes and an entire novel set over the course of a Ramadan—I immediately fell in love with celebrating them through the pages and the authors sharing their experiences.

What's more, I realized how much I didn't know—and how much I *wanted* to know—about these precious celebrations. And I knew I wanted to share some of mine, too.

Holidays are about tradition, and community, and coming together, and there's nothing quite like being welcomed into someone else's festivities, enjoying new food and music and decor, and feeling infused with the spirit of their joy. In *For the Rest of Us*, we open our own celebrations to you, the reader, and invite you to enjoy the tastes, sounds, sights, and meanings behind the days most special to us and our loved ones. Thank you for joining us.

—*Dahlia Adler*

for the the rest of us

This Is How It's Always Been

BY KELLY LOY GILBERT

It's seven minutes to five, and my mom has been in her tight-lipped, jaw-clenched, company's-coming mode for two hours now, stalking through the house with bleach spray and towels and barking orders at me and Liam. Or, more accurately, to me through Liam—*Liam, tell Olivia to pick up the sweaters all over the living room! Tell Olivia I expect the bathroom to be spotless!*—because she and I still aren't speaking to each other directly.

Usually Liam is on my side, but it's his first time home from school since Christmas and I think in his way he probably missed her. He's a junior at UCLA, where he lives off campus in a barren, dingy two-bedroom apartment with four other boys from the fellowship he joined freshman year. One of the guys is from the city, the Sunset District (he went to Lowell), and he was coming back for Lunar New Year with his family, too, so he and Liam carpooled on the way up. I'd had this fantasy of flying down to visit him and then us driving back home together, talking the way we used to, and telling him everything. I haven't told him about Laurel yet, and I don't know how he'll take it.

I had asked my mother yesterday, shyly, if I could bring Laurel to dinner tonight. Laurel is the kind of person who cares about every part of your life and also genuinely loves people. She's delighted by everyone, and she's heard so much about my family and has been dying to meet them. And I want to show her this part of me, this part of my life. I want the people I love to know her, to see how when I'm with her I feel myself expanding. And since Lunar New Year is my favorite holiday, it just seemed like the right time.

For months, I'd been having anxiety attacks picturing how this conversation would go with my mom. She isn't as conservative as the rest of her family—she's divorced, for one thing, and sometimes we have dinner with her high school friend who's gay—and we don't go to church nearly as regularly as everyone else does, but I didn't know what to expect. I guess you always hope. I had realized that somewhere along the way I'd stopped telling her things, and with Liam gone, I felt so alone in the house, and so part of me hoped that maybe this would be the spark of something different. Maybe we could be like Auntie Linda and Evangeline, who always went shopping together and went on boba runs and stayed up late watching TV and giggling together. Evangeline has always told her mom everything.

"She's, um, really special to me," I'd said. My palms and temples were sweating. "Actually, she's kind of—she's my girlfriend. Um,

I've realized that actually I'm bisexual, so I like girls also, and Laurel is the person right now that I—she's—" God, I should've prepared this better. "We've been dating."

"And you want her to come to Chinese New Year?" My mother had stared at me as if I'd suggested we just order McDonald's for the whole meal. "No. Absolutely not. What are you even thinking?"

Something calcified inside me, some knot in my stomach. In retrospect, of course this was how it had gone: Of course she'd jumped right past what I'd wanted her to know about me, skimming completely over the part where I opened up, and leapt immediately instead to how it would look to the family. How it would affect her careful preparations.

"My cousins bring their girlfriends all the time," I said, but I could hear the lack of certainty in my voice. I hated myself for that a little bit.

"Olivia, this is the time for family, not the time for—for some kind of political statement. Gong Gong is not doing well and it might be his last Chinese New Year with us."

"Lunar New Year," I muttered. You're supposed to say Lunar New Year to be more inclusive. It's not like Chinese are the only ones who celebrate it. But my mom always either forgets or just doesn't care: probably the latter.

"And I don't know why you think you need to make this political."

"It has nothing to do with politics, Mom, it's about—"

"How is this not about politics? Didn't you just say you were bisexual? If you want to bring a boyfriend, that's fine, you're young, but bring a boyfriend. You don't need to prove something."

"But I don't—"

"You know every single one of my siblings is going to disapprove. And your grandparents, absolutely. And what do you expect from everyone? What is it that you want? Some stamp of approval? Just to make a scene?"

Do I want to make a scene? That is literally the last thing I want, have ever wanted. I hate the spotlight. I don't want everyone staring at me, everyone speculating about what kinds of things I do with my girlfriend, wondering if I'm lusting after every girl I'm friends with. I don't want quiet or outright disapproval.

But still—but still. I want to be able to talk about Laurel. I want her to meet my cousins, come to one of our game nights or go with me to my little cousins' soccer and softball games. I want to take pictures of us at prom and show my grandparents. I want my grandfather to tell her all the stories he knows about the ancestors, those mythical people to whom I owe my existence.

And yes, I want my family's approval. Is that so wrong? I want my mom to hug me and say she's happy for me and she's proud of me. I want them to embrace Laurel. I want them to multiply my joy.

"It's completely inappropriate to want to monopolize the night like this. A holiday isn't about one single person. It's about family."

We both said more. Mostly we screamed at each other: She called me selfish and said we obviously needed to go to church more, that I needed to pray about this; and I screamed back that she was the selfish one and that maybe I should just live with my dad full-time instead. I said it because I knew it would hurt her, and it did.

After we fought, I locked myself in my room and called Laurel in tears. But she didn't pick up right away—she was taking a shower, and by the time she called back I had composed myself. I couldn't tell her about this fight. Instead we talked about a book she was reading and I said it sounded depressing and terrible and then she teased me about how much I always love happy endings, I'm addicted to people's joy, and we were both laughing and I remembered how I'm the best version of myself when I'm with her, the bravest version, and before I knew what I was doing I told her it would be great if she came to dinner and I'd call her when everyone was there.

She was thrilled. "Oooh, I'll make a key lime pie!" she said. "Does your family like pie? What should I wear? Do you guys dress up?"

I'd stopped myself from telling her not to do those things, just in case, because otherwise it would be too easy for me to back down. Now I'm committed.

And now here we are; the party is starting. The doorbell rings.

My mother looks directly at me for the first time since our fight.

"Behave yourself," she says, her voice low, and then she puts on a smile to open the door for her family.

I feel myself wavering immediately as soon as all my relatives come pouring in. We all fuss over my grandfather, who recently underwent chemotherapy for kidney cancer. He looks frail and thin, but happy to be here. There are thirty-eight of us now, four generations living—the five oldest cousins have children of their own. Our family gatherings are like a paean to heteronormativity. Everyone over the age of thirty is married. No one except my mom is divorced; no one is a bachelor. We have bridal showers and baby showers, girls' trips, men's golf games. In our grandparents' hallway there are two long rows of family wedding portraits: the bride and the groom. It's part of how we're so respectable: a sixth-generation Chinese American family, the kind of family where the boys are all Eagle Scouts and the moms all volunteer for the PTA and the dads teach Sunday school at the Chinese Presbyterian Church on Jackson Street, next to where my great-great-grandfather opened his grocery store and three generations worked after school and weekends. I've pored over all the photos, listened to my grandparents' stories. I know the model I was cast in: generations of strong and devoted wives who bore their husbands' children and scraped together food for their families against all odds, during war and famine and discrimination, in overseas villages I've never been to and across the Pacific and in whatever housing here they could find.

Tonight my cousins have brought boyfriends and girlfriends, a few we've already embraced and incorporated into all our inside jokes and potlucks, but a few we're just meeting for the first time: Brandon's new girlfriend, Aileen; Katie's new boyfriend, Joe. I watch as they bring them first to my grandparents, who insist on standing up to shake their hands and hug them, exclaim over them. "Where's your ring?" my grandmother says mischievously, grabbing Aileen's hand, and Brandon pretends (maybe doesn't pretend) to be mortified. Brandon is nearly thirty, and everyone's been gossiping for years about when he'll finally find a girl and settle down, because that— both the gossip and the straight marriage—is what my family does. Has always done. Katie is twenty-four and has been through a lot of boyfriends, so her bringing Joe isn't as monumental.

But I want this, too. I want to bring my person to be ogled over and presented to my grandparents. I want the gossip and the good wishes and, someday, the shuffling of the family to make room for one more and all the teasing about what a mistake it was to get married because now we have to be the ones to hand out lai see.

I left my phone upstairs because I can't bear seeing what Laurel might be texting me, waiting eagerly at home for me to tell her to come.

I hug my grandparents, put on a smile, say, "Gung hay fat choy!" a million times to everyone as they come in.

"Let's eat!" my grandpa says. "I'm hungry."

The house is full, four generations' worth of voices bouncing off the walls and tile floor. Our kitchen counter has disappeared under all the bowls and dishes and spare rice cookers, and my mom set up folding tables for the overflow and the desserts. Sometimes at my grandparents' house I like to thumb through their recipes, and it's a mix of twenty-ingredient lists and painstaking steps for wonton and then things like "1 bottle Yoshida sauce (Costco). Cook for two hours with pork shoulder and ginger" and "spaghetti Bolognese: mix 1 lb ground beef with 1 jar ragu sauce." Which is to say, basically, food for my family is a free-for-all. Anything goes. Today there's lap cheung– and shiitake-studded nuo mai fan, a whole steamed fish, an aluminum tray of salt-and-pepper fried chicken from the place our grandparents like in the Richmond, Auntie Michelle's Chinese chicken salad, a lasagna, gai lan with oyster sauce, one of those bagged salad mixes from Trader Joe's, a tray of Spam musubi, the crispy roasted pota-toes my cousin Evangeline made once and everyone begged for every holiday forever after. On the dessert table there's a coffee crunch sheet cake in a pink bakery box, Pyrex pans of mochi, Auntie Linda's two-tone Jell-O made with heavy cream, and a few pie tins of my grandmother's nian gao, speckled with sesame seeds and topped with bright mandarin oranges with the leaves still on. Someone, probably Auntie Helene, brought a two-pound box of See's Nuts & Chews, and there's a tray of Rice Krispie treats and almond cookies and a platter of orange slices.

I put a few of my grandfather's favorites onto a plate for him, even though it's not dinnertime just yet, and bring it to where he's sitting at the table. It's good to see him eating. When I make my way over to where everyone is crowded around the appetizer table, Uncle Garrett is telling a story about how Auntie Linda was gone for a week on a trip to Palm Springs with her girlfriends and he had to fend for himself, which is how he found himself one night eating spaghetti with mayonnaise and oyster sauce.

"That is vile," Emma says, wrinkling her nose. Emma is five years older than me—she goes to Davis—and when we were kids that was enough of an age gap that I didn't know her well on a personal level. "That is literally a hate crime, Uncle."

"Stop Asian hate," Micah says, swooping in for the sushi casserole.

"You know what, though," Uncle Garrett says, "it wasn't bad. Kinda creamy. Kinda—"

"No," Emma says, "please stop. I want to eat tonight."

Uncle Garrett laughs. He points at Micah with his clam-dip-laden chip. "Micah," he says, "you gained some weight, huh?" He motions toward his stomach. "What happened, no soccer this year?"

"You can't say that," Auntie Helene, my grandfather's sister, says from across from me. "You'll turn him anorexic. You can't tell kids about their weight. Not like in the old days anymore."

"Yeah, Uncle, instead why don't you tell us more about how you're too smart to get any of the vaccines your doctors want you to get," I say.

"Or just start snoring," Emma says. "You know we all love listening to that, too."

Uncle Garrett hoots with laughter. "You kids think doctors know everything. But you ask them—trust me, you ask them—they don't have answers for you. You just have to think for yourself. That's the important thing. You kids have to learn to think for yourself instead of just whatever the Facebook or your phone is telling you."

We all have roles in life. I feel it more strongly in my family than anywhere else I've ever been. The problem, I guess, is that I love them. I love the noise and mess and spectacle and chaos they come with. I love that we exist, against all odds, all those ways our ancestors almost didn't survive. In a big family, everyone waits for those first clear traits to rise to the surface during childhood, and from then on they're tagged to you for the rest of your life: Jared is clumsy, Emma is bossy, Liam is hotheaded. You're not yourself, not completely—you're a part of a larger fabric. I'm okay with that. I love my family. How well can you really know a big group of people, anyway? Maybe it's not the worst thing to hide behind their image of me.

I can lie to Laurel, maybe—I can tell her I got sick and missed the party. I could tell her no one else brought a significant other after all. I think she'd let me get away with it. She's not the kind of person to push. She's the kind of person who wants to believe the best in you.

"You know," Auntie Linda says to me, using two spoons to lift the spine off the fish, "in Chinese the word for fish is supposed to mean abundance. So you're supposed to eat a whole fish for New Year."

"Oh yeah?" I say. None of us except my grandparents speak any Cantonese, minus a few words and phrases here and there—siu yeh for a late-night snack, ma fan for something troublesome. I look like my dad, who's white—my family never tires of telling me this—and so I hoard these small phrases as proof of something in my life. Sometimes I feel like I'm cosplaying at being Chinese. When I was in elementary school, we used to have International Day every year and you could dress up and be in the parade to represent your country, and the year when I wore a cheongsam, I overheard one of the other parents hissing to another that I was being culturally appropriative: *Does she think it's just a costume?* I'm already different from my family; I feel it every time we're together.

"Right, Mom?" Auntie Linda says, turning to my grandma, her mother-in-law. "The word for fish?"

"And noodles," my grandma says. "Noodles for longevity."

"That's what Garrett needs," Auntie Linda says, rolling her eyes. "I can't get him to go do his checkups. He'll have to rely on the noodles instead if he has any hope of meeting his great-grandkids someday."

"When are we getting those great-great-grandkids, huh?" my grandfather says, and then everyone's talking all at once, and underneath the noise Liam turns to me and says, his voice low, "What's going on with you and Mom?"

I hesitate. "Um, just fighting about stuff."

"Yeah, I can see that. What are you fighting about?"

His fellowship at school is very conservative—I've looked it up, read their statement of faith: "We affirm that marriage is between one man and one woman, and anything outside of God's perfect design for marriage is sin." I imagine losing him. We used to refer to ourselves as Oliviam, so many times that eventually even our parents adopted it. I'll be dropping Oliviam off at five! Don't forget I have Oliviam for Christmas Eve this year!

Is it worth it? I imagine telling Laurel no, she isn't.

"I wanted to bring someone today," I say finally, softly.

Liam raises his eyebrows, a huge grin spreading across his face. "Wait, what?" he says loudly. "Do you have a boyfriend?"

"Um. Not exactly, I—"

"A situationship?" Emma says, overhearing. "Is it complicated? Ooh, Olivia, how did you not tell me? Who is he?"

"Olivia's in a situationship?" Micah says, and the grown-ups turn to look at each other as if to say, *What on earth is that?*

"No, no," I say. My face is turning red. "Nothing like that."

"Does Olivia have her first boyfriend?" Uncle Garrett says. "Finally?"

"Over my dead body," my mother says, playing her part perfectly. You'd never guess that we were screaming at each other right before this. How did we all get so good at hiding? "Come on, everyone. Let's pray and eat."

We all gather in a big circle and hold hands, and Gong Gong prays: "Heavenly Father, thank you for gathering us all here together. We ask that you bless this food and be with us in this new year. In Jesus's name, amen."

While everyone's getting food, I slip upstairs for my phone. Laurel has messaged me: how's dinner?? I can come anytime, I'm just at home! And a picture of the pie she made. She candied little slices of lime. It must have taken her hours.

No one's here yet, I write back, and quickly press send. And then immediately I wish I could take it back—because now what, I'll ask her over and she'll realize we all ate already and I lied? I turn off my phone. I feel sick.

I didn't want this to be the kind of thing we lied to each other about. I don't want it to seem like I'm ashamed of her. She brought me to meet her family right away; her mom had a rainbow bumper sticker on her car, and her parents both introduced themselves to me with their pronouns. It was a little self-satisfied, maybe kind of showy, but they were nice people. I don't think Laurel would understand my

11

family. They wouldn't translate for her. I can't ask her here just for them to reject her.

But maybe if she were here, it would be all right. Maybe it would feel like it does when we go out, just the two of us, how she has this way of slipping her hand into mine and making it feel like this little cocoon around us, everything else suddenly mattering less.

And also—this is one of the few things I've never told her—I'm afraid she'll leave me if I can't be brave about this. It's such a small thing in the grand scheme of things—it's dinner; it's my family. My ancestors crossed oceans and carved tunnels from granite mountains; they survived when it didn't matter if girls lived or died.

I turn my phone back on. Laurel hasn't responded, which is somehow worse.

I go back downstairs where everyone's eating. I manage to choke down some sticky rice and laugh along when one of my cousins starts a game of Would You Rather, but I don't make it twenty minutes. I keep checking my phone—after the seventh or eighth time, Emma teasingly asks me about it—and finally I escape to the bathroom, where I can sit and stare at the phone, willing a message to come in and also dreading it. Liam finds me in there a few minutes later. I forgot to lock the door, and it flies open, almost banging me in the face. He takes one look at me, then closes the door behind him and locks it.

"Whoa whoa whoa," he says. "What's happening here?"

I wipe my eyes roughly and try to smile. "Nothing. I'm fine."

"Yeah, let's not do this." He rips some toilet paper off the roll and hands it to me. "Is this about Mom? Or the guy you're seeing? What's happening? If he's making you cry, dump him. It's not worth it. You need me to talk to him?"

"It's not like that."

"What's it like, then?"

I think about all the ancestors before me, everything they endured. The famine and wars in the old country, the ocean, the inexorable railroad, the burned Chinatowns. How could I even look them in the eye?

"It's—" I wipe my eyes again. "It's actually not a guy."

His expression doesn't change. "I see."

But then he doesn't say anything else. All the muscles in my chest twist into knots. We sit in a heavy silence. Finally Liam clears his throat. "So who is she?"

"Her name is Laurel."

"Does she go to your school? Or what?"

"Yeah."

"She's your grade?"

I nod.

"Ah," he says. "Wow. Okay."

There's a knock on the door.

"Who's in the bathroom?" Uncle Garrett yells. "We've been waiting!"

"Go upstairs," Liam calls back.

My phone buzzes again. It's Laurel: Are you okay? Is everything okay? I would really love to meet your fam!! No pressure tho! If you don't want me to.

"She's really kind," I say. "I think you'd probably like her."

"No, yeah, I'm sure she is," he says a little too quickly. "Just—yeah."

"Just what?"

"Just—" He stares at the door. "I don't know, I mean, you're young, Olivia, and you're probably confused about who you are, and trying to—I don't know, experiment or whatever."

"I don't think I'm confused," I say, but without conviction.

Am I confused? What does that even mean here? That I don't know myself, that I shouldn't trust the way she makes me feel? Do I have to know myself perfectly already, possess some innate unchanging steadiness, before whatever I can build with someone else counts as real? Because I am confused. I don't know what I'm doing. I'm here freaking out while Laurel and her pie are waiting for me to figure everything out.

My brother laughs, not unkindly. "You're in high school. Of course you're confused. You don't know yourself. That's what high school is."

"Maybe," I say.

"Yeah," Liam says. "Sometimes it feels like that in high school, like you get really close to someone and then, I don't know, you think it's something it isn't. But you can be close friends. It doesn't have to be something it's not."

I understand then that I was wrong about this conversation, all that time I worried about coming out to him. I don't know why I was afraid that—what, exactly? That he'd storm off and drive back to college, stop taking my calls? I was never going to lose him in the moment. I should've known to fear this instead: him radiating emptiness where what I wanted so desperately was welcome, approval. I feel myself on the verge of some unraveling.

I take a few long breaths, try to fill my lungs. Maybe all along the thing I should've been most afraid of in telling Liam was the way I myself might waver and crumple in response. Maybe I was afraid to learn this about myself, that I'll let other people poison what they think I'm not allowed to want.

I stand up. What am I doing? Why am I sitting on the bathroom floor waiting to find out whether my brother thinks it's okay to feel

14

the way I feel? Why am I trying to decide how much I care about Laurel, actually, as if I can somehow weigh what I feel for her against what I've always believed I needed from everyone else around me? I push the door open and go back out to where everyone's eating.

"Just so everyone knows," I say loudly, my heart pounding, "I have a new girlfriend. Her name is Laurel."

There's a long, stunned silence. My mother speaks first.

"I told you not to do this," she says. But her voice is different this time—less angry. I understand when she looks around, frantic, for everyone's reaction, and then takes a helpless step closer to me. She wanted to shield me from this.

There's a moment of suspension, no one speaking. My grandmother is holding noodles between her chopsticks and they dangle over her plate as she stares at me.

Then everyone speaks at once. Uncle Garrett asks my mom, "Did you know about this?" his voice dripping with disapproval, and Auntie Linda whispers something to my other aunts, and Emma tries to give me a hug, and my cousin Evangeline's seven-year-old looks up at her, concerned, and says, "Is Auntie Olivia going to go to hell?"

"This was totally inappropriate to say in front of the children," Evangeline's husband, Noah, says to me, his voice hard. "This is a conversation you should've had with the adults first."

"Yo, watch how you talk to her," Liam says sharply.

"Did you know she was going to say that?" Noah demands, and then they're arguing.

I want to disappear. I want to not exist anymore. I open my mouth but close it when there's nothing to say. My face is burning.

"Okay, but this is all seeming super homophobic?" Emma says loudly. "Maybe we can all just knock it off and everyone can keep their bigotry to themselves and we can just celebrate Lunar New Year and—"

"You think we should be silent?" Auntie Miriam says, whirling to face her. "What would our ancestors think? All these generations of listening to the Word, and God working in our lives, and you think we should deny God's Word and—"

Over the din, Gong Gong raps his chopsticks on the table.

"I want to tell everyone a story," he says, and has to repeat it three or four times. "About our ancestors."

His voice has gotten shakier with illness and with age, and we all go quiet so we can hear him. My heart is pounding. I can't look at Auntie Miriam. I don't know if I want to hear this. Of course, if my ancestors could see me, see my life, they would be amazed and disappointed. Isn't it enough to have thirty-seven living family members rejecting you? Liam glances at me, sympathy in his eyes, and I look away.

"Once upon a time," Gong Gong says, "there was a little girl who lived in Canton. Her parents were poor and didn't want her because she was a girl, so they sold her very cheap to a man who promised to take her to America and marry her. The man put the gold in the girl's hand and she gave it to her parents. Then they sailed together to America. When they arrived, he told her that he had lied to her and he had purchased her as a prostitute."

"One of our ancestors?" Brandon says, shocked. This is not the respectable, pulled-ourselves-up-by-our-bootstraps story we have known all our lives. "Who was that? Our great-great-great-grandmother? Our ancestor was a prostitute?"

"Who, the girl? No, I don't know who the girl was. She died, probably. Girls didn't survive very long in those conditions. They got sick or they got pregnant and they died. That was your great-great-great-grandfather. He was a very bad man who did very evil things. He purchased girls and sold them into sexual slavery. He died of tuberculosis in his forties and now he is suffering for all eternity in hell."

Everyone is shocked. I don't know what I'm supposed to make of the story. It's a threat, maybe: We have worked hard to come this far; we have buried our past to become the kind of family we are. It's my job to not threaten that.

Or maybe that's not it, either. Maybe it's a different kind of threat: Now he is suffering for all eternity in hell. I swallow hard.

"What kind of seedy stories are you telling us, Dad?" Uncle Garrett says gently. "I don't know if this is appropriate for—"

My grandfather waves him away. "No, no," he says irritably. Then he looks at me.

"Olivia," he says, "who cares what the people who went before you think? Your great-great-great-grandfather did unspeakable things and now he's in hell. I'm old. I don't understand the world anymore. Everything is different now. But now it's your world. That's why we all did everything we could. So all of you could have this world now. Every generation has to make its own way."

Auntie Miriam presses her lips together. Gong Gong adds, "I don't want anyone to say anything unkind to Olivia."

It's not outright approval, but it's more than I ever imagined. My eyes fill with tears. My mom, who never hugs him, who never hugs anyone, wraps her arms around him and murmurs, "Thank you."

He pats her arm. I can see how weak he is, and I think how when I lose him, hopefully not for years and years, I will carry this with me. But I'll carry the rest of today, too: the look of judgment and disgust in my aunts' and uncles' and cousins' eyes, that subtle way they rewrote who I am to them. Liam's silence on the bathroom floor. The way I learned that shame can corrode you, even when it shouldn't be yours to carry.

But there will be time to deal with that. I take out my phone.

Hey, I write. Still have that pie? Ready to come over?

P.S.: I (DON'T) LOVE YOU

BY LAURA POHL

There are two truths that are absolutely universal, no matter where you come from on planet Earth: The first is love makes people stupid, and the second is art class is the most useless subject in a high school schedule.

The second is confirmed on Monday when Mrs. Collins, our art teacher, hands us heart-shaped red cards for us to write confessions on during class so we can put them in a ceremonial pyre later. The first truth is one I've been living through for the past three months ever since Kevin Li, my best friend, decided he was unconditionally and irrevocably in love with Christopher Dunne, captain of the basketball team. He even postponed our movie Fridays indefinitely so he could attend every single game.

"I don't get why the hippies love burning stuff so much," I say, picking up a silver Sharpie. "It's bad for the atmosphere. Aren't they supposed to love the environment or something?"

"You're distracting me," Kevin answers. "I gotta make this perfect. Maybe *this* is what will convince Chris to give me a chance. The Valentine's Day dance is *this* Friday."

"As if I could forget," I grumble. "Wait, you're thinking of giving this to him?"

Kevin looks up, mortified, his fingers full of the pink glitter powder he's spreading around the edges of his heart. We'll be finding that stuff in his bag until graduation.

"Jesus Christ, no," he says, his face draining of color, even as he turns back to add a few more hearts around Chris's name. "Why are you acting like this is not fun? Do you not have Valentine's Day in Brazil, Elis?"

Kevin likes saying my name when we talk about Brazil, just so he can enunciate it properly, instead of butchering it like all the teachers. Everyone in school just says Elis like Ell-is, with focus on the first syllable, instead of like it's supposed to sound, Eh-*lees*, emphasis on the second.

Kevin's not an exchange student like me. The only other exchange student in the school is this huge German kid built like a brick wall who shot up in all the popularity lists because he can kick a ball really far across the field or something. (Look, it's been eight months but I still haven't figured out all the rules of football, because there's only one true futebol, and Brazil's got five stars on our shirt to prove it.) Kevin was born in California, but his parents emigrated from China, which means he usually remembers that Brazil is just south in this same continent and not on Mars.

"Sure we do, but it's in June because Doria's dad didn't like that there were no commercial dates that month to boost sales," I reply.

"Who's Doria?"

"Infamous politician."

"You sure have a lot of those. And his dad seems to have very sincere motivation."

"Every celebration date under capitalism is a sales date. You're American, you should know that."

Kevin makes a face, because he can't argue with that, working again to flourish a card that could probably compete in a *RuPaul's Drag Race* challenge.

"Besides, a card doesn't cut it," Kevin mutters, turning his head to look at his work from another angle. "I need something dramatic. Life-changing. Soul-wrecking. What would you do?"

"I can push him into the train tracks so he gets into a coma and loses his memory, and then you can pretend you're his boyfriend to his family, so when he wakes he inevitably falls in love with you," I answer without looking up, finishing up my little heart and folding it.

"Why are you like this?" Kevin emits the most exasperated sigh in the history of humankind. "Also, in *While You Were Sleeping*, she ends up with the brother of the guy in the coma."

"All right, then I can push *his* brother into the train tracks."

"You've got to stop thinking movies have all the advice you need to live your life," Kevin says with an air of superiority. "You're turning into your dad."

"A phrase every girl loves to hear."

Kevin finally stops adding stuff to his heart. It's likely unreadable at this point, and he pouts unhappily, swiping his black hair from his forehead. "I just need him to see that we're made for each other."

I roll my eyes. "Kevin, it's just a school party and he's just some guy. In a year, you won't even remember what you were going on about."

"In a year, you'll hear me go on about how you almost ruined the week I invited the love of my life to the ball by pushing his brother onto the train tracks."

In a year, I won't be here to actually hear him, but I don't say that out loud.

"It's not a ball, and I don't think you have the balls for it."

Kevin makes an outraged sound, but he also knows I'm right. He can talk all he wants about how gorgeous and funny and incredible Chris is and I'll listen, but he won't do a damn thing to make a relationship happen. That's a problem.

But maybe it's a problem I can happily solve.

San Francisco greets us with a little chill in the air as we head out of the school for the day. The students stream into the parking lot, and I brace myself tighter in my jacket. The weather here is pretty much like São Paulo in July, so it's not a big deal, except I'll get two winters this year in different hemispheres. Hooray for me.

We pass through the huge sign at the front door, which has a countdown for the Valentine's Day dance: *4 days, people!* A couple of cheerleaders are leaning against it, making eyes at people who pass, and Hayley—Haylea? Haleigh?—a redheaded junior in our class with whom I've exchanged precisely eight words during the whole school year, smiles at me. I smile back.

Kevin walks by my side, completely oblivious, gaze fixed on

where the basketball team gathers. I don't know what standard their uniforms follow, but believe me when I say probably no one should see that much of anyone's thighs. Kevin fervently disagrees.

Kevin makes it past the boys without stumbling.

"My time is just running out," Kevin mutters as we head toward the bus stop. "I don't want to be a loser senior who doesn't have a boyfriend in the last year of school. I need to live a little before going to UCLA."

"Like that's the worst problem to have in the last year of school," I mutter, seeing if he actually realizes that the school year is ending and that actually means something.

I wait for what feels like an eternity, hoping the sky will break open, some light will shine down from the heavens, and the angels will trumpet, *Behold! Your best friend is leaving the country forthwith!*

The sky doesn't cooperate, and neither does Kevin's memory.

"Can you believe we're in the second gayest city in America and I can't even get a *boyfriend*? Does God actually hate me?"

I suppress a sigh, the gears in my head turning endlessly as Kevin's words echo back to me. Time is running out. I should do something, for me, for him. For the both of us.

I can be a good friend and play the matchmaker for Kevin, so he has something once I'm gone. That way, he won't be the loser senior with no boyfriend *and* no best friend. That way, we can all be happier and I won't have Kevin reduced to pining for his crush until the moment I get through the door of the plane that will take me home.

And then, as if struck by lightning, I suddenly have a very good idea of how to manage that.

"You go ahead," I tell Kevin. "I think I forgot my water bottle in the English classroom."

Kevin shrugs. "Sure."

Mrs. Collins didn't lock the classroom. She didn't even lock the box where all the juniors stuffed the little hearts with confessions. Anyone could just waltz right in and take them.

There are about sixty of them, which isn't that many. So it's kind of easy to sneak the box out and read each one. Some of them—like mine—aren't for people in the school, but a good solid forty are. Which just makes me conclude that Valentine's Day does affect people's brains in an irreversible and miserable way. Maybe it's not just Kevin who needs a nudge.

So one by one, I find people's lockers and slide the little hearts in.

On Tuesday morning, Kevin's next to my locker, looking tense. His thick black hair is impeccably styled, and he's wearing tight jeans and a shirt that accentuates his lean frame.

"Elis, you won't believe what happened," he says when he spots me.

I'm still drowsy, having nodded off on the bus on the way to school. "What?"

"This is the worst day of my life," Kevin says. "Look around you."

I look around, spotting other groups of people talking and whispering and just looking normal. Then, as if on cue, a girl in our year gives an earsplitting shriek. Startled, I look at what she's holding—a red heart.

"That happened," Kevin says, pointing. "Word is, the red hearts we made yesterday in class ended up in people's lockers. The *people who the cards were written for.*"

I give him a blank stare, trying my best to keep my face neutral. "Uh, okay." I yawn.

"Why are you not concerned?" Kevin asks, his voice high-pitched now.

"Because I made mine to Taylor Swift, like a levelheaded person."

"*Elis, for the love of God, Chris Dunne has my heart.*"

"I know, you've been saying that for the past month."

"*Elis!*"

"Kevin!"

Kevin grabs my shoulders and gives me a little shake. "Elis, look at me. You're acting so blasé that it almost looks like you knew this was going to happen."

I shake him off me, turning to my locker. "Well. Look here. I got one too."

Gotta admit I hadn't seen that one coming when I got to the bottom of the pile, but by then I'd already been in way too deep, and I was committed.

It was kind of a cute card, filled with other little hearts, and no glitter, thankfully. On it was written, *Elis, you're the beautiful dream I dream.* "Fascinação" is one of Elis Regina's most famous songs. My parents had named me after the singer. It surprised me that someone would do basic research and put the lyrics through Google Translate to make a card using that reference.

"Let me see," Kevin says, snatching it from my hands. "This sounds gay as hell."

"Thanks," I mutter dryly, seizing it back.

"What are you going to do about it?"

"Nothing," I reply.

I should have figured out I was aromantic on Valentine's Day in the fifth grade, when a classmate came up to me with a stuffed bear with an "I love you" heart attached, and I tried to hand it back to him, saying it wasn't mine. When he insisted it was a gift, I said, "No, thank you," and promptly shoved it back in his hands. If I'd known then, it would have certainly spared me from the relationship problems that led me to want to move to another hemisphere.

"I'm so glad you're all romantically resolved in your life, but *we* need a plan to retrieve my heart before Chris Dunne knows I'm the one who sent it. I can't let him see it. I just can't."

"No one will know it was you, relax," I tell him, even though partly, I hope Chris can recognize the calligraphy. All I wanted was for Kevin to get a push, the right kind of adrenaline to make him act, and then he can thank me for fixing his life.

I turn my card in my hands, but then I see something on the other side. It wasn't written with the same pen as the card. It's on the back, too small for me to have noticed. It's a name. The name of the person who wrote the card.

I stare at it for a moment, the implications turning in my mind. I couldn't care less about *my* card and the girl who wrote it, but considering everyone in school who's gotten one of them . . .

Chris will know it was Kevin.

Because what I hadn't realized is that Mrs. Collins did the worst-possible thing—she wrote every student's name on the back of their cards. Probably to make it easier to hand them back to us for the burning. I just hadn't thought to check before shoving them through people's lockers.

It turns out the angel on my shoulder who whispered this plan to me wasn't Cupid—it was probably Satan.

By the time homeroom is over, everyone knows.

The school is thrown into utter chaos. Even the seniors, who are usually determined to rise above the petty squabbles and rumors of junior year, have joined in. Honestly, Chris Dunne should be the least of my concerns—apparently, the quarterback wrote his note to his girlfriend's best friend, and the corridors have turned into a festooned, heart-decorated war zone.

Kevin and I head to lunch, and I look over to see if anyone is looking at us funny when we enter the cafeteria, but as usual, the school is more concerned with their main characters than the untalented gays of year eleven. At least everyone is too focused on the drama to ask the crucial question: Who the hell could have done this?

Kevin passes by the popular table, then spots the basketball team and tries to hide behind me, which only half works. He's too tall to go unnoticed. He puts his tray down on our usual spot.

There's some kind of showdown starting in the cafeteria, led by the quarterback who's cheating on his girlfriend. Everybody who is anybody turns to watch, but Kevin's too absorbed in his own spectacle.

"Look," Kevin says, leaning over the table, face serious. "There's only one thing we can do at this point."

I don't know what he's thinking, but—I could come clean, but I have a feeling Kevin's too panicked to appreciate my efforts on his behalf.

"Chris wasn't in class before break, so I don't think he's seen the card," Kevin says. "We have to steal it back."

Kevin makes me down my lunch in record time and then we slink off to Chris's locker. Kevin doesn't ask me how I know it's his when I lead the way. He could connect those dots if he wanted to.

"How can we be sure it's even here?" I hiss, jangling the lock.

"We just have to get this open and then get it out," Kevin says with his back to me, standing as a lookout. "It's hardly a crime, Elis. The heart is mine, anyway."

The school should have changed the locks years ago, but these are so old they barely close on the proper combinations. I twist it again. "You should take this opportunity to actually *talk to him*."

"I'm not going to embarrass myself like that."

I look over my shoulder to stare at my best friend's nape. "What's the worst thing that could happen?"

Kevin turns to me. "It isn't about the worst, or the best."

"How isn't it?"

Kevin's face darkens. "It's easy to put pressure for things to work when it isn't *your* heart on the line."

That phrase makes me freeze, and something in my stomach churns.

I didn't do this so Kevin would hate me—the opposite, really. I'm doing this *for* him. So he gets the stupid boyfriend he wants so much, and things can go back to normal before I leave.

Before I can argue, a voice asks, "What are you guys doing to my locker?"

Kevin and I jump.

Chris Dunne is standing on the other side of the corridor (the one Kevin wasn't looking at), a late note in his hand. He's nice-looking, I guess. Sandy-brown hair. Some freckles on his nose, which is a little large for his face. Nice shoulders from exercising. And taller than Kevin, which I guess is eighty percent of the appeal here.

"Is this your locker?" I finally ask, like an idiot.

Kevin throws me a scathing look.

I shove my best friend. *Talk to him*, my eyes say. *Now's the time.*

Never, Kevin's eyes return. *Not in a million years.*

I kick him in the shin. Kevin stands stoically, unmoved, like the mountains of old.

"You know, if you dropped something in here—" Chris approaches and starts opening the locker, and I slam my shoulder against it so hard that I feel it reverberate in my teeth. I look at Kevin, significantly. Kevin looks back at me, imperiously.

Chris Dunne stares at us both, confused as hell.

"Actually, the janitor said to inform you that the locker is out of commission," I say. "There's something wrong with the—"

Chris doesn't let me finish. In a much nicer gesture than could be warranted in the situation, he moves me aside and opens the locker. I turn around to look at Kevin and then, to my astonishment, realize that he isn't even there anymore.

Kevin just *bolted*—I only see the sleeve of his jacket disappearing around the corner.

I stand there stupidly as about five different red hearts flutter out of Chris Dunne's locker—he's popular enough to get a few—falling at his feet. He picks the most extravagant one, full of glitter, turning it in his hand, his long fingers holding it carefully.

"Oh, uh, I gotta go," I grumble. And without waiting for a response, I follow Kevin out of there as fast as I can.

When I get home from school, the Moms—my host parents for this year in San Francisco—aren't back yet. After their only daughter, Christine, left for college, Tracy and Gina signed up to host different exchange students to keep the empty-nest sensation at bay. They're a pair of effusive, overenthusiastic lesbians, and so different from my biological parents that it often feels like I've crossed a portal and now my supervising guardians are extras in *My Little Pony*.

The Moms are cool, but since my stay here has always had a

deadline, their approach to any problem is just patting me on the head and saying, "It'll pass." Since part of the problem *is* that I'm only here temporarily, I don't think they'll be much help.

So I decide to call my dad earlier than usual and immediately start with, "Dad, do you think I can come home?"

On the video chat, Dad quirks an eyebrow. "Hm, no. That ticket was expensive."

"God, I wish you weren't so honest," I say, throwing my head back on my pillow. It's on the queen-size most comfortable bed ever in the room I've been given, in a spacious attic with a perfect window that is all round and transparent glass, letting the afternoon sunshine through. The house is not near the bay enough that I can look at the water, but I feel the brine in the breeze when it blows through on good days.

"I just don't want you coming home early because of some avoidable circumstance, like boy trouble. Is that it?"

"Ew, no."

"Girl trouble?" he suggests.

"Congratulations, you can name more genders if you try," I say, feeling mean-spirited. "It's not that. I was trying to nudge Kevin along and—well, it went badly."

Dad waits patiently, so I sigh and finally tell him the whole story. Taking the Valentine's Day cards, putting them in people's lockers, the school turning into chaos because of me.

"Kevin is going to hate me when he finds out," I finish weakly. "And then I'm basically going to lose the only friend I have left."

I say that last part like a confession and then immediately feel embarrassed that I have to tell *my dad* this. But Dad is the only person I talk to daily while I'm over here. Mom only calls once a week.

It was Dad's idea for me to go on this exchange. I never had a lot of friends growing up—always just one or two. I had friends at school, sure, but they weren't *best* friends. They didn't invite me over to their houses for sleepovers. Up until seventh grade I had Olivia, but then her parents moved to Manaus and our friendship became restricted to liking each other's Instagram posts and meeting up maybe once a year if she came to visit. Then there was Lucas, but after the whole Debacle, well . . . spending a year in the USA going to school to get more fluent in English seemed like a great idea.

"Do you want advice?" Dad asks, his tone gentle.

"If it's movie advice, no, thanks."

"There's nothing wrong with movie advice," he says defensively.

"The last person you gave movie advice to was Mom, and then she decided to get a divorce."

Dad considers this for a moment. "You know, I always thought you were going to be meanest when you were thirteen. I'm happy to see my daughter surpass my expectations."

I snort an irritated laugh. It's too easy to talk to him, to pretend the situation is ridiculous and out of hand and that I'm not . . . well, afraid. That's the word. But I don't know why. Something about Kevin's eyes this morning, when he said it wasn't my heart on the line.

I wasn't scared after my parents' actual divorce. It was amicable, and Mom moved out to the country to live with her sister, and I stayed with Dad, which was the right choice considering he's always been the responsible parent. That first couple of months, when we were feeling strange to see the house so empty, we'd sit down on the couch and watch a movie from his extensive collection. Every single night. Recent releases or black-and-white pictures from the forties,

Marvel or Scorsese. It was comforting, watching life unfold in the movies. It made me feel like everything was always going to turn out fine, which is maybe the reason Dad also liked them.

I wasn't even scared when everything fell apart with Lucas. I just felt—defeated.

But that small inkling of fear stirs something in me. My time here is running out. I'm leaving in just a few months, in July after school ends.

I don't want the best friend I've made here—the one person who likes me even when I'm mean and angry because he's also mean and angry—to hate me just because I'm trying to leave him something after I'm gone. Because I *will* be gone. I have a ticket home already, even if Kevin seems to pointedly forget it.

"You're just going to have to tell him," Dad says after my long pause. "He's your friend, he'll forgive you. You can fix things."

He's right about something. Maybe I can fix this.

On Wednesday, peace talks between our beloved quarterback and the star cheerleader started and ended as abruptly as they began. Wild accusations have been thrown around the school corridors. Both the quarterback's and the cheerleader's former bestie's lockers have been painted red. Everyone has declared their allegiances, gazes throwing daggers as they cross paths. The arrows puncturing the hearts on the decorations now seem decidedly dripping with blood.

"I can't believe you just left me there," I tell Kevin as we walk to homeroom.

"What else did you want me to do? I couldn't bear for him to see. And he did, right?" he asks, his voice half hopeful. "So I guess he knows now," he finishes, sounding miserable.

"Can you decide which emotion you actually want to explore? I'm getting whiplash."

"Elis, this is all your fault," he says, and I freeze, but then he carries on. "You could have just opened the locker faster, and then—"

"Then you could have invited him to the party like you wanted to," I interrupt. "He was right there. Talking to us."

"More like thinking if he should call the school therapist for interference."

Fair point, but still.

Kevin sighs, frustrated. The cheerleader squad passes by us in a united front. The redhead locks eyes with me for a moment as she passes, looking at me in expectation. I turn back to Kevin.

"You miss one hundred percent of the shots you don't take," I tell him.

"What despicably old movie is that from?" Kevin asks, disinterested, and I'm not even sure.

"Even if it's movie advice, it's solid. Chris has seen the card now. You can just ask."

"You make it sound so easy."

"Because it *is*," I say, walking through the door. "If he rejects you, you just listen to a lot of Sabrina Carpenter and then move on."

Kevin presses his lips together and then sighs.

"Valentine's Day is going to be the end of the world," he concludes dramatically.

Since Kevin won't talk to Chris Dunne, I am running out of ways to make my plan of getting them together work. So in the end, I guess I'm the one who has to talk to Chris.

The problem is, Chris already left school, and I stayed back to try to get his address from the school secretary, but that was a bust. She wouldn't give it to me even after I told her that Chris had left his wallet and I'd picked it up for him.

I bump into the redheaded cheerleader when I'm almost to the door—I'd seen her name just yesterday but was too worried about the implications of my screw-up to remember the correct pronunciation—on the way out of school. She looks up at me, a little flushed. "Hey, Elis."

"Hey," I say back. An idea occurs to me. "Do you know where Chris Dunne lives?"

That seems to take her by surprise. "Oh! Sure. He lives on the block up from the Starbucks, in the red house."

"Perfect, thanks," I say, and start walking.

"Look, I just wanted to—"

"Sorry, I really gotta go!" I say, looking over my shoulder. "See you tomorrow!"

I leave the school grounds and head in the direction she pointed me to.

Before I came to San Francisco, the only thing I knew about the city was from that one scene in *X-Men 3* where Magneto is being gay, saying that Professor X always liked building bridges before he rips apart the Golden Gate Bridge. (Dad loves that movie. He's a Magneto apologist.) Right after Kevin and I became friends, in one of our first movie nights together, he showed me *The Last Black Man in San Francisco*, which is possibly one of the best movies ever made, and I fell right in love with the city. The houses, the streets, the people, the history. And there was something about that feeling I'd only shared with Dad before—Kevin showing me his home, the place he loves, in the way I'd understand it best.

Chris lives in one of those old town houses not far from the school. As I near the house, I see that the paint had been a vivid red once and now it's a murky brown, and the white eaves are chipped. It's got charm and personality.

I pass through the gate, which has been left open—Americans, please, I beg you, lock your doors and gates—and ring the doorbell. I hear rustling on the other side, and when the door opens, Chris is standing there. He blinks at me, confused.

"Look, I already voted for Hearts King and Queen," he starts saying, "and I can't take it back, so tell Chloe I can't—"

"I'm not here for that," I interrupt, befuddled. "Who's Chloe?"

"The cheerleader whose boyfriend has been cheating on her with her best friend for the past four months."

"Oh, right," I say. Another name that should be familiar. "They're really making a big deal out of it."

Chris throws his hand into the air, helpless. The gesture makes him sweet. "So what are you doing here, Elis?"

I blink. "You know my name."

"You're Kevin's friend."

"Yeah. It's kinda about that." I don't know where to actually start with this. "Do you have a date to the Valentine's Day party on Friday?"

Chris tilts his head. "Are you inviting me?"

"No, I'm trying to ask whether you'd invite Kevin," I say.

Chris blinks at me for a moment, still standing in his doorway. Then his shoulders relax, and he opens the door wider. "Come on in."

I notice Chris is wearing shoes inside, so I don't take mine off. I follow him to the kitchen, where he gets two glasses of water and slides one over to me, sitting on a bench at the kitchen island. I do the same.

"So," he starts. "You're here because Kevin asked you to?"

"No. I'm here because Kevin is an idiot and he won't talk to you. You've seen the card, right? I mean, his card. You got more."

Chris nods. He maintains a very neutral expression.

"It was hard to miss," Chris says. "With all the glitter . . ."

Then he takes the card out of his pocket, like he's just been carrying it along the whole time. Some glitter floats to the floor.

"You know, I kind of waited years for this," he says, a small smile tugging at one corner of his mouth. "Kevin and I have been in the same class since preschool. I spent half of my time in middle school hoping he'd notice me. Then I realized it wasn't because I just wanted to be his friend. But he never even looked at me. By freshman year, I'd given up and decided it was time to move on."

He puts the card on the kitchen island between the two of us.

"Well," I say, clutching my glass of water. "Kevin's the most self-absorbed gay guy I've ever met. I'm glad God didn't make him white or he'd be unbearable."

Chris laughs. His eyes crinkle when he smiles. Maybe Kevin has good taste, after all.

"Now if you don't mind me asking again, why are you here?" Chris asks, looking up at me. "Why are you trying to get us together?"

I drink some water. There's some feeling lurking in my stomach, the fear I felt when I talked to Dad but didn't know why. I still don't know what's wrong, but if Chris invites Kevin to the party, then no harm done.

Everything is going to turn out great, and Kevin will thank me.

"I'm going back to Brazil once the semester is over," I tell him at last. "I just wanted to leave something nice for Kevin. For his last year of school."

There's something like understanding in Chris's eyes, in his tight-lipped smile.

"Kevin's not going to do shit," I go on. "He's been talking about you nonstop for the last couple of months. And maybe it took him a while to notice, but if there's a part of you that still likes him, now's your chance. Maybe you'll have more sense than he does."

"Not like that's hard."

We both laugh. Chris meets my eyes again.

"Thanks for coming here," he says. "Maybe I needed the extra incentive."

I smile back at him.

The plan is back on track.

On Thursday, things are looking up for everybody. Chloe has officially dumped her quarterback boyfriend and made up with her best friend. A girl in homeroom whispers insistently that they were actually secretly dating too this whole time. The countdown now reads, *1 day, people!* It sounds more like a threat than ever.

Kevin seems mollified. Almost at peace with the party being tomorrow and not having the date he wanted. That is, until we leave history class and Chris is waiting in the hallway with a fresh bouquet of wildflowers. Kevin immediately freezes.

"Hey," Chris says, opening up his—dimpled!—smile. "Hi, Kevin."

The three of us stand there awkwardly in the ensuing silence, jamming the door and waiting to see who moves first.

"I got your card," Chris continues. "And I thought it was really nice. I wanted to ask if maybe you wanted to come to the par—"

"No," Kevin says.

Time seems to slow down.

"What?" Chris and I ask in unison.

"No," Kevin repeats. "Thanks."

Then Kevin practically sprints down the corridor. Chris looks at me, and I look back at him.

"I thought . . ." Chris trails off, still clutching the bouquet.

"Me too," I say.

Chris looks down at his feet, all the confidence of minutes ago disappearing. *Damn it, Kevin.*

"Give me that," I say, snatching the bouquet from his hands. "I'll see if I can get him back."

I run after Kevin with the flowers in hand, entering the empty music room. I find him pacing in circles, frantic.

"You okay?" I ask, shutting the door behind me.

Kevin looks up. "I just said no to Chris Dunne. What do you think?"

"That you have a serious cognitive dysfunction," I tell him honestly.

"It wasn't like I imagined it would be," Kevin says, almost as if he's thinking to himself. "Like, he suddenly decided to notice me? After a card?"

"Why can't you accept that as a good thing?" I ask, impatient. "Kevin, this is basically all you wanted." I gesture with the flowers. "He got this for you. I didn't even have to tell him to do it."

As soon as it's out of my mouth, I realize the mistake I've made. Kevin whirls around so fast he almost does a ballet spin. *"What."*

Carefully, I set the flowers down on the teacher's table. "Let's say that, er, maybe I talked to him. After you refused to."

Kevin looks outraged. "I refused?"

"You ran away and then said you would never actually invite him," I say defensively.

"So you thought asking *him* to invite *me* would be fine?"

I resist the urge to roll my eyes. "He likes you. I didn't force him into anything."

But Kevin's already too caught up with his own scene to listen.

"Why do you have to interfere? Like I'm some pathetic charity case?" Kevin practically shouts in the empty room, and I wince. "I am perfectly capable of doing things on my own. I don't need your help."

"If you did, then I wouldn't have to do something drastic just so you can talk to some guy."

Kevin's whole body tenses like he's about to vibrate out of existence.

"Elis," he says, my name so sharp it threatens to cut, "did you steal the Valentine's Day cards so I had an excuse to talk to Chris Dunne?"

The question hangs in the air for far too long. This is a bad time for confession, when we're both impatient and exploding with each other. It should happen after everything has worked out, when the happy ending is in sight and my idiotic scheme would just feel like a victimless crime.

"Oh my God," Kevin says, mouth agape. "I can't believe you'd do that to me. You *listened* to me talk about it all the time and still you decided the better way to go was to *humiliate* me—"

"I was trying to help! And you're not the only one who's been affected by this—"

"Who the hell cares about Chloe? I'm your friend and—"

"Yes, you're my friend and I've had enough of you acting stupid, like this crush is the most important thing in your life when I'm right here!"

That stuns him into silence. I shut my mouth, wishing I hadn't said anything.

The fear comes crashing back, only this time I understand it. I don't have to pretend anymore that I did it to be altruistic, so I could help Kevin and do this fantastic thing for him, because it's what friends do. Sure, of course I want him to have all the best things he wants in life, all the good things he deserves.

But all this time, I also wanted my friend back. What I've been feeling all this time is jealousy, because Kevin dedicates all his attention to Chris and none to me. I didn't do it for him, I did it for me. I made the selfish choice. And I decided that he could afford the heartbreak, because I couldn't afford mine.

"Well," Kevin says. "Nice to know this is what you think of your *friends*."

He exits the room. When he slams the door, all the instruments rattle like a sad, splintered orchestra.

Maybe the reason I don't have any friends is because I am a bad friend.

"Smile for the cameras!" the Moms say in unison, holding up their phones.

"Ugh," I say, smiling anyway just so they can take a picture.

The Moms take several, making me do different poses.

"So who's coming to pick you up?" Tracy asks, putting her phone away.

"No one. I had a fight with Kevin."

"Oh no, baby," Gina says in her most consoling and sugary voice. "I'm sure you're going to make up with him."

"If he doesn't hate me forever for ruining his love life," I say, heading for the door where my shoes and purse are. Gina found me a very ridiculous dress—a pink monstrosity with ruffles and red hearts stamped all over it. The bag is also hers—heart shaped with a huge glittery arrow crossing it. She's got a whole room of the house dedicated to the clothes she kept while working at the Orpheum Theatre costume department.

"Nobody can ruin anybody's love life," Tracy says, pursing her lips. "That's entirely up to ourselves. You can just mildly interfere."

"Is that what you call kicking your ex-girlfriend's date out of your house on a whim and then deciding you should date her instead?" Gina teases with a raised eyebrow.

They start discussing the story of how they met once again. I've heard it about a million times. They still love each other so much that sometimes it hurts my ears. Dad says this is "child of divorce syndrome," but I think it's just who I am.

I open the door, and Gina puts a hand on my shoulder, adjusting the ruffles. "Elis, Valentine's Day is a magical day. Love is in the air. It's impossible to deny it."

"That sounds dangerously ominous."

Tracy appears by my other side. "She just means that no matter what happens, you're going to work it out. Love always wins."

I don't feel like love is winning anything when I get to the school. The decorations, which seemed brighter early this week, look deflated. Some hearts have been shredded by the wind, and the balloons look decidedly sorry. The party is happening at the gym, and I head in that direction, unsure whether I can make it all the way there. I convince myself that I can try it, just for the food. They promised cheese balls.

I linger at the pink, red, and silver balloon archway. The party inside is raging already, the music blasting over the speakers. Before I go in, though, someone else stops in front of me. I'd completely put her off my mind this whole week.

"Hayley," I say, trying to recall the exact spelling on the back of the card I got. Her red hair is falling in waves over her shoulder and her red dress, which is a bold choice, but it works for her.

I should have talked to her earlier about the card. She clearly wanted to talk to me when I was in a hurry to get to Chris's house, but I figured whatever was going on with her, a girl I barely spoke to in school, could wait. I guess since now Kevin isn't my life's sole focus, we might as well talk.

"It's actually Halley," she says, amused. "Like the comet."

"Cool."

We stare at each other for a moment. Then she finally says, "Did you get my card?"

"Oh," I mutter. "Yeah. I got it. Sorry, I've had a busy week."

She tilts her head, her red hair brushing over her shoulders. "So . . . ?"

"Look, I'm leaving in July," I say. "You know that, right? I don't want to break anyone's heart."

Halley blinks. "Wow, presumptuous much."

I laugh, and so does she.

"I know you're leaving," Halley says. "I'm not here declaring anything at all. I just like you, and I think it's kinda hot how you seem completely oblivious to everything that isn't what you want at the moment."

That makes me grimace and cuts far too deep for someone who doesn't know me.

"If that's your type, it's going to land you some fuckboys in college," I reply, and she laughs again. "But it's not—it's not you, it's me. I can do friends. I don't do romance." I don't have a better way of explaining it, and this cuts to the heart of it. "That actually fucked up my last friendship. He said he couldn't be 'just' friends."

I still remember Lucas's insistence. How he said that maybe we should just *try*, and I couldn't know what I liked unless I tried it first, and it seemed better than losing a friend. Only to lose Lucas either way, in the end, because whatever I tried, it just wasn't enough.

"I don't think there's anything bad about being 'just' friends," Halley says after a moment. "I don't think it's anything 'just' at all. And if you want to try kissing sometime, I could work with that too."

She grins at me. She's got a really nice smile.

"Favorite movie set in San Francisco?" I ask, because knowing a person's favorite movie in a random-but-extremely-specific category is really the only way to judge a person's character. (Maybe I *am* turning into my dad. Ugh.)

"*Vertigo?*" she says, almost as if she's asking me, evidently confused by the random change of subject.

"Did you know it's called *A Body That Falls* in Brazil? They basically give away the ending. Twice."

"Huh. Weird." She tilts her head. "I don't love you or anything, Elis. But maybe you'll have to trust me in making that decision for myself."

I blink in surprise and then turn back to the balloon archway, watching the party through the opening. I spot Kevin on one end,

dancing. Chris, on the other, trying his best to pretend he isn't looking at my best friend.

"I gotta go," I say to Halley. "But come and find me later. I
just have to do this thing first."

I walk up to Chris. "You're coming with me," I tell him, and then
drag him by his tie across the gym floor until we're face-to-face with
Kevin. He protests all the way, but I ignore him. Kevin looks at us
and the scene that we're causing, but I hold my victim tight.

I stop in front of Kevin and take a deep breath.

"You can be mad at me all you want," I say, forcing my voice to be
even. "You can be mad at me for the rest of your life. And I did it
because I'm selfish, yes, and I wanted to go back to us being normal,
because no matter how much you want to ignore it, I'm going away
in a few months. I'm not going to be walking with you to the bus
stop, or trying to ditch stupid art class, or stopping by Starbucks to
get coffee with you at lunch. I'm going to be four hours ahead of you
all the time. I'm *leaving*."

Kevin's face goes slack with shock, and then something else in
his eyes. Not worry. Just utter . . . despair. Maybe I hadn't been looking at his face when we talked about what was going to happen after
the school year ends, because I was too afraid of what I'd see, or
wouldn't see. In case he wasn't as heartbroken as I was.

But now I look at him, and I see, in his tear-filled eyes, that he
knows. He's always known.

"And you can be angry with me until then and after," I force
myself to continue, swallowing thickly even when I feel tears pricking my eyes. "But now that I've already turned the school upside
down for you, can you please just kiss this guy so you don't become

44

a loser senior who doesn't have a boyfriend in the last year of school?"

I shove Chris's tie in Kevin's direction. Chris blushes so hard that I can see his red cheeks even under the neon lights.

"Fine," Kevin says. "Fine."

And then he puts both hands on Chris's face and pulls him down. Applause and whistles ring around us. Chris relaxes after a minute, pulling Kevin by the waist to bring him closer. When they finally break apart, Kevin's dark eyes sparkle like the night sky.

"I'll just be a minute," Kevin says to him. "I still got my priorities."

He lets go of Chris, and then he pulls me by the hand to the other side of the gym, marching us away from the crowd and the music and back into the school corridor where I was a minute ago.

Kevin is flushed, breathing hard like he's just run a marathon. I notice he's wearing a pin over his black shirt collar to match my dress. He still wore it, even though we weren't talking.

"I needed to say that to you," I start before he can go on a tangent. "And I'm sorry I said you were acting stupid, but you *were*. And I was just worried that I'd spend the last couple of months here having to listen to you ramble on about Chris and just . . . Our friendship is the most important thing in my life."

Kevin's still breathing hard, like he can't find his words, so I just power on.

"Kevin, I love you," I continue. "You're my soulmate. And now I'm going to have to spend the rest of my life knowing that you're a continent away."

"Same continent, technically," Kevin corrects, his voice hoarse and eyes teary. "*Now* who doesn't know geography?"

"Shut up," I say, pulling him into a hug.

He hugs me tight, and it's like the whole party fades away.

"I love you too," he says. "As if I'm not forcing you to apply to UCLA with me, whatever it takes. I'm not leaving you behind, Elis."

"You could come to Brazil."

"I can't believe you're telling me to come to Brazil like I'm some sort of celebrity," he says above me, not letting me go. "I got something for you."

"What?"

Kevin releases me just enough to pick something from his pocket. It's another red-heart card.

"I made this one so you'll forgive me for being the most obtuse gay ever," he says, handing it to me. "Who says I never listen to your cheesy movie advice?"

I take it from his hand, still sniffing. It's got so much glitter that future archaeologists will find it under my nails when they dig up my coffin. In it, there are just two names. KEVIN + ELIS.

I turn to the other side, and Kevin scoffs.

"I didn't get to finish it," he says.

"So finish it now," I say, opening my purse and handing him a pen.

"Fine," he says, taking it and starting to scribble on the back. "Here."

Elis, not a single movie in the world could capture with its lenses my love for you. You are my best friend/soulmate/pathetic cinephile partner.

P.S.: I DON'T love you for making me write this.

"Satisfied?" he asks.

"No," I reply, taking the heart and shoving it in my purse with the pen. "You just kissed the love of your life or something because of me. You owe me forever."

We start bickering again, and then we walk hand in hand all the way back to the dance floor. I guess love does make people stupid, and I'm the stupidest person of all for thinking my best friend wasn't as brokenhearted as I was about me leaving.

But maybe two broken hearts get to make a whole. Maybe we're the answer to mending each other's half.

Holi Hai!

BY PREETI CHHIBBER

ऐ हे जी रे!
उड़े उड़े मन उड़े,
पर लगे तेरे संग जुड़े
मन उड़े पग बढे तेरी ओर बढे,
जग छोड़ बढे

When she steps off the A train and onto the platform at Ozone Park–Lefferts Blvd., Vritika imagines that she can already feel the bass thread of "Rang Barse" rumbling in the concrete below her feet. Of course, it might be the train rolling in across the way, but a girl can believe what she wants to believe. She starts humming the minor chords as she moves toward the exit with the rest of the commuters—from the look of the brown skin and light-colored clothing around her, the crowd is heading in the same direction she is. She keeps her gaze forward, just in case. She doesn't think she can stand seeing *him* today.

"Girl, I *know* you're not already humming that song; we're going to hear it eight thousand times today." A heavy arm comes down around her neck, and Vritika grins, already turning to the speaker.

"Hey, Avantika." Vritika eyes her best friend, taking in her white sweater and jeans, an outfit reflecting her own. Avantika sighs dramatically and pulls away as they get to the stairs, flinging a long dark braid behind her as she goes.

"Holi is supposed to be the beginning of spring, so remind me why it is fifty-five degrees today?" she grumbles as they take the steps down to the station exit.

"You'll warm up once we get started," Vritika says, trying to hold in laughter at Avantika's theatrics.

"Yeah, yeah. Oh, did you bring powder from home, or do you want to buy some?"

"Buy some."

Vritika follows Avantika onto the streets of Richmond Hill, heading down Liberty Avenue to where the Phagwah Parade will start. Avantika isn't wrong; the air that hits Vritika's face is cool and dry. But she knows from experience that all she needs is the crowd and music and dancing that's just a short time away, and she'll be fine. She will be *fine*. As they get closer, the energy starts to ramp up—there are little kids running around shooting each other with water guns full of colored water, and old aunties singing in the street. They stop by a street vendor and buy a couple of bags of bright powder in an array of colors—red, green, purple, orange, blue.

"Is Reisha meeting up with us?" Vritika asks, dropping the powder into the cross-body bag slung over her shoulder and hoping her question sounds nonchalant.

"Yeah, later, she's here with her cousins. She'll see us at—" Avantika stops short, realizing what she's just said. "Uh, I mean—"

Vritika sighs and waves Avantika off even as her stomach drops to the ground.

"It's fine," she says, moving by her friend. "I assume that means Aman's coming."

In answer, Avantika shrieks and Vritika whips around to find a splatter of pink across the back of Avantika's sweater and a group of small children running by screaming with laughter.

"Happy Holi!" one of them yells as they retreat farther down the street.

"I wasn't *ready*!" Avantika yells back, ripping open a bag of orange powder and pouring a healthy amount into her palm. "But now I am," she says, closing her fist around the pile.

"Holi hai!" a woman's voice crackles out from a speaker a block or two away, and Vritika speeds up her steps.

"Come on!" she calls back, forcing the thoughts of her ex-boyfriend, Aman, out of her head.

"Why do you care so much about this dinky parade?" Avantika laughs, gasping a little as she hurries to catch up. "It's like seven floats and they're all playing the same song." A huge gust of wind snatches away Vritika's answer, pulling up her hair into a frenzy of whips. Colors picked up from the sidewalk surround her, a particularly robust shade of indigo catches her across the chest and blooms, stark against the white. The gust suddenly settles back down a second later. She almost thinks she heard someone talking, but she couldn't quite catch the words. Her eyebrows come down low over her eyes as she frowns.

"That was weird."

"The universe just said you looked too clean," Avantika says, still laughing. "Now let's go see some little kids dancing poorly to 'Soni Soni.'"

The parade is as silly and fun as Vritika remembers. She'd been coming to the Phagwah Parade in Ozone Park since she was little, and this would be her last before heading to college in the fall. She wanted to experience every bit of it. She especially wanted to write over *last year's* memories of spending the day with Aman. At the thought of him, Vritika shakes her head as if trying to physically kick Aman out of her brain. It was Holi, and she wasn't going to let him ruin this.

They'd followed the parade down Liberty and were ready to turn and make their way to Rizzuto Park, where the main festivities would be held. Just from the short walk alongside the parade, Vritika and Avantika were both already sporting several dyes to their clothes and skin and hair. Avantika's braid looked like it had been dipped inside the sky, it was so blue—that was courtesy of an auntie sporting a particularly large neon-green water gun with a massive pump and tank attached.

"Okay," Avantika says, looking down at her phone, "Reisha's waiting at the corner for us. Aman's not there." But there's something in her tone that implies *more*. Vritika ignores it. That *more* is not her problem any longer.

"Chalo, chalo, chalo," someone says in her ear, and Vritika stops and twists her neck around in surprise. But there's no one there. She stares at the empty space beside her, bewildered.

"Vri?" Avantika asks, several feet ahead of her. "You okay? I know I should have said something about Aman earlier, but honestly, I didn't think he'd—"

"No, no, it's fine," Vritika says, distracted by Avantika's mention of Aman. "Let's not even talk about him."

Avantika's wide dark eyes and downturned mouth are an open book of questions and concerns, but Vritika isn't spending Holi thinking about her ex-boyfriend of two years dumping her through a text message and then *immediately* starting to date someone else. She thought she'd gotten the Phagwah Parade in their breakup, but apparently not. With a start, Vritika realizes that Avantika is staring at her with concern *and* pity now.

"Let's just get to the freakin' park," she says, and pushes by her friend.

"Okay . . ." she hears Avantika trail off behind her. There's a hint of discomfort in her tone, and Vritika's stomach twists with guilt. But she doesn't say anything more.

Rizzuto Park is already a mess of people in various states of rainbow transformation by the time they get there, and some of the excitement seeps back into Vritika's bones. The stage at the front of the park is full of people—local business owners, a group of musicians, and she thinks she sees someone's dog. From the speaker, a steady stream of Bollywood music is pumping out. A group of elementary kids ahead of them are screeching and running from a few dadis throwing powder at them. The older women were covered head to foot in color themselves, their gray hair disguised by reds and blues and greens. It was a welcome sight, and something unclenches in Vritika's chest. But the feeling is short-lived.

"Avi!"

Avantika's girlfriend Reisha is waving to them. Vritika lets Avantika rush ahead of her and slam into her girlfriend, wrapping her arms around her and pressing her cheek against Reisha's. Reisha pushes her off, laughing.

"You're getting your color all over me!" Her eyes shift to Vritika, and she can actually see the moment that unease slips into them. "Oh, hey, Vri, how are you?" The question gets Vritika's hackles up, but she refuses to succumb to the irritation. She pushes it away somewhere deep down inside of her.

"Ready to play Holi!" she responds, tossing a fistful of yellow powder directly at Reisha. As if on cue, a loud voice from the stage shouts out into a microphone, "*Holi hai!!*" and the crowd erupts as the musicians kick off a dhol beat. The effect is instantaneous and *chaotic*. The three of them break into the crowd, shouting and singing and dancing.

"*Rang barse!*" She sings the off-key melody directly into Avantika's face. "Rang barse bheege chunar wal—"

"I cannot hear that song *again*!" Avantika laugh-cries, interrupting Vritika's terrible singing with a dousing of purple. A stranger nearby throws an entire bag of green into the air, coloring the skies viridescent. She closes her eyes and smiles, tilting her chin up to the sky. This is what she'd been waiting for. Avantika laughs again, pulling Vritika back into the play, and they dance and tease their way farther into the crowd. And she doesn't think of Aman. Well, she tries very hard not to think of him and how much her chest still aches.

A dark-skinned man in a white hoodie and sweatpants combo points a small, plastic water gun at Vritika's face. His widening grin is the only warning she has that she's about to get hit with a stream of brightly colored water. She closes her eyes tightly and brings her hand up in retaliation before the liquid even hits her shirt. She has everything she needs held in her fist. Once she lets it fly, a shower of deep red powder cuts through the air and lands in a slash across the man's hoodie, and he laughs in delight and cries out, "Happy Phag-wah!" before turning to find his next victim.

Vritika watches him go, but he's lost in the massive crowd within seconds. She probably couldn't find the guy even if she wanted to. Frowning in sudden realization, she looks around at the people near her and then groans. She doesn't recognize *anyone*. Where are Reisha and Avantika? Vritika brings a hand up to rub at her eyes, as if that will magically make a face she knows appear, before remembering the eyeliner she'd put on that morning.

"Damn it," she curses to herself.

"Language!" a deep, playful voice curls into her ear just before someone presses a palm against her cheek, leaving behind the familiar texture of the fine colored powder on her skin. There's a sheen of yellow caught just in the corner of her eye. She whips around to find out just who was teasing her.

"Who—" she starts to say, but the sentence falls away as she realizes the culprit has already melted back into the crowd. Again.

"Vritika?"

Every inch of Vritika goes cold at the familiar sound of Aman's voice saying her name. He sounds *exactly* the same, with a voice that used to make her feel safe and loved and warm. She fixes a wide smile on her face before turning to find him standing just behind her, holding hands with a pretty, fair-skinned girl in a white sweater dress. They're both completely covered in color from top to bottom. The joyful expression on their clothing is a jarring juxtaposition to the clear awkwardness on their faces.

54

"Hey, Aman," she says, and hopes that her voice isn't shaking. But before Aman can say anything else, someone grabs her hand and yanks her backward.

And then she's not in Queens anymore.

The first thing she registers is the heat. It is *hot*.

"What the—" Vritika stares around her in shock. She opens and closes her eyes several times and then rubs at them, eyeliner be damned. But when she opens them again, the view is still the same. It's not the Phil "Scooter" Rizzuto Park she'd been in moments before, and it's certainly not full of a massive crowd of people dancing to 1980s Bollywood songs.

She's in a green meadow, surrounded by a circle of neem trees with their outstretched branches covered in thin, pointy leaves. There are large metal pots about with the kumkum, sindoor, and chandan powders she mostly knew from holiday pujas. On the ground are two gold cylinders with long, thin rods sticking out of one side and knobs on the end. They almost look familiar. She steps toward the pots, and the grass is soft under her feet. Vritika pauses at the realization that she's *barefoot*. She looks down at herself and sees that that's not the only thing that's changed.

"What am I doing in a lehenga?!" The skirt is a pale pink and the dupatta is blue, cutting across the choli and her bare midriff. "What the actual hell is happ—"

"You're here!"

Vritika jumps and screams in surprise. She twists around to find a tall, brown boy grinning at her, his hands behind his back and mischief in his eyes. His hair is a mess of thick black curls, just long enough to cover his ears. He's bare chested under his colorful vest and has a white dhoti slung low on his hips. There's a long, heavy gold chain around his neck. Like her, he isn't wearing any shoes. Vritika ignores the little flip her belly does as she takes all this in. Instead she focuses on her confusion.

"Who are you? Where are we? What is going on? I was in Queens, like, five seconds ago, right?" The questions spill out of her almost faster than she can think of them.

His grin never wavers. Instead of answering, he brings one of his hands up to his chin and opens his fist, revealing a palm of deep red kumkum powder. Then he puckers his lips and blows—the powder explodes forward, covering her.

"What the—"

"Holi hai!" he says. It's the same voice that had spoken to her in the streets, and the—

She gasps and points at him accusingly.

"You're the one who told me to watch my language!"

He laughs, and the sound is like the *chum-chum* of a dancer's payal. It's playful and melodic and welcoming all at once.

"I did," he admits, his hands raised so she can see his red-and-orange palms. "You looked like you needed to be teased."

"Where are we?" she asks again, ignoring his clear flirtations. "And who are you?"

"You can call me Darshan." He pauses here like it's a name that should mean something to her, but Vritika has no idea why it would.

"Okay, Darshan, where are we?" She swings her arm in a wide arc to encompass the space around them. "I know I woke up this morning in Forest Hills, and that I started Holi in Richmond Hill, so . . ."

"Don't you just want to play?" he asks, bypassing her questions again. "It's Holi! A celebration of spring, and defeating evil, and divine love, and *joy*."

Each word is punctuated with a little half step away from her, until he's landed right next to one of the gold cylinders she'd noticed earlier. He leans down to pick it up, and it suddenly occurs to her what it is.

"No, wait—" she says, holding up her hands. But it's too late. He holds the pointed end toward her and pushes the thin rod forward with all his strength and she gets absolutely covered in red water.

"Rang rang mere rang rang mein!" he sings, dancing away from her furious sputtering. "Rang jayegi tu rang!"

The pointedness of the lyrics is just too much to ignore, and Vritika dives for one of the pots, shoving both her hands into the yellow chandan, cupping them to pull up as much of the color as she can.

Then she gives chase, running after Darshan.

It doesn't take her long to catch up to him, and she tosses the chandan his way. He doesn't even try to dodge, just lets the powder coat him like a fine dust of pollen. The spattering makes his skin look even darker, and Vritika has the passing thought that if she stares at him too much longer, it's going to get weird.

"Send me home," she tells him, pushing away that part of her brain.

"No, wait, what did you just do?" Darshan looks at her inquisitively, something uncomfortably studious in his gaze.

"What do you mean? I threw powder at you and now I'm asking you to send me home." She needs to get back and—it occurs to her that he'd pulled her away the second she ran into Aman. There's a quick wave of pain at the thought of his name, but Vritika ignores it.

"No, you decided *not* to say something." He shakes his head. "You decided to think *practically*."

"Obviously." Her reply is dry. "Although, if I was really thinking about this *practically*, I'd probably assume this is—you are—a hallucination."

The sound of light laughter cuts through the air, and Vritika goes stock-still as a group of gopis come through the trees. It's a scene straight out of one of the ancient prints her mom has hanging on the walls of their home—women in a range of lehengas, all different colors and patterns, holding on to their own golden rods and colored powder to play for the holiday. She turns back to Darshan, her face a few shades paler than before.

"Should I be asking *when* are we?"

He gives her a coy smile and then lets out a loud whoop. The gopis hear him and call out a mess of greetings in answer. Darshan tilts his head toward them in a clear question to Vritika.

"Shall we go? Would it be practical?" His lips turn up, teasing, and his teeth are white and a little crooked inside his mouth.

She'd been trying so hard to *not* think about Aman and the anger and pain she'd been feeling all day. Maybe this was just a respite from all that. Maybe she should let this cute boy give her the gift of a smile and a joyful game.

"Okay, okay. Show me what I'm missing."

Darshan laughs and grabs her wrist, pulling her toward the other women.

Turns out, what she'd been missing was sheer abandonment of all her anxieties. The women were welcoming and kind and, most of all, *ready*. When she and Darshan had joined the group, one of them stepped forward holding out a golden rod and gestured for Vritika to take it.

"A pichkari, for you," the woman says. Vritika thanks her and examines it. In her hands, she sees that it's actually brass and not gold. The weight is light, and she grins. It's just a water gun. She immediately turns on Darshan.

"Revenge." Her smile is impish as she adds for the women behind her, "Chalo, let's get him!"

Their answer is a resounding "Haan!" and Darshan cackles, speeding off away from them all. Vritika loses herself in the action and fun of it all—she doesn't have a moment to think about anything else lest she become the target.

They lose sight of Darshan at some point, and one of the other women, Deepa, thinks they should split up to find him.

"He always wins," she complains, but there's no malice in it. "Let's get him this time."

That's how Vritika finds herself on her own again, but her entire focus is on figuring out where Darshan could have gotten to. After stepping under one of the neem trees, she stops for a moment—the hair on her arms goes up and she can't stop the feeling that someone is watching her. Looking right and left reveals nothing, but it hits her that the space around her isn't entirely quiet. The soft shaking of leaves hovers in the air, and then she gets it and looks up.

Darshan is grinning down at her from a spot in the branches, and Vritika doesn't hesitate, lifting the pichkari up and pressing the rod in with one swift motion. Bright orange water sprays out and up into the branches, causing Darshan to squeal as he jumps from branch to branch before finally making his way down to the ground, a sweaty orange mess.

"You're having fun, yes?" he asks Vritika, and she's not surprised to find the answer is yes. What she is surprised to find is that the paragraph of pain that's been written into her heart has turned into an asterisk. Her anger at Aman is no longer the full text of her. She's turned it into a footnote of a broken heart.

Vritika falls backward into the grass, her dupatta flung out beside her. There's an ache in her legs from all the running, and she's sure her hair is caked in a red-yellow-orange mixture, but her heart feels light in a way it hasn't in a long time. With a start, she realizes that she had to let herself feel this way. It was her choice.

Next to her, Darshan has an elbow flung over his face, but she can see his lip curved up at the corner.

She turns her head so she's looking at him directly and tentatively reaches a hand over to tap the back of his hand. His skin is warm, and she can feel heat rushing to her cheeks as she pulls her hand away. He uncovers his face before turning to look at her.

"So, your big plan was just to play around in this fantasyland until we both got tired, and I stopped feeling bad that my ex-boyfriend didn't care enough to have a conversation before ending our relationship?" she asks. "And then I remember the magic of Holi?"

"My big plan," he says, his voice soft and pensive, "was to play Holi with you. That's it."

Vritika rolls over to her side and rests her head on her hand.

"Seriously, who *are* you?" she asks, but when Darshan opens his mouth to answer she surprises herself by interrupting him. "No, wait. No, hold on. I'm not sure I want to know. I think maybe I don't. Not yet."

His eyes light up and he pushes his palms against the grass, moving into a sitting position. He reaches a hand out to pull her up next to him. She lets him, and when they're seated together, she leans slightly so their arms are touching. Out of the corner of her eye, she can see him glance at her, but he doesn't say anything. She drops her head, resting it against his shoulder.

"I'll send you home soon," he says, and she can feel the low tenor of his voice vibrating out from his body and into hers.

Vritika *could* just leave. She could let this exist as an experience she had once. But she doesn't want that.

"Let's go together."

Darshan tenses under her, but she doesn't regret asking.

"That's . . . not an option right now."

"Right now?" she asks. He shifts to turn to her, and his smile is rueful.

"Happy Holi," he says in lieu of an explanation.

"Happy Holi—" Vritika starts to reply, but the words are barely out of her mouth when she's standing back in her sweater and jeans, in the middle of a partying crowd in Richmond Hill, directly in front of Aman and his new girlfriend.

"Uh . . . Happy Holi to you, too, Vri . . ." Aman says, as if she'd been talking to him. She's thrown, and there's a hot spike of irritation in her gut at, well, *everything*. She opens her mouth to tell Aman to screw off, but just as the words start bubbling out of her, she snaps her jaw shut. He's just a *footnote*. She closes her eyes for a second and searches for joy again, choosing to center that part of her. The feeling flows through her, in her blood, her veins, her thoughts, overwhelming the fleeting irritation she felt.

Her eyes open, taking in Aman and his girlfriend and their uncomfortable expressions. Then she looks at the wider picture around them, of all the people still shouting with happiness and throwing bright spots of color into the air, and Vritika grins. Darshan's crooked smile flashes in her imagination.

"You know, Aman," she says, her gaze darting to the people over his shoulder, searching for her friends, "the way you handled ending things between us really, *really* sucked. You could have just talked to me instead of hiding behind a screen."

"Wha— I—" Aman's voice is shocked. *Of course* it is. "I'm . . . sorry?" He asks it, like he isn't sure he should be, or he isn't sure if it's the right thing to say. Vritika waves it off.

"I just wanted to say it out loud, so you heard it. You can listen, or not. Have fun today!" she adds, and then repeats with genuine feeling, "Happy Holi!" Vritika doesn't wait for Aman to respond, just turns on her heel and shoves her way back into the melee of people. She knows she could have walked away from Aman without saying anything, but centering her own happiness didn't mean *ignoring* the other parts of her. If she hadn't said anything, the hurt inside would have festered. And maybe it will come back, growing big and small in measures until it stays steady as a piece of her history. But right now, she's happy. And she'll hold on to that happiness.

As if there's a guiding hand on the small of her back, Vritika walks with purpose and isn't at all shocked when she runs directly into people she actually wants to be around, Reisha and Avantika.

"There you are!" Avantika laughs, punctuating the sounds with water spritzes from an opaque, tiny plastic water gun she must have found somewhere.

"Here I am," Vritika says, her smile so wide she wouldn't be shocked if her cheeks hurt later. Avantika gets distracted by a tall, teenage girl dropping fistfuls of blue powder into her hair from above. Vritika reaches into her pocket for a fresh packet of powder and tears the plastic open with her teeth. Tipping a small amount of yellow into her hand, she sees it splashed against dark skin for a moment and only refocuses at the sound of Reisha's voice.

"You seem . . . different."

Avantika's girlfriend is giving Vritika a speculative look, and she doesn't shy away from it.

"I feel different," she says easily.

"Good different?" Reisha asks, barely even reacting as a small kid runs by, pressing bright fingers against the bottom of her shirt and leaving a streak of pink behind. Vritika throws her own handful over the spot and the yellow overlaps the pink, turning into a welcoming saffron color.

"Very good different," she replies, and then amends slightly, "very welcome different." Because more than good, it was welcoming. Comforting to know she had a choice in the chaos of it all.

"Perfect place to have a serious conversation, I guess," Avantika interrupts, her tone teasing. "Let's get closer to the stage. That junior bhangra team is gonna perform after the puja." Reisha rolls her eyes, but it's good-natured rather than irritated.

"Yeah, yeah," Reisha says. "Can't miss ten-year-olds dancing to 'Dholna' again." But she follows when Avantika starts to push her way toward the front of the crowd. Vritika takes a step forward, intending to follow, when she sees something out of the corner of her eye. She turns her head, catching sight of a familiar head of curly black hair. "Darshan!" she calls loudly. The head turns and she sees his face, but the second their eyes meet, he starts to fade and Vritika's heart pounds in her chest. "Not an option right now," she repeats his words to herself. Fingers curl around her wrist and Vritika starts, her body already getting pulled along as she turns to find Avantika.

"Don't get lost again!" her friend says without looking back.

"We'll see . . ." The corners of Vritika's mouth turn up in a small, secret smile. Avantika's fingers are tight around her wrist, and around her the celebration is reaching its zenith as the people onstage start to kick off the holiday's prayer. Vritika barely registers it, her mind already whirring on how she'll make it back next year. "Right now isn't forever."

A New Day

BY ABDI NAZEMIAN

"I'm officially begging," I plead as my mom turns toward my school. "It's our senior year. Next year, I could be out of state for Nowruz. *He* could be out of state. We could be broken up by then."

She glances my way. "If you're planning on breaking up, then why introduce him to the whole family?" she asks, returning her eyes to the road.

"Because maybe, if he meets everyone, if he *really* knows all of me . . . all the cultural bullshit—"

"Our culture is only five percent bullshit," she cracks.

I stifle a laugh. "Yeah, and at least half of that five percent is the homophobia, so please let me bring him."

"Your grandmother . . . She . . ." The look she gives me tells me that we're allies, a progressive island in an ancient ocean. At least that's what she wants to believe about herself. "I just don't want her to hurt you, that's all." She stops at a red light. Runs a gentle hand through my messy hair. Her eyes offer me comfort, but I reject it. I know it's not my feelings she's concerned about. It's her family's judgment.

"Someday, Maman and Khaleh Goli and Amu Hassan and the Straight A's are going to find out I'm gay," I say. "We might as well rip off the Band-Aid."

"I'm just trying to protect you. That's a mother's job," she counters. "You don't know what it's like when my mother disapproves of you. My sister inherited that same quality from her. They can cut you down with one look. One word. One—" She brakes hard behind a bro on his cell phone at a green light. She honks. Loud. *"Ahmagh."* I smile because I love when my mom road rages in Persian. Of course, I know that it's her family she's really angry at, and I share that anger. Her harsh mother, who doles out her love conditionally. Her extravagant sister, who convinced her to move to Los Angeles when my dad overdosed, and who technically owns our apartment, which is probably why my mom feels like she owes them her gratitude and my secrecy.

"I guess it feels . . . sometimes . . . like the person you're really protecting is yourself," I stammer.

She turns on the radio in an effort to end the conversation. The local station announces that the Archdiocese of Los Angeles is halting all masses. She quickly turns it off. She's already been demoted from server to delivery driver. I know she doesn't want to hear any more about the virus.

"It just feels like you want their approval more than you want my happiness," I continue.

The fact that she can't even look at me means she knows I'm right.

My mom, Vida, can't compete when it comes to money, 'cause we live paycheck to paycheck. She can't compete when it comes to career, 'cause she works at a Mexican restaurant while her sister charges people unspeakable sums of money to choose art for them. She can't compete for choice of husband, 'cause Uncle Hassan invented an app that disrupted the health care industry and saves countless lives while my dad, he's dead. And she can't compete when it comes to beauty because her sister has access to Los Angeles' best doctors. The kind of beauty my grandmother and the Persians appreciate is the kind money can buy. My mom and her sister used to look alike. Now my aunt is a yassified version of my mom, a living reminder of what she could have been if she had made different choices. The only category where my mom stands a chance is children, because the Straight A's—my cousins Ava, Amir, and Abbas—are more like B minuses. Which means that on Nowruz, I must look perfect and act perfect so that my mom can brag about me. And in both Tehran and Tehrangeles, gay is imperfect.

"Okay, let's compromise. We bring him, but we just say he's a friend?" I suggest. "The Straight A's always invite their friends to the Nowruz party."

"But Shawn is not your friend." She parks her car at a meter outside my school.

"No one has to know that," I argue. "It's not like I'm gonna make out with him in front of the Haft-Seen."

She manages to laugh. "I know that, but . . . The way you two look at each other . . . It's so obvious you love each other." Her face opens into a warm smile. "And I'm happy you have the kind of love that can't be hidden. I really am." I close my eyes and feel her warmth. Remind myself that for the rest of the year, she's the mom I need and deserve. Supportive. On my side. I just have to get through one more new year. Nowruz is the only time our whole family gets together, which means that next week, I'll get my real mom back. "You deserve love," she says. "Not my family's judgment."

Right on cue, Shawn knocks on my window. I feel myself bloom when I see him, like he's the sun and I'm a grateful flower. I roll the window down. "Good morning," he says. "Is our guest speaker ready for her big presentation?"

"I'm not a teacher," my mom says to my classmates once they all quiet down, though of course she's taught me everything I know about how to live and when to hide. "But I'll do my best to tell you a little bit about why Nowruz is special for the Iranian people."

Before my mom can go any further, class overachiever Emily Gibson raises her hand. "Nowruz isn't just celebrated by Iranians, though, right?" She knows she's right. "It's celebrated by Afghans, Kurds . . . um . . ." She opens her notebook and reads from detailed notes. Shawn thinks she has the handwriting of a serial killer, and I don't disagree. "Tajiks, Turks . . ."

Shawn leans over. Whispers in my ear. "Someone studied the Wikipedia Nowruz page in anticipation of your mom's visit." I smile, enjoying the feel of his lips near my ear. Last night, his lips were on my neck, my chest, my mouth. I'm still running on the energy he transmitted to me.

Emily's list of countries is long. She's still going when I turn my focus back to her. ". . . Syrians, Uzbeks. It's celebrated by the Uighur people in western China, where, by the way, there's currently an ethnic—"

Before Emily can educate us about the persecution of the Uighurs,

Mr. Montaña gently interrupts her. "Emily, while your knowledge and empathy never ceases to amaze, Mrs. Moshiri is here to tell us about how your classmate Nader's community celebrates the holiday and what it means to them."

Everyone's eyes turn to me, their only Iranian classmate. Maybe if this were some westside private school, like the one my cousins go to, our class would be littered with the shahs and shahbanus of Sunset. But this is a public school in the 818. I'm one of one here. My mom and I have that in common, always standing out wherever we are. Me, gay and Iranian. Her, a single Iranian mom who works for a Mexican restaurant. Vida's a Persian name, too, by the way. She literally is life, my mom. Except when she's around her family, and then she's pure insecurity.

"Nowruz is the most important festive occasion of the year for Iranians," my mom begins. "It embodies a wealth of ancient rites and customs." She eyes the Haft-Seen table we set up together in my classroom, all the traditional items on it. The irony is we never have a Haft-Seen table in our home. We're usually too busy to bother. "If you look at the table over—"

"The Haft-Seen!" Emily cuts my mom off, which makes her flinch. In our culture, you don't talk over your elders.

Mr. Montaña shifts in his chair. "Emily, you're not being graded on this. This is a family share."

"Thank you," my mom says. "Why don't we all turn to the Haft-Seen table your teacher has let us set up in your classroom?" The whole class turns to the beautiful table.

"Is that, like, your Christmas tree?" Cooper asks.

"Persian culture is way older than Western culture," Shawn says defensively. "But by all means, let's use our traditions as a point of reference."

My mom smiles. "I wouldn't say it's like a Christmas tree. We don't put gifts under our table."

"But there are gifts, right?" Pia asks. "I mean, what's a holiday without presents?"

"Some families do give gifts," my mom says. I can see her debating whether to tell them about her sister Goli's husband, my Uncle Hassan, who hands out gold coins to any child under ten at their annual Nowruz party. She chooses not to. "But in most Iranian homes, Nowruz isn't about what you get. It's about setting your intentions for the year. A fresh start. Often, we clean out our homes and donate the old to make room for the new. Nowruz literally means 'new day.' It's timed to the exact moment of the vernal equinox, which is when the Earth shifts into spring. This year, that means we'll bring in the new year at exactly eight fifty p.m. in three days, on Thursday. There have been years when the moment comes earlier, or much later. One year, we all stayed up until the middle of the night at my sister's house—"

My mom is interrupted by the dings of a whole lot of phones. "Phones off," Mr. Montaña orders. But when he looks at his own phone, there's a look of panic on his face. He stands up. "I'll be right back. Mrs. Moshiri, why don't you tell the class what the items on the table represent until I'm back?"

My mom nods. She can tell everyone is distracted by something. Out in the hallway, doors swing open and closed. Teachers march out of classrooms into the hallway. "Every Nowruz, we create a Haft-Seen table," my mom explains hesitantly. "Haft means seven, and seen is the letter S. We choose seven items beginning with the letter S, each one symbolizing some element we want to bring into the new year with us. The mirror represents honesty. The candle is for enlightenment. The apple is for health."

"I don't get it," Cooper says. "Apples? Vinegar? Garlic? They don't start with the letter *S*."

My mom looks at me, then at Shawn, and then we all laugh.

"What's so funny?" Cooper says.

Emily rolls her eyes. "Cooper, seriously? The items start with the letter *S* in Farsi. Hello?"

Cooper comically slaps his head. "Okay, I'm an idiot. But also, I'm a little distracted. Like, are we all going to pretend that the world isn't ending?"

My mom finally looks at her phone. Then her eyes find mine, a familiar worry on her face. She's a master of barely hiding her anxiety. I pull my phone out too. I have a news alert. Los Angeles County just ordered the closure of all bars and gyms. Last week, we were told to avoid large gatherings. Clearly, things have gotten a lot worse.

Awkwardly, my mom keeps making her Nowruz presentation. "Some people will put a holy book on the table," she says. "A Quran or another holy scripture. Others will use a book of Persian poetry. Rumi or Hafiz or—"

She's interrupted by the ring of the school bell. Our principal's voice comes over the loudspeaker. "This is an emergency announcement. School will be shutting down at the end of the school day. We will send further instructions to your parents via email, but please don't leave anything in your lockers. Stay safe, everyone."

Shawn and I turn to each other, our eyes panicked. I know he's thinking the same thing I am. How will we figure out a way to spend our days together if we're not at school?

No one stays at their desk after the announcement. A chaotic force sweeps over the class. From the hallway comes the sound of students firing questions at any teacher they can find. How long will school be closed for? What about the spring musical? And next week's basketball games? Everyone has something they've been working on, rehearsing for, looking forward to.

I had something I was working toward too: finally convincing my mom to let me bring Shawn to Khaleh Goli's Chaharshanbeh Suri party on Wednesday, or to the big Nowruz party on Thursday, which will probably both be canceled now.

"We are not canceling Nowruz!" Khaleh Goli insists, her feline voice coming from the speaker of my mom's phone. "I'm so over cancel culture. It's destroying the world." Yes, she voted for the current president and still loves him, even as he tried to ban her own friends and mother from entering the country. Most of her Tehrangeles friends also voted for him. I think they only care about their taxes. My mom thinks they may be genetically predisposed to authoritarianism. It's probably a bit of both.

From my bedroom, I can hear my mom trying to stay calm. "That's not what cancel culture is," she tells her sister in Persian.

"I don't need you to educate me," Goli snaps. "I need you to pick up food for the Chaharshanbeh Suri party. Our caterer quit, and you have contacts in the restaurant business."

My mom laughs. "I *was* a waitress. Now I deliver burritos. I have no *contacts*, just sore feet."

Shawn is lying next to me on my bed, doom-scrolling through social media. He takes a break to ask, "What are they saying?"

"My aunt is refusing to cancel her parties," I explain.

"Did you ask your mom if I could come to one of them?" he asks.

I feel myself tense. "Yeah, I mean, it didn't go well, and now . . . with school shut down . . . I mean, would your parents even let you go to a party?" I feel guilty for trying to shift the blame to his parents, when the problem is clearly my family.

He shrugs. "I don't know. Maybe. This is all happening so fast."

"How long do you think school will be closed?" I ask. "Weeks?"

"Hopefully less than that," he says. "Is your grandmother still in Iran? I hear it's really bad there."

"She's in Tucson visiting her brother," I say. "She lands the morning of Nowruz."

"If they don't shut down the airport by then," Shawn says.

"You think it's going to get that bad?" I gaze into his eyes. They don't have an answer. "You'll still come to Nowruz if they let you, right? I don't want to keep fighting my mom if your parents won't even let you come in the end."

He laughs. "You have to admit it's kind of funny that we've been trying to convince your mom to bring me to Nowruz for years, and in our last year of high school, this happens."

"We should definitely alert the CDC that this pandemic is happening just to keep you from meeting my extended family." I laugh too. What else can I do? "But you will come if she lets you, right?"

He nods. Then he asks a more important question. "Does this mean we can't kiss until it's over?"

I feel my heart sink. "I don't know . . . Is kissing how you get it?" I smile. "Or is kissing each other the medicine we need?"

His eyes brim with the same dread I feel. When we left school, the tree-lined Burbank streets felt different. Ominously empty. Panic in the air. I think about my grandmother flying in to see us for Nowruz on Thursday, and my whole body fills with anxiety. Sure, we all laugh about how cutthroat and harsh Maman can be, but we still love her. We still obsessively crave her approval. Even me. But what my mom doesn't understand is that I want Maman to approve of the real me, not some fake straight version I perform for her once a year as spring arrives.

My voice is haunted as I ask, "We'll still see each other, right? If this gets worse."

His eyes flutter. It feels like a gust of wind. Everything feels heightened. "I won't last a day without you," he says. He runs a hand through his hair, pulling it back and revealing the dark roots under the bleach.

We stare into each other's eyes for a few breaths. I move closer to kiss him, but before my lips reach his, my mom barges into the room. "Nader!" she yells out, shocked. It's not like she hasn't seen us kiss before. She hesitates but finally says, "Maybe don't kiss? Just in case that's how it's spread."

Shawn gets a ding on his phone before I can respond. "It's my mom," he says. "She wants me to pick up toilet paper on the way home. Apparently, people are hoarding it and she couldn't find any."

"I'll give you some," my mom offers. "I always stock up at Costco."

Shawn and I blow each other comic air kisses until my mom emerges with one of those mega-packs of toilet paper. "Ooh, ultrasoft," Shawn says. "You're spoiling us."

"It's the least I can do," my mom says. "Given that it's unlikely we'll be able to bring you to Nowruz this year."

"Is the party canceled?" I ask.

"You know she won't cancel unless she's forced to, but we have to be safe," my mom says. "I'm sorry, Shawn. But it might be for the best. And whenever Nader does tell my mother he's gay, you don't want to be in the room. She can be so harsh."

Shawn puts an arm around me. "But that's why I *have* to be in the room when it happens," he explains. "So I can give him the love and support he needs."

My mom's face softens. "He's so lucky to have you." I wonder if, like me, she's remembering how I came out to her just as we were entering Khaleh Goli's Nowruz party four years ago. It felt like perfect timing. Because she wouldn't be able to freak out in front of everyone. And because Nowruz is all about new beginnings. She took my hand in hers. Held it tight. Told me she loves and accepts me just as I am. And then begged me not to tell anyone else in the family. "We don't want to give your grandmother a heart attack and have her death on our conscience," she said. "Just do this for me." And I did. And I still do.

"Nader, we're late!" my mom yells on Wednesday evening. I throw on my one blazer. When I find her, she's already dressed for Khaleh Goli's Chaharshanbeh Suri party, in one of Khaleh Goli's hand-me-downs, of course. A part of me wants to suggest we should stay home to be extra safe, but we take family really seriously in our culture. Family is everything, and we don't bail on them. Family is so important that we have to hide who we are from them.

My mom races toward her sister's house, her stiletto on the accelerator. Those were also handed down from Goli. My mom works on her feet all day. She hates heels. But she knows the rules of her sister's home. No sneakers or jeans at parties.

I ring the bell of Goli and Hassan's Persian palace and wait a long, long time. My mom rings again. Finally, a light turns on and we can see their maid, Gloria, at the foot of the winding marble staircase. There's a lot of marble in their home. Also a lot of gold. And chandeliers. My mom and I live in Los Angeles. My aunt, uncle, and cousins live in Tehrangeles. It's a totally different place, a city within a city, with its own rules and customs. In Tehrangeles, unpleasantness is repressed, manners trump emotional honesty, and everyone is hiding something under their luxury fabrics. Tehrangeles has no borders. It exists on certain strips of Los Angeles' most exclusive zip codes and a few of its not-so-fancy ones. You will know you're in Tehrangeles by the scent of turmeric, cardamom, and rose water and by the fact that every woman above fifty has the same haircut and many of them have the same nose. The denizens of this fabulous universe vacation in the same spots and dine at the same hip restaurants, always looking for an opportunity to one-up each other as they exchange kisses. Everything in Tehrangeles is a competition: clothes, homes, cars, travel, but especially children.

"Where is everyone?" my mom asks when Gloria opens the heavy door.

Gloria sighs. "Your sister didn't tell you."

"Tell me what?" my mom asks.

"Tonight's party is canceled," Gloria announces.

"And tomorrow's Nowruz party?" I ask.

Gloria looks confused by how little we know. "Miss Goli didn't tell you anything?" she asks.

I watch as my mom's face sinks. "My God, is she sick?" she asks. "It's not one of the kids, is it? If it is, you shouldn't stay in this house. You could come with us, or—"

Gloria quickly says, "No, no, I'm sorry to worry you. They're all in Hawaii."

"Sorry, what?" I blurt out. "They're in . . . Hawaii?!"

My mom pulls out her phone and calls her sister on speaker.

Goli answers on the fifth ring. She was probably deciding whether to ghost us or not. "I'm so sorry," she quickly says. I can almost hear the ocean breeze wafting through the receiver. "It all happened so fast."

"What happened so fast?" my mom asks.

"School shut down, and a few of the parents put together a pod in Maui."

"A pod?" I echo. "What does that even mean?"

"This is serious," Goli says. "We made a spontaneous decision when Pearl's parents invited us to their compound in Maui until it all blows over. They've flown in two teachers, so our kids won't fall behind. I'm so sorry we forgot to tell you. I panicked. My hot yoga studio is closed. My hairdresser is closed. I didn't know what to do."

"What about Maman?" my mom asks. "She's still landing tomorrow. Did you tell her?"

"Can you explain it to her?" Goli pleads. "You're so much better at difficult conversations."

"Goli joon, your loco moco is getting cold," my uncle calls out from the same direction as the crashing waves.

"I have to go," Goli says. "Let's FaceTime tomorrow when you're with Maman."

"Yeah, sure," my mom says.

"We'll see you in a few weeks," Goli says. "This can't last long. Hang in there, you two. If you need anything, let us know, okay?"

Before we leave, Gloria gives us each one of the swag bags my aunt and uncle had already prepared for the party. When my mom and I get back into the car, we burst out laughing. "'My hot yoga studio is closed,'" I say, trying to imitate Goli but sounding more southern than Persian. "'I didn't know what to do.'"

We open our swag bags at home. Inside each bag, there's a

gorgeously packaged baggie of esfand, a rose-water-scented candle, a Starbucks gift card, and a beautifully illustrated copy of the *Shahnameh*. We light the candle and place it on the floor. On Chaharshanbeh Suri, the last Wednesday before Nowruz, we leap over fire. Usually for us, it's a bonfire in Khaleh Goli's backyard. This year, we leap over the swag bag candle and chant the traditional words, "My yellow is yours, your redness mine." It's about purification. About saying goodbye to the darkness of winter and welcoming the sunshine of spring. But it's also about letting the red of the fire heal the yellow of sickness. This year, as I leap over the candle in our apartment, I close my eyes and pray the chant works. That the whole world might be healthy again.

"*Nader, wake up!*" my mom yells on Thursday morning. "We have to go pick up your grandmother from the airport." She rips open my curtains in a dramatic swoop that lets in the California sunshine. "Hurry up, Maman hates lateness."

I roll myself out of bed and throw on whatever I was wearing the night before. I grab a cold brew from the fridge as I follow my mom into her car. She always changes when her mother is near. Her breathing becomes labored. Her stomach rumbles in anticipation. So does the car. It won't start. "What the hell?" She slaps the steering wheel. She tries again, but the old car just won't start. "I'll call an Uber," she says. "We'll deal with the car later. If car shops are even open." She gets on her phone and opens the Uber app. But there are no drivers near us. Same with Lyft. She calls a local cab company. It rings and rings.

"Mom . . ." I say gently. "Maybe I could call Shawn. His dad lets him drive his car."

"No." She shakes her head a little too aggressively.

"But you can't find an Uber or a cab," I argue. "And even if you miraculously do, think about it. Any cabdriver has been in their car with countless people who could be sick. It doesn't seem very safe. We've already been around Shawn. Shouldn't we limit the number of people we're exposed to right now?"

She turns to me slowly. "Okay. Call him." She sighs, defeated. "Please warn him about my mother. I don't want him judging me because of her."

Shawn drives us to the airport. We park on the curb and wave from the sidewalk when we see Maman Parvin. She has a plastic shield over her face. "Hi, Maman. How are you?" I ask.

"I'm fine," she answers curtly, as if asking how she's doing is an offensive question because of course, she's always fine. Better than fine. She's perfect. "Here, wear these." She hands us each a plastic shield. Including one for Shawn. She explains that her brother in Tucson gave them to her. My mom and I put our shields on. "Can you tell the driver to wear it?" she asks us.

But Shawn doesn't need to be asked. He gets the social cue and puts the shield on. We're all speaking through a plastic barrier now. "It's nice to meet you," Shawn says to Maman. He bows. I'm not sure why. Maybe because we're not supposed to shake hands or hug anymore. Maybe because he correctly assumes my grandmother likes to be treated like royalty.

Maman rolls her suitcase at Shawn. It crashes into him. "Please tell the driver not to talk too much," she says to my mom in Persian. "I hate taxi drivers who talk, talk, talk. All the cabdrivers in America always think they're my best friend because we come from the same region of the world. But this one isn't, thank God."

"What's she saying?" Shawn asks me.

"Nothing important," I say.

Shawn drives us home. My mom and Maman sit in the back seat. I sit in the front. Shawn plays Spotify's "This Is Googoosh" playlist on the way home. From the back seat, I can hear Maman ask why an American cabdriver is listening to Googoosh. "He's not one of those light-skinned Iranians, is he?" she asks. "Can he understand me? I hate not being able to speak behind Americans' backs. The only good thing about Americans is that they don't understand us."

"I think he's trying to make you feel at home," I explain in Persian. "Because he's not just a driver, he's also—"

"Tell him to switch to the radio," Maman says. "I don't even like Googoosh since she made that disgusting video about lesbians."

I can see my mom's eyes through the rearview mirror. They offer me both steel and sympathy. I turn the music off and switch to the radio, which informs us that the governor has issued a statewide stay-at-home order. Of course, the world is ending on Nowruz.

When we get home, Shawn pops open the trunk and carries the suitcase inside. "Why is the driver coming into the house?" she asks. But she doesn't wait for an answer. Instead, she asks, "Where is the Haft-Seen?" as she moves her eyes across the living room.

My mom shrugs. "We thought we'd be spending Nowruz at Goli's before she went to Hawaii, so we don't have a Haft-Seen this year." Or any year.

"What kind of Iranian doesn't have a Haft-Seen? Don't you grow your own sprouts in preparation?" Maman asks dismissively. "How will your son learn our traditions?" Maman looks at me with a unique blend of scorn and pity. Then she grabs her suitcase and announces, "I need a nap. I really wish you had a guest room. I hate sleeping in your bed, Vida. Perhaps if you had chosen a better husband or a more viable career, you would have a guest room like your sister."

"My sister has six guest rooms," my mom jokes.

"Too many, but better than none" is the last thing Maman says before leaving us.

When we hear the click of the door closing, we breathe a sigh of relief. "I'm so sorry," my mom says to Shawn. "She had a very hard childhood. Not that it's an excuse."

"Is there something I can do to help?" Shawn asks.

"Can you whip up a Haft-Seen table for us during her nap?" my mom asks with a laugh.

Shawn thinks for a moment. "Well, stores are closed so I can't go scour the city for sumac or sabzeh," he says with a smile, proud of himself for remembering the Persian word for sprouts. "But . . . well, aren't traditions meant to evolve?" he asks.

"Not Persian ones," I say.

"But like . . ." Shawn thinks. "What if we just . . . found other objects that start with the letter *S*. It's better than nothing, right?" Shawn digs into his vest pocket, where he always keeps a little candy. "Skittles!" he yells triumphantly, holding up a small bag of candy.

I laugh. "That's an English *S*."

"Oh really." Shawn raises an eyebrow. "And how exactly do you say Skittles in Persian?"

Putting on a thick accent, I say, "Skee-tehls."

"Still an *S*," he says as he throws the candy on our small dining room table.

My mom grabs a framed photo of the two of us at a lookout point on Mulholland after a rainstorm, a shockingly clear Los Angeles skyline behind us. "A selfie!" she yells out, placing it on the table.

"Which in Persian is an eh-sehl-fee," I joke.

The mood turns giddy as we scour the apartment for anything that might start with an *S* in both languages. Items that defy language. I open the fridge and pull out some supermarket sushi. "Does supermarket sushi count as a double *S*?" I ask.

"Definitely," my mom says, just as Shawn says, "One hundred percent."

I put the sushi on the table. The three of us run around like whirling dervishes. Shawn snatches my mom's dog-eared copy of *Sense and Sensibility*, another double *S*. I run to my room to grab the photo of Beyoncé and Solange that's taped to my wall. I cut Bey out and put Solange on the table. My mom finds a plastic-wrapped hunk of salami in the bottom of the fridge. "Sah-lah-mee," she declares. Then she fingers through her small vinyl collection, an eclectic assortment of international music that says more about her than anything else we own. She carefully pulls out *Dónde Están los Ladrones?* "Shah-kee-rah!" she yells out triumphantly.

"Oh wait," I say. "I thought that words that start with *sh* wouldn't count because in the Persian alphabet, *sh* is its own letter, right?"

"Technically true," my mom says. "But I think we can bend the rules for the one and only Shakira-Shakira." My mom's voice is bright. This is who she is at her best. Playful. Spontaneous. Fun. "And also, the ancient Zoroastrian tradition was a Haft-Sheen, not a Haft-Seen table," she explains.

"Wait, really?" I ask.

"I bet Emily knew that," Shawn cracks. "And is really pissed she didn't get to show off that knowledge in class."

"It's true," my mom says. "It was sharab, which means wine, of course. Shir, which means milk. Sham, which means—"

"Shawn!" I blurt out giddily. I pull out my thin wallet and grab the Instax photo of Shawn I keep crumpled up in there. "We can put Shawn on the table."

"You keep a photo of me in your wallet?" he asks, moved.

"I do." I place the photo on the table. Lean it against the salami.

My mom's eyes go from giddy to concerned. I know what she's thinking. That Shawn can't still be here when Maman wakes up. And that his photo can't be here either. But before she can verbalize her concern, Maman's voice rings out from behind us. "Why is the driver still here?" she asks. "And why is there a picture of him on the table?"

There's a long, awkward silence. Finally, my mom exhales and speaks. "Because he's not a driver," she says. "His name is Shawn and he's . . ." I'm afraid she's going to come up with some elaborate lie. But instead, she turns to me and says, "You know what? This is your moment. Tell her."

I breathe in my mother's surprising defiance. I turn to Shawn and breathe in his love. And then I turn to Maman. "I'm gay, Maman," I say in English, because she can comprehend the language perfectly well and I want Shawn to understand me too. "And this is my boyfriend. He's not a driver. Or maybe he's *my* driver. He's driven me to be a better person. To love myself. And to—"

Maman waves her hand in the air. "It's just a phase," she says in Persian. "You'll get over it, like a flu. But you . . ." She turns to my mother now. "I hope you're not encouraging this. You're most likely to blame, of course. Boys who are too close to their mothers always end up confused."

"He's not confused," my mother says in English. "And neither am I. I love my son and I won't let anyone hurt him in my home, not even you. If you plan on saying one more cruel word, you can book

83

yourself a hotel since your preferred daughter deserted you. What'll it be, Mother?"

I turn to my mom, impressed. Shawn approaches me and places a hand around my waist. I clutch him tight. Watch as Maman works to hide her disapproval. Perhaps even her disgust. But she has nowhere to go, and so she simply says, "I brought some barbary bread from Tehran. It's in my suitcase. I'll go get it." Then, in her accented English, she asks Shawn, "Have you ever tasted barbary bread?"

Shawn, confused, answers, "I don't think so."

With that, Maman disappears. My mom puts a hand on my cheek. "She'll have more to say later," she warns me.

"I don't care," I say. "At least it's not a secret anymore."

"An *S* word," Shawn says.

I smile. "Maybe every year, we can write a secret on a note card and put it on the Nowruz table. Like, if there's anything we've been holding in all year, we know Nowruz is a safe day to reveal it."

"I like it." My mom's face glows with pride. "A new tradition."

"A new version of an ancient tradition," I say.

From the bedroom comes the sound of Maman's voice. Screaming in Persian at her preferred daughter. "How dare you desert me like this?" Maman bellows. "This is a disaster. If you hadn't disappeared to Hawaii, none of this would have happened."

"What are they saying?" Shawn asks.

I smile. "She's taking it all out on my aunt."

"As she should," my mom says, laughing giddily. "I'm sorry, it's not funny." She covers her mouth to stop herself.

"Don't be sorry," I say. "Laughing and crying are the only acceptable responses to whatever's happening."

"But I am sorry." There's an aching sincerity in her voice. "I shouldn't have stopped you from telling her. We should've gotten this over with years ago."

From the bedroom, Maman screams, "What about your kids, Goli? Are any of them gay? Just tell me now and make this the worst Nowruz ever."

I join my mom in laughter now. Maybe the tears will come later when I process it all. Or maybe they won't. Because I already know that this will always be my best Nowruz ever.

EID—1 SHAWWAL

Without a Plan

BY KARUNA RIAZI

Knowing whether or not a date is the perfect date is just one of my talents.

No, I don't mean the fruit, though I do have a few opinions on those as well. (Let's be honest here: Medjools are totally overrated. Not satisfied with a normal, not weirdly plush and overly sweet date and want something sweeter? Get a Medina date, smear some almond butter on it, and dip it in melted chocolate. You're welcome.)

And before the great auntie community that is, was, and always will start wagging their tongues and fingers admonishingly—I don't mean romantic dates, either. At least not outside my head, where they can be as ridiculous and elaborate and improbably starring my favorite K-pop star, who is inexplicably Muslim, in the Mafia, and bound to me in a weird contract marriage decided on by our grandfathers to end a family feud, as they want to be. (Yes, I read a little too much Y/N fanfiction on Wattpad. It's not a crime, is it?)

No, my obsession is with setting up the perfect day, starting from the actual calendar *date* it falls on and moving on to every single gorgeous detail, no matter how small. Give me the time frame you need me to work within and a set of aesthetic highlighters, and I can make it all align: perfect vibes, perfect weather, perfect moment.

I'm very good at figuring out how to make things fall into place for other people. I'm an excellent errand girl. I don't mind distracting the babies that tug at my lehenga during wedding receptions, if it keeps them away from the bride during the perfect photo op. I'm who friends turn to instead of apps to know what the weather will be several days in advance, where the graduation party should be held for the best vibes, and how to get stubborn bangles off a wrist at the end of the night.

But when it comes to making things align just right for myself? The gift flounders. Like a spark against an ill wind, it gutters out without so much as a protest. My planner magically eats my homework reminders, and I'm always scheduling appointments on days doomed to disaster both likely and incredible. The one time our dryer broke and we had to old-school clothesline our laundry out the window, it was the day before the PSAT and the outfit I was going to wear was in that load. And then it started raining right when everyone else's clothes were in and mine were out.

It's not even fair at this point—and considering that I'm recovering from white-knuckling the armrests of a battered Airbus while massive turbulence greets my arrival into White Horse, Pennsylvania, my luck is only getting worse instead of better.

"You okay, honey?" a kindly woman asks me from a safe distance. I don't blame her. I didn't throw up as I thought I would when I stumbled off the plane, but it was a close call. She anxiously spins a greeting sign between her fingers as I lift my head wearily from my hands. "Do you need me to call anyone?"

"N-no, thank you. I think I'm good now."

I'm still wobbly, though, and glad I didn't pack a full-size suitcase for this misadventure, since the bag carousel—close enough in this dinky little airport that I can see it—is already swarmed with everyone who was on the same flight.

Is White Horse this much of an attraction?

So far, I can't see anything worth the excitement in coin vending machines, a closed airport convenience store, and nothing outside the large bay windows but a concrete parking lot.

There has to be something charming about it, though. After all, this was where my grandmother unexpectedly spent three years, going from an artist-in-residence in what my father hand-waved as some "experimental commune for retiring hippies" to buying the hosting property from its former owners and running the residencies herself.

Not for the first time, I feel a twinge of guilt. She always wanted me to come out to White Horse and see what she loved about it, when she had the energy and the strength to show me around. Maybe, with her eyes guiding me, I would have been able to see some magic waiting in the lackluster gray terminal.

But now she was back in Boston in a rehabilitation center and was probably moving to assisted living after that.

And I was here, doing my parents a favor "since it's not like you're doing anything else with your gap year" (per my mother, the sharpshooter who never fails to hit the target for emotional damage), and packing my grandmother's things up to make the transition a little easier.

And I'll be honest, again. My mother is right.

It wasn't like I *was* doing anything with my gap year, except making things fall into place for people I loved, and standing in the back as the photos were taken and the smiles were wide and bright, wondering why I couldn't snap my fingers and make my life make as much sense the way that my sister could so easily find her soulmate while backpacking across Asia, or my cousin seemed to be thriving in a film MFA program where she made soulful documentaries about her childhood cats.

And then, if I told any of these people I didn't know what I was doing, either they felt the same way my mom did—that I wasn't applying myself—or they would ask me why the party thing couldn't go further.

Like I didn't wonder that myself. If this was supposed to be what I was doing the rest of my life: making fun occasions happen for people who actually seemed to be doing cool things.

It takes me a moment to realize that the kind, older lady from earlier didn't peel off with the other few passengers in tow. She stands behind me as I fumble with my cell phone, trying to find the contact information for Grandma's friend—"Chef Anna," she said. No last name, no further details beyond a phone number.

Great.

"It looks like you're waiting for someone," she prompts when I finally look up to give her a nervous smile. "Maybe I can help. Everyone knows everyone around these parts."

"Oh, um, well, my grandma used to live here. I'm trying to get in touch with her friend, Chef . . ."

"Chef Anna?" The woman's face creases into a welcoming smile. "Well, now that's just perfect. I was wondering if you were who I was waiting for. It's me, honey. I'm Chef Anna."

"You? Chef Anna? But . . ."

My voice trails off. I don't want to admit that my dad's constant refrain of "retiring hippies" has gotten to me and I was expecting a much more colorful individual to be charged with collecting me.

My grandma has always rocked a dyed Afro, large hoop earrings, psychedelically patterned wide-leg pants, and scarf-belts tied at the waist in a style that can only be described as a yoga instructor who definitely misses the seventies.

Chef Anna, on the other hand, looks like she would be comfortable passing hors d'oeuvres at some swanky gala at an art gallery. Now that I'm actually looking at her closely, all the signs are there: elegant, graying updo, color-coordinated blouse and slacks, and . . . is that a pearl necklace?

It is. And not one off the Macy's jewelry sales rack, either.

I snap my mouth shut, not sure what else to say, but Chef Anna just chuckles. "Oh, it's okay, dear. I guess I'm not what you expected. But I'm glad you are exactly what I was hoping would walk off the plane. Goodness, you're the spitting image of your grandmother!"

Really?

I assess myself: wrinkled tunic, jeans stained with the water I'd asked for on the plane and promptly spilled on myself, hijab loosening from its neat folds.

I was pretty sure Grandma never had looked so disorderly in her life, but . . .

"Thank you," I manage.

"Do you have anything else besides that backpack?"

"No. It felt better to travel light." Especially considering everything unseen I was currently carting around with me, from my internal nerves about being here to Mom's parting words at the airport: *Try to look into how long your deferral period is for Mountmarie College on the plane, sweetie. I know you don't feel ready, but sometimes you just need to dive headfirst and make a change. The change of scenery may help with that.*

I wasn't so sure, particularly since—as Chef Anna ("Just Anna is fine, sweetie") ushered me out of the terminal and into the parking lot, air glossy with heat and exhaust, and I craned my head to figure out what time it was—I couldn't see a single clock in sight.

"Um, what time is it?"

She turns and blinks at me, as though I've asked her something in Simlish.

"What, hon?"

"What time is it? I haven't checked . . . I'm sorry, I was trying to plan out what I should do first and—"

"It's midafternoon," she interrupts gently.

"But what time, exactly?"

"Does it matter?"

Matter?

It matters more than anything. But at my incredulous look, she continues.

"At least, here. I know it feels like there's so much you need to do, and such little time to do it—and in a lot of ways, that's true. But the Barn runs differently. White Horse runs differently. While you're here, take the time to experience things as they happen, not *when* you think they should happen. It might give you some of the answers to questions you have about what you might like to do, and how you should go about doing it."

I can only stare at her. Do I look like I'm having some sort of ridiculously early midlife crisis? Is it written all over my face for more people than my mom to detect?

As if reading my mind again, she chuckles. "No, I'm not psychic, if that's what you're wondering. Everyone who finds their way here is searching for something. And believe me, they usually leave . . . well, not with all their answers, but at least a sense of what they need to do in order to find them."

I mull this over as I'm steered through the parking lot toward what is—surprisingly—a battered dark blue pickup. I was really expecting something equivalent to my equally dreamy friend Nahla's car, a serene teal Bug with Coexist stickers on the bumper and a lingering smell of incense.

It smells of the last exhale of a nearly burnt incense stick and spilled pumpkin spice latte, and I love it instantly. It feels like one of those perfect moments when something special should be happening, and even though . . . just Anna . . . and her admonitions about experiencing things as they happen are ringing in my ears, I can't help but wish I had something, anything, to fall into place at this moment.

And then, as we're clearing the road from the airport and merging onto another toward an exit that reads, "White Horse, Propolis, South Riverbanks" (all names of locations that sound like I should expect to see wandering Hobbits through my window, grazing on handheld cheese slabs and crumbly bread as they meander by), it happens.

Or rather, *he* happens.

It's a boy, standing on the side of the road.

Of course it's a boy, when I'm in the middle of a Hallmark movie montage made up of my own uncertainty, my fingers itching for a phone to scroll through and ask any of my friends if they have a proposal or important announcement to make against the golden skies and gauzy clouds of White Horse, Propolis, or South Riverbanks—or better yet, all three—and Anna's distantly playing a Fleetwood Mac CD.

"Dreams," and he's a dream.

Tall, black hair drifting back on the breeze like corn silk off the fields the plane angled over during descent.

Strong arms, the type of arms you want a guy to have during a meet-cute when you stumble over his feet at a coffee shop.

Not much else to make out from a passing car, except for the fact that his pants are rolled up to the shins and his head is turned upward to the sky.

Watching a kite, I slowly realize, and then, there's more than one.

Just one, in his outstretched hand, trembling on the breeze like a full-winged butterfly, but there are others around him.

I see all that, inexplicably, in a brief flash. He's there, and then we're whipping past. And my heart is in my mouth, trying to get a second glance when the opportunity's already gone.

"Ah, a kite festival," Anna muses next to me. "It's definitely a nice afternoon for it."

I look at her. "A kite festival? So there's more than one?"

"Festival days can be any day you want them to be, and there's no rule that says you can't have more than one of the same," she assures me. "We do try to have an officially scheduled kite festival near the end of the month, but . . . some things just can't be scheduled. A good wind and clear skies are one of them."

That's true, but . . . I can't help but rub my palms together. Spontaneity has never been a good thing for me, or to me. The best-laid plans are what come together well—or at least, that's how it's always felt, so I've always done it that way.

That's how it should be, right?

Of course, in White Horse, away from parental expectations and friends hitting milestones you only just realized you were hurtling past, they had the luxury of impulsive festival days and kite festivals.

I didn't have that luxury. Or at least, I thought I didn't. My lack of college plans might beg to differ. Just the thought of them made my gut twinge. And then, Anna tosses another shocker at me.

"Well, to be fair, though some things can't be scheduled, others should be on time. That's why I was so glad to hear you were coming. I hear you're good at that, too."

Wait . . . what?

"Good at that, too?" I voice aloud.

"Like grandmother, like granddaughter, right?" Anna winks at me as she makes a turn. "Your grandma was quite the event planner here, though she always told me it was nothing like the miracles you could make happen. She would align a great deal of local events with the Barn's residencies. It was part of the draw for people: Guest artists would find a niche and an audience to perform to or display their work to, and the local community would gather and enjoy a good evening out."

I absorb this for a moment. It's not like I expected that my gift came from nowhere, but I feel a little cheated and stunned that Grandma never took credit for this being shared between us. Why hadn't she ever said anything?

"She probably wanted to let you shine," Anna says, reading my mind. Again. "Don't take it to heart. Most grandmothers like it when their granddaughters get the lion's share of attention, and they can just stand back and be proud. In any case, it's a good thing that you've got the same knack with it she did."

"Oh?"

"You have a special month coming up in the winter, right? Ramadan?"

I nod, not sure why this confident knowledge of Islamic holidays surprises me. After all, Grandma and Anna were collaborators for years, and if they ran events together, knowing to schedule around the moon as much as the sun's waking hours probably was important enough to pick up quick.

"Yeah, we do. Why?"

"Well," Anna says slowly. Carefully. Easing me into something as much as one of my cousins trying to spring a "last minute, totally low-key" function on me.

My stomach lurches.

"Every year—well, at least, since your grandma arrived in town—we've always held an iftar on one of the nights projected to be Laylatul Qadr. Well, you know, iftars happen every night—because everyone breaks their daily fast every night—but this one always tends to be a bigger one for that reason, and if anyone's missed the usual communal dinners, they have this one to look forward to most. We call it our Harvest Eid Festival, since Ramadan's been in the fall up until now, even though it's not quite Eid, and not quite the full harvest season yet. Really a marketing draw more than anything, and an excuse to break out the tractor and get some kids fired up for a ride through the fields."

Laylatul Qadr, the Night of Power. Anna really wasn't pulling from the basic Wikipedia Ramadan know-how here, another sign of how close she and my grandmother were. Laylatul Qadr was the most sacred night of Ramadan, being the night on which the holy Quran was revealed.

At home, that was the night where—even if their family hadn't had time to attend all the taraweehs at the masjid, long prayers in which, over the month, the imam recited the entirety of the Quran—they would make the effort to attend prayers and participate in the additional supplications and hopefully blessings that would be shared.

95

That was why the Harvest Eid Festival oxymoron was weird, but it wasn't the only thing bothering me.

"Wait, but the whole thing about Laylatul Qadr is that we don't know what night it is."

"I know," Anna allows. "That's why we aim for one of the odd-numbered nights and hope for the best—usually the second to last, because our Muslim community here is small but still takes pride in holding their nightly taraweeh prayers, and the last odd night is usually the most crowded."

There's a charming twang to the way she says "taraweeh," but I can't fully enjoy it. I'm too stuck on the fact that if Grandma always ran this event . . .

"So . . . you want me to arrange it? I mean, I don't think I'm going to be here that long . . . and besides, I don't think I've ever planned anything on that scale. In any case, Eid will be in the winter now. Why are you having it so early?"

A half-truth.

Of course, I've semi been responsible for community iftars, though my aunts were at the helm of the ship. My expertise was usually relegated to correspondence with the imam to ensure our names were pinned to the appropriate night, and then carting our supplies down to the masjid basement, rolling up my sleeves, and dragging spoons through trays of white rice and numerous spiced bhortas and curries while neighbors and friends stood in line for their meals after the Maghrib prayer so that everyone could have dinner before the call for taraweeh. My feet always ached at the end of the night, and so did my cheeks from smiling and nodding at community elders as they asked if that was Mom's special curry, and I never ate on time because of serving duties, but it did always feel worth it.

But that was different in a way. All my events were different. Even if the hosts thanked me profusely, referred me to their friends and family, who would ask me to pull strings behind the scenes to make everything fall into place just right for their own shindigs and celebrations, the credit ultimately rested with whoever first dreamed up the event.

And that was fine with me. I didn't have to take credit for all the big decisions.

And that was probably why I had such trouble with my own.

Having to take over something that Grandma was apparently amazing at, and be so visibly, obviously, trying my own hand at it?

I couldn't.

I wouldn't.

Anna seems to read my expressions. She smiles, eyes crinkling at the corners.

"You don't have to say yes, or think about it too hard right now," she says as she pulls up to the weathered old cottage on the far end of the property that I recognize from the pictures Grandma would attach to her emails. She puts the truck in park but doesn't toss her door open yet.

"We're having it earlier than usual as more of a . . . welcome Ramadan event, something like . . . Christmas in July, let's say. Some members of the community are snowbirds and won't stick around once the first frost happens. It'll be nice to let them get some pre-celebrations in; our local vendors can sell decorations and people can connect. Just think about it. You don't have to say yes right this minute. Now, let's get you settled in."

Think about it.

Thinking and I are not the best of friends—not to say I don't think at all, but I've never been a girl who likes to spend too much time in her head mulling over stuff and poking it from every direction. There's too much in there that's heavy and unpleasant and hard to hold for too long.

My approach to thinking? Kick it in the corner with the other junk and poke at it gingerly every few days, the way I've seen my mom approach a medical bill: take it out of its envelope, wince, shove it back in with a loud, discontented crunch. *That'll keep for another day. Payday's Friday, anyway. Nothing I can do with it today.* Ironic that she calls me out on avoidance while modeling it so well herself.

Grandma's cottage is a good place to not think about things, too. It's fun-sized and charming, with a bright sunflower theme and a little herb garden on the kitchen sill I've been having fun harvesting from every morning to make tea.

I see why she stayed here and made a home here.

I wish I could think of a way to feel as confident in my next steps.

So when Anna gives me a flyer announcing the Harvest Eid Festival, I take it out to the communal event board next to the small store that acts as post office, general store, and deli, and I tack it up— just to try to feel like I'm doing something with myself.

I think about it as I pack up boxes and fight down odd flurries of emotion upon seeing pictures of Grandma at every single festival this town offers—which, apparently are a lot—grin wide, dimples deep.

(Why had it always been so hard to answer her invitations to come out and join her here?)

I think about it as Mr. Dream Boy—whose name, as it turns out, is Khalid (not that I ask him, his mom just volunteers the information with a knowing smile as I somehow get roped into shelling peas at their kitchen table and holding a cousin on one hip—the Desi older cousin in me falling into line at this hint of familiarity)—always happens to be around when I need to figure out something like the old hose at the back of the house or why my mailbox won't seem to open when I need it to.

"Thank you," I manage without flushing as a little elbow grease (and his fist landing hard on the side) solves the issue.

He doesn't smile. Doesn't even smirk. Just cocks his head and fixes those intense, warm eyes on me in a way that makes me feel the ridiculous urge to giggle into my dupatta like a Bollywood heroine.

(Eww. But also, wow.)

Like all he's thinking about is me. And trying to figure out what I'm thinking about, too.

And then he ruins it by saying, "Heard you're lining up the Harvest Eid Festival this year. I'm not usually big on hanging around—Mom tries to rope me into babysitting—but if you've got some new ideas, I'm eager to see them. Here, let's exchange numbers."

"I . . ." But before I can say anything, he's slipped out his phone from his pocket. I numbly pick the right numbers to put into his contacts. He gives me a sweet, friendly smile.

"It'll be nice to see what you plan to do."

"We'll see. I . . . I got some packing to do."

And then I run back into the house like a coward.

Of course I do. I can't talk properly with him. I can't talk properly with any of them. The residents—both those in town and those attending the most recent residency—are all so nice. So encouraging. So believing that I could actually pull this off.

And I know I can't.

I can't even get the words out to Mom—*I need more time, I'm really not sure what to do*—when I make the mistake every evening of exacerbating both my nerves and my homesickness by FaceTiming during iftar and being propped up against the napkin holder on the table so they can all call out their greetings and send their love while letting me soak up the distant chatter and laughter.

And then, a few days later, I get yelled at by the mayor.

Not yelling, really. It just feels that way. I happen to be walking past the bulletin board when his raised voice holds down my shoulder like an extended hand.

"Any updates on that?"

I turn. He's supposed to be addressing the owner, but they're both looking at me.

"The state rep comes out for that every year, you know," he says to the owner, but really to me. "He called last night. Wondered where his invite was. I told him we're still working things out. I hope I was telling him the truth."

"I . . ." My tongue feels heavy in my mouth.

"I'm sure we'll have news for him in a day or two," the owner says to him, but actually to me. "I'm sure it's being worked on."

There are other people pausing nearby—or maybe they are fumbling with bags that need to be adjusted, or maybe they are just actually continuing their walk past. But it feels like they are all looking at me and realizing that I'm still sticking out like a sore thumb when they expected me to just fall in line.

I've been avoiding the iftars, I've been sitting in the last row on Jummah days and slipping out, I've been here but not really here the same way I am at home when I arrange the events and can just . . . duck out.

But here, everyone can see me and size me up to Grandma and

know I'm not enough, and suddenly I need to turn back and rush full tilt into the house, even though I just came outside.

I stand by the door, shoulders slumped, panting.

I'm not doing anything with my gap year except what I did before. Ramadan is supposed to purify your heart and give you direction through controlling your desires and not letting them control you, and giving to people rather than indulging yourself.

The nearness of Eid, after this long sacred month, should be filling me with joy and new hope.

But I don't feel either of those things. I feel just weary.

And wrong.

What am I doing *wrong*?

What am I that I feel so *wrong*?

And then, I hear the distant buzz. My phone, buried somewhere under my stack of laundry to resist the temptation to fidget with it when Khalid is nearby so he maybe asks me (in my most ridiculous dreams) for my baba's number so this routine of his not-smiling but just giving me those intense, warm eyes and my blushing and looking anywhere but his face can keep going for eternity.

Mom always has good timing, so of course it isn't her.

It's Grandma.

"How is it going, baby?"

She sounds so faded, like one of those vibrant pictures of her has been put through the wash accidentally after being forgotten in a back pocket.

I sink to the floor, fighting tears.

"I don't know how to do this without you."

"Oh, sweetheart. Isn't Anna helping? I hope the community is supporting you like I asked."

"They're being great. It's . . . it's just me. I don't know how to do this."

"That's normal, baby. That's how it is for everyone. Even me. You think I went out there and it was just so easy for me to make friends and knit that community together? Even I dropped a few stitches here and there, and goodness knows that mayor doesn't make it easy for a girl to feel good about herself if she doesn't format the flyer just right and remember to cc the state rep. Like our lives depend on his getting good publicity off our backs."

That gets a damp laugh out of me, and she chuckles knowingly.

"If he's been saying anything, ignore him. The state rep will come no matter what night it is. He won't miss it. And you won't miss it, either. You always hit the mark with your plans. Just give yourself time and space, the way you do when it's meant for anyone else. You've always been so good at setting boundaries with everyone but yourself."

I think about that for a moment as she sighs, and I can hear her shifting and making herself comfortable in her armchair.

She's actually right. Maybe my thinking isn't so much protective, as I've always thought, as it is antagonistic to myself. I would build up the pile I was trying to ignore, then drag myself over it and practically rub my nose in it to shame myself for building it up in the first place.

I didn't give myself space.

I didn't give myself grace.

I just expected it to feel right and blamed myself when it didn't.

"Thanks, Grandma," I whisper. It didn't fix everything. But maybe I should stop myself from expecting a good eye for dates and some interior designer skills to do that for me.

Maybe I just need to let myself be.

102

"I'm always here when you need me," she hums. "But I think you've got it from here."

"How can I be so sure?"

I don't need to see her face to feel the warmth of her smile seeping through. "Why would I doubt the hostess with the mostest, the event planner extraordinaire?"

The words sock me in the stomach. I don't think I've ever told her about my proud little slogans for myself.

But she just knew.

And she's right.

I do have it from here.

Even if it isn't everything it was in Grandma's pictures, the Harvest Eid Festival can and will happen.

I steel myself and dial Khalid's number.

He picks up on the second ring.

"Hey," he says breathlessly. "I mean, salaam. I mean . . . are you okay? I heard you had a run-in with the mayor. Whatever he said, don't mind him. He's resentful that even after your grandma moved away, no one considers him in charge of things here."

"No, I'm fine," I manage, and actually mean it. Well, mostly. "I just . . . think I'm ready to start planning. And I need some hands on deck to make this happen."

"Amazing." His voice is warm and excited. "What are we doing?"

Armed with the right date, a weather forecast (from Khalid's aunt, whose knee can predict a rain shower, since the apps don't work as well as they should out here), and some help from very kind community members, the Welcome Ramadan (Way in Advance) event manages to happen.

And it looks pretty darn good, if I do say so myself. I'm not sure who thought of the sparkly glitter snowflakes alongside hay bales and baskets of apples, but it works. Somehow.

The mayor mumbles something as he passes me about "forgetting the string lights on the tractor" that I try to ignore.

The food is rushed, the collective effort of a flock of aunties who give me tight smiles as they take foil away from hastily folded samosas and pilaf studded with peas. I've given myself grace for evading their gossipy inquiries into my family and pastimes and school plans, and sat on the last row for prayers if I felt like it and timidly moved up if I didn't.

I'm breathing through it. I'm letting myself mull over things, without shaming myself for choosing to move something to the next day.

I'm letting plans fall into place as time passes. And I've been able to have a call with Mom and work on a spreadsheet with her for the next application cycle.

"I'm proud of you for facing this," she tells me. "I don't want you to do this when you don't feel like it. I just want to make sure you don't let it pass you by entirely. You have good timing. I trust that your timing will be right. When you're ready."

I'm trusting in my timing, too, to step out and thank someone for coming, to step back when the state rep is approaching the table after greeting him and let the mayor do his thing.

I spend some time snuggled up to Anna, her arm around my shoulders like the surrogate grandma figure I need while everyone else is strolling by with family, and she draws me into her quilting bee group (I didn't even know those still existed) while they chatter and discuss patterns and look at Etsy on dated phones.

And when Khalid and his siblings beckon me over with loud calls (theirs) and a tilted chin (his) to hop on the hayride, and I tilt my head back and break my fast with a date as the adhan drifts over my head, and stare up at the crescent moon as it shines as brightly as the smiles around me and the scrubbed-clean floors and walls of the cottage I'm starting to make a little more my own as much as Grandma's, I do.

Knowing whether or not I'm making the right move is kind of my thing.

And I think I am.

Elijah's Coming to Dinner

BY NATASHA DÍAZ

Passover seders are living time capsules. We may get older, our uncles get balder, my Great-Aunt Bea gets feistier, but this night, every year, has always been the same. On Passover, we gather at my grandmothers' house and sit banquet style at the giant table to read through the Haggadah, the guide of blessings that weave the tale of our ancestors' quest for liberation. Then, two-thirds of the way through the story, almost as if God knew we would all regress to our toddler forms and throw a hunger tantrum at this very point in the story, the Haggadah tells us to pause our readings and eat dinner in abundance. I finish the last bits of brisket on my plate and glance at the clipboard in my lap before looking at the clock on the wall. We're right on schedule, and yet something feels off.

On Passover, we tell the same jokes, we listen to the same stories, we watch Nana and Savta get tipsier on kosher wine and their pride that they made this beautiful rainbow of a family. The point is, seders never change, at least they didn't until two years ago. When Covid hit, we had our seders virtually, and even though Savta belted the blessings like she was still on Broadway and my dad fell asleep with his head leaning against the closest flat surface halfway through the Haggadah, and even though each home had identical seder plates, Passover just didn't hit the way it does when we get together in person. Even with our mics on so the mouth sounds were amplified as if we were chewing right beside one another, we still felt so far apart. But now, after a few years of waiting, we finally are back in one room again, which is why I have taken it upon myself to make sure tonight goes back to *exactly* how it is supposed to.

Spoons and forks clang against the bowls and plates as they scoop up the remains of roast chicken and potatoes and kugel and brisket amid side convos and bites and sips. I check my clipboard again; dinner will be wrapping up shortly, which means it is almost time for me to walk straight into my own disaster. Because after dinner, the Haggadah says we welcome the spirit of Elijah the prophet to join our celebration and that the youngest at the table is the one who opens the door. In this house, that happens to be me, which means every year on this blessed day, somewhere between the seder table and the front door, my cousins prank me into oblivion.

The Cohen cousin prank war is a multigenerational rite of passage. Our parents and aunts and uncles did it to one another and passed the torch to my cousins and me to do the same. I mean, the great fridge smoothie of five years ago ruined Muenster cheese for me forever. I've been frosted-and-feathered on the way to the door and then syrup-and-sprinkled on the way back. Love it or hate it, it's a Cohen thing. Normally, at this point in the night, I would have sweated through my cardigan at least twice, anxiously dreading what may befall me, but tonight I'm fresh and clean because so far, no one has even bothered to tease me. In fact, they have barely looked in my direction.

Sorry, but no. Not acceptable.

Covid took enough from me, so if they think I am going to give up the fight to outsmart them when I have had to give up the last few years, sitting alone in my room—they are very wrong. Aviva Cohen is back at the seder table, and I came ready. A snore ripples out of my dad's nostril from where he has, on brand, conked out against the chest full of fancy plates and cups no one is allowed to open under any circumstances. The interruption to my spiral is welcome. I can't lose my grip now.

"Ahem." I clear my throat.

My cough doesn't make Dad flinch, so I kick his foot underneath the table, inadvertently slamming my heel into my cousin Toby's toes beside me when I bring it back. Toby bangs his knees on the table, then slides back in his chair to hug his leg, snarls under his breath, and stomps away. My cousin Nadine's eyes flick toward me for one-eighth of a second before they windshield wiper back to her twin sister, Sage. This whole night, I've been waiting for the taunts and the burns and the warnings that always lead up to the big finale, but there have been none. Not a single threat, almost like they forgot.

"Aviva." Nadine says my name from across the table.

Finally, I turn to her, ready for whatever snark is heading my way. I may be stuffed to the brim, but my appetite for the playful jest of competition never wanes.

"Yes?" I try not to sound too desperate for the attention, but she ignores me.

"Um, hello?" I lean over the table and wave in her face.

Nadine gives me a glare that could make the brisket slice itself.

"Come on, Nadine, you just said my name. You said Aviva."

"No, I didn't."

"Yes, you did!"

The adults stop their banter and focus on our argument as Nadine rises from her seat to bend over the table toward me.

"I said, *Aunt Bea* is going to let me shop in her closet before I leave for Wes-le-yan."

Nadine draws the word out like we don't already know she is going to Wesleyan. None of us could forget it. She makes sure to say the word "Wesleyan" in every sentence she utters, including on the cousin WhatsApp group chat where they have all spent the last couple of years too wrapped up in their own social wins and academic achievements to acknowledge me, a mere high school freshman, as being worthy of the spotlight. My face is a hotter purple than the horseradish sitting in a pool of its own juices on the edge of my plate. I just heard what I wanted to.

Oh yeah? Cool, me? I'm doing great, thanks for asking, I say to myself.

The thing about being the youngest cousin is that no matter how old I get, I'm still the youngest. It was silly of me to think they may take me seriously one day; I'll always just be their baby cousin. But, well, I am not a baby anymore. I'm a fifteen-year-old who had to spend the last year of middle school and half of freshman year alone in our apartment while my parents were at work. It might have been nice for even one of my cousins to consider that maybe they should take their elder-cousin-hood seriously and guide a cuz through the coming-of-age pains. Like, I don't know, maybe if they saw me as more than a prank target, I could have asked for advice on how to survive high school—that would have been nice! Perhaps if anyone had thought to check on the baby in the last two years, let alone since the Kiddush at the beginning of the seder, they would know that things have been getting better. I'm figuring it out myself without their help, and I finally don't feel like my chest is a box filled with helium forcing my rib cage to float closer and closer to my skin every time I walk into a room of people. They might even know that their little cousin has been half kissed once by Martin Schoenfeld in the hallway outside the school dance by the purple lockers on senior row. If they ever asked about my social life or how I was doing, they would know it could have been a whole kiss with Martin, but he sneezed midway, and it was hard to come back from that. I hate to break it to them, but I got my braces off in the middle of a respiratory pandemic with a dentist who couldn't see what he was doing inside my mouth because his face visor kept fogging up every time he exhaled. I've been through things.

Savta whispers in my ear, "They are off their game. Don't lose your chance."

The reminder hangs outside my ear. She's right. I can't get distracted. I have a job to do.

Ahem.

Savta gives me a smile and whispers, "Are you ready?"

Each Passover, the adults bet on who will come out the winner in the prank war. Savta is the only one who puts her money on me without fail. And every Passover, she loses.

I nod at Savta. *I was born ready.*

Maybe it was silly to try to make things the same when I'm the one who has changed. I may still be the youngest, but over the last two years, I got smarter and faster. The one-woman rally in my head is enough to hype me up. I look around the table at my cousins Toby and Nadine and Sage and Jonathan, all of them going about their business, barely engaged. They want to act like I don't exist; well, maybe they will start to pay attention when for once I don't get got, because I am not going to make it easy or pleasant for them when I win.

"I'm ready," I say.

Savta hands over the dark blue glass goblet. "For Miriam."

We offer the water to Miriam the way she did when the Jewish people fled from Pharaoh. The story of Miriam, Moses's sister, like that of so many other prominent women, has in some retellings been whittled down, but in this house we do it right. We thank Miriam for her part in our quest for liberation. Nana and Savta share a peck once the cup has been filled to the top. Savta rises and I see the pain in her face.

"Let me, Mom—" My dad tries to offer her a break, but Savta shoots him down.

"Hush," Savta says, and limps to the kitchen to retrieve the other goblet, which she fills with some wine for Elijah's cup and places it beside Nana. My grandmas have been a couple for sixty-five years, but they only got married eight years ago when same-sex marriage was legalized. Savta looks at me with a wink and a nod. The time has come. The door has to be opened for us to welcome Elijah. I look back over to my right. Toby's gone, and across the table from me, my cousins Nadine and Sage and Jonathan are as well. Finally, things are falling into place like they are supposed to.

It's on.

I grab the go bag I packed to ensure success and throw it over my shoulder and rise to walk into the hallway. With each step toward the front door, I grasp the foghorn I packed as my first line of defense, ready to blow my cousins away, but I come up empty. This is the redemption story I will hear about for the rest of my days. Every speech, every post, every anecdote, until I die will fall back to this moment when Aviva finally dodged the bullet; even with my cousins' lackluster behavior I'm ready for my moment.

I tiptoe down the final hall of the bottom floor and to the stairs. My cousins have to be up at the top, there's nowhere else for them to hide. Halfway up the staircase, I run and jump up to the top.

"Gotcha!" I shout, poised like a bear on its rears, to no one. My finger loosens from where it has started to push down on the foghorn button.

The house is still, barely alive but for the distant clinking of glasses downstairs, where I'm sure everyone is starting to wager on how it's going up here. A shadow darkens the rectangular windows of stained glass on the other side of the front-door frame. They are outside, preparing to scare me when I open the door. How basic, unoriginal, and frankly sloppy. I'm offended. Where are the cousins who once used a voice-changer app to call me while I was walking to the front door and pretended to be a booking producer for *Tween Jeopardy*, which they recorded and played on TikTok and all other social media platforms they could tag me in? Where's the gusto? I get they are going to elite colleges and going to parties and finding themselves, but this is a tradition—we can't just forget about that.

Well, even if they have, I won't. I'm ready to win this thing. I march up and open the door to step out. The cone of the horn flies up in front of my face and the screech starts to slip out as I push the button on the foghorn down and throw my head back to give my best villain laugh.

"Ha!"

A set of footsteps backs away, but no cry or complaint or name-calling rains down on me. The silence falls over my pride and dulls the initial squeak of the horn. I lift my finger and pull my gaze to the bush to my left, where a figure appears.

"Hello?"

The voice is gentle and kind. I love my cousins, but none of them sound like that. Especially not Toby—he must have purchased one of those voice-changer apps again.

"Very funny!" I shout into the night, and lower the horn, but I don't put it away, not yet.

"Um, what is funny?" a young man close to my age asks as he steps back onto the porch. He stands just a few inches taller than me, with honey-brown skin like Nana and Aunt Bea and Daddy.

"You can come out now!" I shout to wherever my cousins are hiding, but he seems to be the only person out here with me. His eyes are trained on me as I turn in a circle, searching for my cousins. No one comes. The only sound is from a TV that floats out of an open window across the street. Otherwise, there isn't so much as a leaf willing to rustle. I drop down to my knees and try to spot them in the bushes from the railing.

"Who exactly are you talking to?" the stranger asks me.

Fine, they want to pass their responsibility off to this guy, I'll make him wish he never took the job to begin with.

I hold the foghorn up like a weapon and interrogate him.

"Oh please, how much did they pay you for whatever it is you are supposed to be doing?"

"How . . . much did . . . who pay me?" he parrots.

However much is too much, I think. *This guy is not selling whatever they paid him to do. I can't believe my parade is getting rained on by how much of a prank-dud this guy is.*

I jam the foghorn behind a potted plant and switch gears because the game is still on. When it comes to a decoy, the point is not to outsmart them and convince them to come over to your side. I step closer and go on my tiptoes to whisper in his ear.

"Whatever they are paying you, I'll double it."

He cocks his head. "I, um . . . what?"

Playing dumb. They must have made tonight worth his while. They must have asked him to get me to step off the porch so they can attack from all angles. I start to rummage through my bag and pull out the hazmat suit, swim cap, goggles, and face visor. He stares at me wide-eyed while I suit up. Once my body is covered, I glance again at his crisp jawline, curly hair, and dark brown eyes that seem to have tiny flecks of gold interspersed throughout. They are the type of eyes that I could fall into if I look for too long. I straighten myself from where I have begun to lean forward, ready to dive.

Keep it together, Aviva, eyes on the prize. I hear Savta's voice in my ear. I hold my arm out, ready for his escort, and point to the stairs.

"Get it over with," I command.

He keeps staring between me and the porch steps. Maybe I misread the situation. Maybe the attack is coming from somewhere else. We stare back and forth silently until he clears his throat.

"I—uh—thought you were going to invite me in . . ."

"Invite . . . you . . . inside?" I repeat.

He nods, giving me and my gear another once-over. "When did you speak to Toby?" I ask.

114

"I didn't."

"What about Nadine? Jonathan? Sage?"

He shakes his head no.

"And you don't know me or have any instructions to, like, dump something over my head or enact psychological warfare?"

He shakes his head again.

"So . . . you are here because . . ."

I start to sweat, and with all these additional plastic layers, I'll be soaked in seconds if I don't act quickly.

"You were supposed to invite me in," he repeats, finishing my sentence.

"What exactly is your name?" My breath comes in tiny spurts, quick and constant. My chest moves up and down. I start to pull off the hair cover and drag the zipper for the suit down. This may be the beginning of a Netflix true crime documentary if I don't get to the bottom of it.

"Oh, right, sorry. I'm Elijah." He holds his hand out to me. "I think you should be expecting me. The lady said there would be a glass and a seat waiting for me."

"The lady?"

"Yeah, umm, she said her name was . . . Sav-yaw?"

"Savta? My Savta? You spoke to her?"

"Mm-hmm, yep. She said everyone would be excited to see me."

The weight of the world plummets to the bottom of my gut. Forget a prank. The literal prophet is standing in front of me, and I don't know what that means. Is he here to deliver me to the next realm or to walk me through different versions of what my future could look like depending on what decision I make? Everything I wish I had done before this moment floods me. I should have apologized to my mom when I told her that I hated her after she said I couldn't go to Marissa Kantor's sweet sixteen because it overlapped with Savta and Nana's anniversary party. I should have told Savta and Nana more often that they are the best. I should have told Toby he had spinach between his teeth.

Elijah steps a tiny bit closer to me, and with him comes a gust of wind that closes the door behind me. The prophet vibes are strong. He is close enough now that I can smell his breath, mint and honey, sweet and deep and fresh. Martin Schoenfeld smelled like Big Red gum and carrots.

"What, uh, were you doing out here?" Elijah asks, his eyes shifting behind me to the foghorn I hid.

"Sorry, I thought someone I knew was out here."

"And you wanted to burst their eardrums?" he asks with generations' worth of judgment.

Sort of.

"Are you going to buzz?" Elijah points to the doorbell.

He wants to get away from me. Great. I can add "meet and turn off a prophet in seconds" to my bingo card.

"Yeah, no . . . because it doesn't work. My nana's been 'just remembering' to fix it for ten years."

I reach my hand behind me to test the doorknob, even though I know the door automatically locks; it doesn't even wiggle. And I left my phone downstairs as well. Guess we are both doomed to wait here.

"You look like you could use a walk," Elijah says to me, "come on."

He starts to saunter toward the sidewalk. It's not like anyone is paying attention to me; they probably won't notice when I'm gone.

Plus, when Elijah commands you to walk, you follow. It's sort of his thing.

"So, uh, where are we going?" he asks.

"Um, this was your idea," I remind him.

"Oh right, well, I'm thirsty."

Right, right. Of course. The cup we always pour rarely gets emptied. I turn toward the closest bodega; he follows my lead.

"It's so quiet here. Not what I pictured New York to be like."

He looks around at the Victorian houses we pass on our way to Newkirk Avenue. These blocks all look like the suburbs, like if you were dropped here with a bag over your head, you'd never know how close you were to Brooklyn.

"So, you live here?"

"Oh no, no, my grandmas do. That's their house. We're all just here for the seder."

The lights of the bodega on Newkirk and Sixteenth appear at the end of the block. The shift back into the heart of the city is sharp. I watch Elijah's eyelids pinch closer as he adjusts to the brighter surroundings.

"So, what has you so stressed?" he asks.

"Oh, um, well . . . my cousins forgot to torture me."

"*What?*" He jumps, alert and in distress.

"No, no, not actually. I mean, it's not malicious, it's done in love. At least, that's what I used to tell myself."

"Um, that's not how love . . . works . . ." Elijah says.

Part of me agrees, but I still don't want to admit it.

"Are you okay?" he asks me.

Loaded question. I'm not just the youngest cousin, I'm the only, only child in the family. So, am I ready to accept that this whole time they didn't really enjoy this game of cat and mouse? No. But maybe the universe sent me the prophet to shake some reality into me. I take a deep breath before I unload.

"My cousins were all born within a year of each other and they had a good thing going. *The cousins Cohen.* They were on a level playing field, they covered for each other and advanced as a unit, no one was ever too sassy or naughty or mischievous. No one was bad or good, they just were. Then five years into it all, I was born. From that moment, they were old and I was young, and my arrival united them further, with the goal of pranking me. This whole time I thought it was a love-hate thing, but now I see that they would have to care to hate me." I suck in oxygen as soon as I spit the last word out.

"Can I ask you something?"

I nod, still catching my breath.

"What's it like, you know, being cousins?" Elijah asks me.

One day you are the victim of annual humiliation in your own home and the next, a prophet materializes before you as a human your age, having no business being as cute as he is, and asks you to teach him about the world.

"When they are not trying to kill you, cousins are that perfect half-friend half-sibling half-person-who-has-a-whole-other-life-between-the-visits-to-the-bubble-of-everything-you-share. Cousins are the perfect type of family, even if they do dedicate themselves to destroying you."

I pause as we enter the bodega and lead Elijah to the beverage wall, where he scans until he sees what he wants: cold apple juice. The kind in the little glass bottle. Classic.

He turns to me with a smile. "I don't care how old I get, I love these. So, tell me some of the pranks."

"The only thing that shifts is their preference between emotional or physical turmoil. I've been chocolate sauced and coconut shredded and then five feet later walked into a wall of Saran Wrap. The worst was probably the time they covered the front doorknob in some rank oil concoction that smelled like ass. It was so bad, Nana made us stop and sniff every surface until we discovered it was coming from my palms. The stench took a month to completely go away."

A muffled snort comes out of him as he smiles to try to hide his laughter. "Brutal."

The twinkle in his eyes is enough to make me melt into a wax puddle on the floor; no wonder he corralled a nation. Elijah pays the guy behind the cash register.

"I think you're wrong," he says as we walk to the front.

"About what?"

"It doesn't sound like they hate you. It sounds like they do care and they are including you how they know best. I think you should give them another chance."

The top of Elijah's juice twists off and he takes a big gulp, then licks his lips. Two things can be true, such as: I have never wished more that I could transform into a glass bottle; and also, everything he is saying out of that perfect mouth causes rage to rush up my belly. I get Elijah is wiser than me, but he doesn't get to take my truth away from me, I don't care how hot he is.

"Actually, you are the one who is wrong. Today was the first time we have all been together in two years, and I waited and waited and waited and it never came. Like they are usually exploding with excitement from the moment I walk through the door. They don't care, they just forgot, or they've moved on. Whatever they want to call it, they couldn't have been bothered to talk to me, let alone prank me."

I stomp out, ready to abandon Elijah the same way my cousins did to me, but I freeze under the awning to prevent getting soaked in the huge wet globs falling around us. Somehow in the five minutes we were inside, a silent storm started and covered the city in slick rain.

"Wait here," Elijah says, still half inside, and runs back in. He reappears a second later with an umbrella and opens it above our heads. It's one of those smaller umbrellas that is only supposed to cover one person, so I have to stand so close to him I can smell the sticky apple residue under his bottom lip.

Get it together, Aviva, he's the prophet, I tell myself.

"The last few years have just really sucked," he says after a few moments of silence.

"Understatement of the century," I agree.

We start the journey back, slow shuffle steps to stay dry under the flimsy umbrella. On the corner, while we wait for the light, he sucks down the last drops of the juice, which leaves an even thicker sticky gloss on his lips. If he was sent here to distract me, he has succeeded in his mission. At this very moment, my cousins could have planned a weeklong trip to Puerto Rico without me and all I care about right now is that I too am overcome by thirst.

Suddenly, Elijah bends down and forward and we stand nose to nose, ready to drink each other up. The rain slows to a halt as the massive droplets land in puddles less and less, but he doesn't lower the umbrella and I don't step back. Is Elijah the literal prophet flirting with me? Put it in my social media bio. My college essay just wrote itself. Martin Schoenfeld, who?

Stop hesitating, I tell myself as I lean forward and up, my lips leading the way. But just as I am about to reach him, he swerves around me and dunks the juice bottle into a bin. Elijah rises and closes the umbrella, unaware he just dodged me. He wasn't flirting, he was recycling.

He turns to me. "The last few years probably sucked for your cousins too. Maybe they just need a minute to settle back in, like for themselves."

Damn, Lij, way to smack down the truth bomb right after I do something silly and try to go for my first whole kiss with the bringer of the Messiah.

He's not wrong, it's not like I called them to check in. Elijah is known for bringing people together; who am I to not answer his call?

"Aviva!" My name bursts out of my grandmas' house the second we step back in front of it, and a horde of bodies flies out of it in our direction. Toby's arms are around me first, then Nadine's, then Sage's, then Jonathan's.

"Where were you!" Nadine says as they continue to pile on their bodies and worries.

"You scared the shit out of us!" Jonathan scolds.

"Aviva, where did you go? You were supposed to be out here," Toby whines.

"Wait!" I free myself and stand before them. "What do you mean?"

"The prank!" Toby shouts, arms flung overhead.

"What prank?" My heart swells.

"Hello? The whole night, making you think we forgot. We were going to run out to get you in the front with water balloons filled with pickle juice that we were going to convince you was cat pee and then you weren't there!" Jonathan cries, exasperated.

"We waited and waited, but then we got worried," Nadine says, and then hugs me again.

"You've been gone for like twenty minutes. Savta has done *two* renditions of 'Tomorrow,'" Sage adds.

"You really care?" I ask.

They all stare back at me, eyes wide and apologetic and relieved.

"What?! Omg, you really bought it? Aw, Veev, there is no single greater joy than messing with you!" Jonathan exclaims.

"But what about the last two years, the cousin WhatsApp was always about you all, never me."

Nadine grabs my hands and squeezes.

"Aviva! We didn't want to be overbearing; we were waiting for you to come to us. And for the record, that doesn't mean we haven't been keeping an eye on you. We all know I'm an amateur sleuth. It's actually what I wrote my essay about to get into Wesleyan. I tracked you on socials, I know what's been going on with Martin Scho—"

It takes me one leap forward to be close enough to clamp my hand over her mouth. I shake my head. Muffled words come from under my fingers, but I push my palm against her face harder to prevent the very real not-prophet with elite bone structure a few feet away from hearing about my almost kiss.

"There you are!" Savta steps outside and looks over all of us. "Elijah! We've been waiting."

My cousins look behind me to Elijah, whom they didn't notice until now. Like he just fell out of the dark Brooklyn sky.

I look between Savta and Elijah, but she steps forward and waves him closer from where he hid behind the bush as soon as my cousins ran out.

"How do you know—" I begin to ask, but Savta jumps in.

"Elijah's parents rented the Airbnb upstairs. They are musicians and mentioned they had a gig tonight, so I invited him to dinner."

The truth overwhelms. My cousins do love me, the prank war is still on, and based on our state right now, uncovered by pickle juice, I won. But even better, Elijah, the extremely hot kid my age, steps into the light pouring down from the porch. Maybe a real, whole apple juice–flavored kiss is in my future.

"Sorry, Miss Sav—" he starts to say to my grandma.

"Mmm-mmm, nope. No 'miss' here, just Savta," Savta corrects him.

"Sorry, um, Sav-tuh. My homework took a while and I didn't realize how late it had gotten. I buzzed, but no one answered, and then I didn't want to interrupt," Elijah explains.

"Nonsense, we've still got tons of food. Now come on inside. I'm old and time ain't what it used to be. I can't be standing around for no reason."

Savta shifts her weight from her left leg to her right and winces, and I know she's holding back the amount of pain she is in to protect us. I have noticed Savta's limp has been getting progressively worse over the course of the night. I knew it was getting harder for her to move around, but we didn't know it was like this. The worst part of not seeing each other for so long is that now, so much of what we love has become a reminder of what we lost because of the last couple of years. Savta holds her arm out to the door, ushering us back inside. The seder isn't over. Nadine's eyes talk a mile a minute: *He's cute, you will need to tell me everything.*

I nod back. *Later.*

Nadine pulls Sage past me and toward the door. Toby follows, then Jonathan.

Savta waits until their heads disappear down the stairs and then flashes a small wad of cash.

"And you! Whatever you did, you got them! Good for you, sweetie. Don't let them push you around! Watch your back tonight, though," she says with a wink.

We always sleep over after seder, all the cousins in the TV room spread out on couches and comfy chairs, fighting over the old quilts and discarded comforters we pull from the closet. Savta turns back to the house slowly, pausing after the first step to take a long, deep breath. She looks steady, so I don't offer to help. I know better. She's not ready for that yet. Once she's hit the stairs, I turn to Elijah.

"You don't have to come if you don't want to. We're . . . a lot."

I say the words and hope he's hungry enough to risk it.

"Oh, your grandmas are something." He rubs the back of his neck. "I like it—them—you, I mean. Your family. I like your family even if they are a lot. And see, they didn't forget!"

They didn't.

In one stride, he meets me at the door, bends over, and whispers in my ear.

"Can you promise not to leave me alone with them?"

His breath tickles my neck. This has to be flirting. I make a mental note to confirm with Nadine.

"I make no such promises. It's every human for themself, except Nadine and Sage. The twins are a package deal."

We walk inside to the warmth coming from the laughs at the extended dining table below us and the chicken broth and the brisket with sweet, caramelized tomato and onions.

"She's back!" Savta sings when my feet meet the stairs. She forces the family to rise for a round of applause and tops it off with a quick falsetto version of Queen's "We Are the Champions" when Elijah and I reach the bottom step.

"Yeah, yeah, we get it. Can we wrap this thing up?" Toby snarls. His eyes meet mine with a death glare as I pull my seat out to rejoin the table. The hunger for torture is back. Savta is right, I am going to have to sleep with both eyes open and avoid them all like the eleventh plague.

Elijah takes the seat beside me and my heart begins to bounce with adrenaline, but even the excitement of brushing the backs of our hands beside one another is washed away by the love I feel as Savta takes her mark on the floor to wait for one of the three spotlights my dad installed in the house for her whenever she needs to have a moment, aka right now.

Savta used to be on Broadway before her osteoporosis made it impossible to keep up. She never got to be a star, but she stayed busy for thirty-five years, which is more than most actors can say.

"What is happening?" Elijah asks.

"This is the blessing to welcome Elijah—well, the prophet, not you," I whisper back.

The room darkens as Sage and my Aunt Bea flip the switch to bright cylinders of light that capture Savta perfectly. She begins to sing from the Haggadah again, and the blessing to welcome Elijah wraps itself from my grandmother's lips around all of us. Once the last word has been sung and her echo quiets, we respond. Multiple generations linked in hope that our cry fills the gap between now and when peace and redemption find us. We have seen miracles before, we know they are possible, we are the product of thousands of years of them. Toby groans, impatient and grumpy with the soreness of his prank loss settling in, and Nana refills her glass with half of Savta's wine, then rises.

"Toby, I believe in you to survive the next few minutes without resorting to toddler behavior."

Toby grumbles, then lifts his body up, glass raised, and the rest of the family does the same.

Elijah's eyes dart around the room. I get it, in a big family like this, it's hard to know where you fit. Once his eyes land on me, I nod my chin toward the cup in front of him, filled with Kedem grape juice and seltzer, then lift mine for him to mimic. His arm leans against mine when he stands, and my heart beats so loud I have to check to make sure it's not a horde of locusts' wings coming to finish the job they started eons ago.

Nana clears her throat, she and Savta hold hands and lift their glasses.

"Just repeat what they say," I whisper quickly to Elijah.

Nadine looks around and we catch eyes, just for a second, from one end of our whole world to the other. The millisecond when we are just kids on either side of the table, unaware how much more we had waiting for us. It's only a blink, but it's enough. Despite the way it can be out there, we've found a way to preserve the magic in us and this finished basement. The whole point of Passover is to take a look back and then to step forward. To remember what we've been through. To say, "Never again means for all of us."

We sit in the unity of our purpose for as long as Toby feels is necessary before he shouts, "Not clearing the table!" and touches his nose.

All my cousins raise their fingers to their noses and repeat:
"Not it."
"Not it."
"Not it."
Their two-word declarations follow each other's tails so closely, they make a round. Any other Passover I'd be devastated, but I look

126

over to Elijah, who sat back down to shovel brisket into his mouth. Maybe it's okay for Passover to change a little here and there.

"All right, go, start the movie." I accept this small defeat and shoo my cousins from the table. "I'll be in after."

Toby collects the plates into a tower and dumps them into my arms.

"I'll help," Elijah tries to say through his half-full mouth.

"She's going to need it," Savta says with a wink. "The dishwasher went kaput last week."

Glossary

Elijah: A Jewish prophet who represents hope and redemption

Miriam: Moses's older sister who helped ensure his safety as a young baby

Haggadah: The text read at Passover seder with blessings and the story of the Jewish exodus from slavery

Seder plate:

　　–karpas, parsley dipped in salt water to represent the tears of our ancestors

　　–haroseth, sweet apples chopped up with nuts and honey to represent the mortar used by the Jewish people in Egypt

　　–the shank bone, to represent the lamb sacrificed as a special Passover offering

　　–maror, horseradish to represent the bitterness of enslavement

　　–a boiled egg, to represent the circle of life and innate hope that sits at the center of our Jewish practice

Hill Country Heartbeat

BY CANDACE BUFORD

I thought I wouldn't understand the land after being away for so long, that I'd lost every ounce of the hill country. I'd been through such a transformation during my first year of college, trading my work boots for lab coats and petri dishes, my dark skies for skyscrapers. The home that had shaped me felt like a distant memory. But as our rental car kicked up that black gumbo dirt, I felt the beating heart of the ranch return to me.

Usually summer saw bone-dry grass baking beneath the Texas sun, making the pastures look almost chalky. But this year was different. A swollen Medina River had recently flooded the valley, and the fields were unusually verdant. Green flourished for as far as the eye could see. Even wildflowers poked their heads between the blades of grass. There was life in this old soil yet.

It didn't look like destruction. It looked like a renewal. But I knew my family was hurting. Even though my parents told me everything was fine, my sister was blunter with her descriptions of the mess, sharper with her criticism of my absence. The water damage to the house and surrounding cabins was apparently more extensive than my parents had let on, and the ranch was struggling to stay afloat through all this change. But I'd had school and then exams and now a summer fellowship with Dr. Riley in Dinosaur Valley. The excuses kept piling up. But deep down, I knew I should have come home sooner.

By some weird twist of fate, the dig site had yielded fresh tracks, so the valley was now swarming with teams of experts. Our student fellowship was put on a brief hiatus until the state park could professionally excavate, leaving a four-day gap in our schedule. And rather than sit in the motel room twiddling my thumbs, I seized the opportunity to make the four-hour drive to my family's ranch. I wasn't sure what I could do to help them, but I was here to lend a hand where I could until my fellowship resumed.

If it ever resumed.

That uncertainty weighed heavily on me, but perhaps more on my dig partner, Matty. He shifted uncomfortably in the passenger seat, then let out a long sigh as he scrolled through his phone, likely checking his emails for the hundredth time.

It was well past eight when we turned down the gravel drive. The sun hung low, beaming through the windshield, making light pierce the edges of my visor. I rolled past the paddocks, squinting at the horses, who flicked their ears at the sound of crunching gravel. They eyed me curiously, their heads turning slowly as they followed my car up the path. Almost like they recognized me. A gasp came from the passenger seat.

"Gosh, you were *not* kidding." Matty's sandy-blond hair whipped in the wind. He rested his chin against the open window and breathed in the evening air. His eyes widened as he pointed at a nearby palomino. "It's like the real country. 'Real America.' I was mostly asleep on the ride to the valley, but now I'm actually *seeing*, you know?"

"I told you." I laughed and shook my head. It was weird seeing him in this context. Matt, who'd only experienced the wilds of Central Park, had never been to the sticks before this summer. He made sense in the city, with his tall, gangly legs and Patagonia vests, with his lightning-fast arms that could flag down a taxi in record time. I wondered if *we* made sense here, if we could maintain a connection through my family's wasteland.

We weren't really a *we*—outside of being lab partners. I was still mulling that over. We'd shared one sloppy kiss after finals, but that didn't make us a *we*. Still, I thought about it sometimes—about the heat of his cheeks against mine, the low chuckle escaping his lips as he pressed his mouth against mine again and again until the lights in the supply room switched on and we shoved away from each other before anyone saw us. Just thinking about it made my cheeks heated and my breath shallow. I cleared my throat, hoping he couldn't hear the huskiness of my voice when I said, "The hill country is a far cry from Morningside Heights, that's for sure."

"Your accent's back." He snapped his head in my direction, his mouth gaping. "I heard a twang."

"Whatever," I said as I rolled my eyes. I drew in a long breath, trying to anchor myself in this strange reality. I was home after a year away. And I'd brought a white city boy with me who couldn't drive and had never ridden a horse. I tapped my palms against the steering wheel. "You wanna try? It's an automatic. Not hard at all."

"I really want to. But I'm exhausted. Maybe tomorrow if there's time?" He turned back to his open window, his gaze following the fence line along the left pasture. My eyes kept darting to the passenger seat so that I could study Matty in this new context. His lips drew into a smirk as he peered out of my window. He cocked his head to the side. "What is that? Are those shoes?"

"Mm-hmm." I nodded with a grin, feeling a weird satisfaction in showing Matty something new. He'd seen everything from the Pyramids of Giza to the shores of the Galápagos, and I often felt like I had nothing exciting to bring to him. But I could tell by the way his eyes widened, he'd never been under a coyote moon or steeped in country superstition. I beamed with pride as I took my foot off the gas and cruised by the fence with old weathered boots turned upside down on the posts. "It's sort of a family tradition to put our old shoes out here. It's good luck."

"Pull over."

I veered the car onto the side of the drive, then eased to a halt. Matt swung his door open before I put the car in park. He skipped over the overgrown grass on his way to the weathered old boots. I followed after him, matching his excitement with my own. Holy crap, this weird trip home was already going better than expected. Matty reached his hand out.

"Careful." I snatched the corner of his T-shirt, bringing him to a halt just before he snagged it on the jagged metal poking out of the fence. "That's barbed wire."

"I bet these were yours." He tapped the sole of an upside-down cowboy boot. Its faded blue fringe wiggled in the wind.

"Please. I have better taste than that. Those were Edith's. But see those down there?" I pointed along the fence line to a faded white boot. "Those were mine."

"Cute boot," he said with a small smile. My stomach did flips as he straightened my weather-worn boot. It had baked in the Texas sun for a decade, was practically falling apart, but he was still so gentle with it. Then his hand wandered to the next post, pawing a tatty work boot with mud caked up on it. Its pair was missing, likely swept up in the waters of the flood. "This one looks really old."

"Some of them are older than we are. Might be my dad's. Or my granddad's." Generations of Williamses had lived on this land. There was something about this place that kept the family tied to it. Maybe it was because my ancestors purchased it only a few years after Emancipation. My dad always said to my sister and me that we were *standing on the shoulders of giants*. I looked around at the rolling hills, at the wildflowers wilting in the evening heat, and shook my head. I felt the weight of my ancestors in the expanse of the ranch. A knot of guilt twisted low in my belly. I'd stayed away for too long.

Matty cocked his head to the side, like he was searching my distant expression. But he wouldn't get to the heart of my thoughts. The weight of generational responsibility on a Black family—well, he could never understand. The struggle was real. Matty and his family didn't know that life. His soft hand inched toward the barbed wire. I grabbed his hand and pushed it away.

"Whoops. I forgot." He chuckled under his breath. Then his phone dinged and he nearly yelped as he fished it out of his pocket. I gripped my chest.

"Jesus, you and your phone are giving me anxiety." I placed

my hands on my hips, raising a reluctantly curious eyebrow. "Well? Anything from Riley?"

"No, it's just my brother. Texting pictures of our family in Tulum." His nostrils flared as he looked across the paddock. "If I'd known the fellowship was going to be delayed, I could have gone on our family trip. It sucks seeing them on the beach without me."

"You've only been here five minutes and already you're ready to leave?"

"Oh, I didn't mean—I'm sorry. It's cool of you to invite me down for the weekend. I would've just been stuck at the motel with nothing to do. You sure it's cool that I crash your holiday weekend?"

"Sure." I shrugged, chewing on the side of my cheek. He looked out of place here with his sweater tied around his waist. And he'd look even more out of place at my family's Juneteenth celebration, when folks from church and the surrounding area would be coming to celebrate Jubilee Day. I wondered if he'd spent much time with so many Black people. I blinked up at him, smiling past the uncertainty. I snickered under my breath. "It'll be fun. Lots of good food. Maybe some fireworks at night. You won't even miss Mexico."

"I mean, technically Texas was part of Mexico." Matty bobbed his head from side to side, his eyebrow raised playfully.

"Yes, it was. And if it had stayed part of Mexico, Black folks would have been freed a lot sooner than Juneteenth. Best not to bring it up to my dad, or he'll go on and on about the fallacy of the Alamo and most lost-cause movements." I gripped his shoulders and peered into his greenish-brown eyes. "Trust me, it's a deep world. And Juneteenth isn't the time."

"Honestly, I've never celebrated Juneteenth." He blinked rapidly, then threw his hands up. "I mean, don't get me wrong, I'd love to

133

learn more. And I'm a total ally, you know. But I've never been to a *jubilee*."

"Why would you? It wasn't a national holiday until a few years ago. Most people had never heard of the holiday outside Black communities, but even then, it was always a Texas thing."

For me, the celebration was in my blood. The delay in our fellowship schedule was like a blaring sign from the universe saying, *Go home. Get back to your roots.*

A rattling came from down the drive. I looked over my shoulder to find the old Chevy pickup dragging the hayride trailer. The crunching of gravel grew louder as the trailer inched closer, and I could see my sister sitting behind the wheel. My excitement waned. I cussed under my breath.

"Speaking of Edith." I cocked my head to the side, signaling her imminent arrival. She took her time driving. That was a rule—make it comfortable for the guests, go slowly so they didn't bounce off the side. Most of the folks who came out here to experience a "dude ranch" were like Matt—city people who didn't usually venture outdoors much. The sort you needed to ease into the wild.

The trailer jolted to a halt. There weren't many people on the hayride, which was odd for summer. In the ranch's heyday, there would have been dozens of folks on there. Now, there was only a handful. In peak season too. Business must have been slow.

"Well, if it isn't my little sis." Edith slapped the side of the truck, her arm dangling out of the open window. She craned her neck to see the folks on the hay bales. "Y'all are witnessing a rare occurrence. Very rare. This is the long-lost Williams sister."

A couple of the people nodded. One even took a picture of me and Matty awkwardly standing in the weeds.

She raised her eyebrow.

"Matt, Edith. Edith, Matt." I waved the air between them as I introduced them to each other. My eyes darted to the people in the back, who listened in on our family reunion. That's what was weird about this place. You were never alone. There was always someone watching. I was a fish in a bowl. And they were watching me in my enclosure.

"Well, you traded up." A sly smile crawled across my sister's face. "The car, I mean."

A blush seared my cheeks. She'd tried to cover it up, but I knew what she meant. She made it sound like I'd left this place behind and found a prep school boyfriend. While she'd stayed here. I was too embarrassed to look at Matt. Because that was *not* what happened. But I couldn't exactly wave my hands and shout, *he's not my boyfriend but we did make out that one time and I'm still trying to figure things out.* Yeah, um, no. Definitely couldn't say that. "It's a rental." I cringed, looking away from Matt. "We should probably get to the house. I'll see you later, okay?"

"If you're still here when I finish work." She shrugged. "Otherwise, I'll see you in another year."

The truck jerked forward as she shifted into drive. Then she slowly eased onto the road, lugging the heavy trailer behind her. It would take a while for her to get up to speed. I wanted to make sure I wasn't stuck behind her. It was still a mile to my family's house, and I didn't want to spend that whole time driving fifteen miles an hour. I shoved my hand into my back pocket, gripping the rental car keys.

"Let's go," I said to Matt over my shoulder. He tiptoed through the weeds and hopped back into the passenger seat.

I pulled onto the road again and veered to the side, preparing to pass the hayride. But then the trailer drifted over in front of me, preventing me from passing. I eased to the left side of the trailer. And what do you know, it drifted to the left. I squinted. Edith's shoulders rumbled, likely from laughter. God, she was probably wearing that same sly grin. My hands gripped the steering wheel tighter.

"Hold on," I mumbled. Then I abruptly turned the wheel in the other direction and pushed the gas pedal almost to the floor. We sped past the truck at a tilted angle, half on the road and half on the bumpy, weedy ditch. And I couldn't be sure, but I thought I could hear my sister's cackle above the churn of gravel. But I didn't dwell on it. I picked up speed, leaving a trail of dust in my wake.

The floorboards of the porch creaked as we walked across. The faded whitewash of the banister overlooked the cookhouse and common spaces. And from the corner of the porch, you had a good vantage point of the first couple of guesthouses. The row of tiny cottages disappeared behind squatty live oaks, whose mangy foliage appeared troubling. Their roots were probably still waterlogged. It would take them some time to shake off the flood.

"Mom?" I called through the door. I poked my head in and was immediately repulsed by the smells of mildew and mold.

The house was empty except for a pile of ruined furniture in the middle of the living room—an overturned chair, a shattered lamp, and a moldy rug rolled up. And along the wall, about shoulder height, was a stain that ran across the wallpaper.

"This must be the waterline," I said in a breathy whisper, tracing the line with my finger.

"You didn't tell me it was this bad." Matty's eyes widened with shock.

"I didn't know." I blanched and turned away from him, stunned that my parents had kept the extent of the damage from me. Even Edith had held back. And there was a part of me that was embarrassed that this was his first impression of my family home. I'd been to his parents' home on the Upper West Side, a solid brownstone with expensive furnishings. I knew my family couldn't compete with that—where they had tapestries, we had quilts; where they had ample room, we were stuffed into a tiny two-story that tilted to the left.

I just didn't expect *this*.

"At least the house is still standing. Must have good bones." Matty craned his head upward as he surveyed the water-stained ceiling. It was a generous observation, but I wasn't in the mood to look on the bright side of things.

"Come on," I mumbled. I linked my arm with his and guided him out to the stairs on the end of the porch. It led to the cookhouse down the hill, where all the food smells were coming from. My family was likely aproned up, helping the guests eat. Maybe my dad was in his cowboy hat, playing guitar, putting on some kind of show for them. Matty and I were quiet for a while. Eventually I broke the silence. "We'll leave the car up here and figure out where my fam is staying after dinner. They're probably all crammed into the large guesthouse at the back of the property. I'm sorry for all the confusion."

"I'll just go with the flow. Don't worry about me." Matty gripped my arm tighter and smiled as he looked down the hill. "I can picture it now—you growing up here. I couldn't before. But I can see you sitting on the porch reading a book, watching the wind blow the leaves."

"I was mostly out there actually. By the creek. Collecting rollie pollies and worms. Getting dirty. Driving my mom crazy." I chuckled softly to myself. Even now, I could hear the river babbling behind the house, sounding fuller and faster than usual. "Not to sound like a total nerd, but prehistorically this whole area was a seabed. You can find all sorts of fossils in these hills. Nothing like the ones at Dinosaur Valley, but still pretty cool. It's what got me into climate science and archaeology."

"Rocks and dirt. Your favorite."

"Mm-hmm. Those were the days." I sighed quietly. The earth science department at Columbia got dirt and rock fragments shipped to the lab in tiny petri dishes. The professor handed the specimens to us to examine under a microscope. I shrugged wistfully. "We don't really get our hands dirty in the lab. It's too bad."

"That's what Dinosaur Valley's for." Matty nudged me with his gangly elbow. "See, I can be optimistic."

"I see that."

"I listen to everything you say about paleontology and the understanding of the past in order to understand the present." Matty nodded slowly, his eyes growing distant, as if he were trying to remember one of our conversations by heart. "And how that methodology could be applied to almost anything. Honestly, you breathed more life back into my passion for the subject."

"Okay, don't at me." I shoved him playfully. "I know I'm a raging nerd."

"Yes, you are." He beamed down at me, his nostrils flaring like he was about to burst out laughing. But then his face changed and he stepped forward, and holy hell I gulped and took a step forward too. Feeling the heat of Matty close by did that to me, drew me in. All those doubts I had about him and whether or not we were a good fit—well, those melted away. But then Matty gripped his stomach. It gurgled through his fingertips. He blinked rapidly, turning to face the walkway, ending the moment. "Oh sorry. I guess it's been a while since that salad."

"Good thing grub is just around the corner." I laughed as I opened the door to the main building.

The cookhouse was connected to the lobby area, which was also connected to the check-in area. A rickety old saloon with swinging doors was tacked on to the edge of the building. It was a patchwork of additions that all looked slightly different. My mom envisioned a future when she could afford to unify all of them into one cohesive building style. That had evidently not happened, with the hodgepodge of linoleum floors meeting tile and wood, with the wood-paneled walls abruptly running into drywall, then cinder block. It was shabby chic. It was home. The heart of our family business.

A wall of apron collided with me as I entered the break room.

"Cora!" My mother squealed as she wrapped her arms around me. She was so close, her dark brown eyes were only an inch or two away from mine. She closed the distance and hugged me tighter, rocking me back and forth. "We heard you was here, but I just couldn't believe my baby was home until I saw it for myself."

"Mom," I said, breathing in the smell of her, feeling that acute sense of home that only her hugs could bring. I stepped back and gestured to Matty, who was grinning from ear to ear.

"Mrs. Williams. I'm Matthew Pembrooke." He grabbed her

outstretched hand and shook it vigorously. "Thank you for having me."

"Okay, nice to meet you too." My mom smiled kindly but coolly, like she was interacting with one of the other guests. She turned back to me, her eyebrows upturned as she took in my flustered expression.

"Mom. The house . . ." My voice trailed off in a breathy sigh. My lips stammered as I tried to find the words. "I just saw it. And it's worse than I ever thought."

"Don't worry about all that now. We're fine. Everything will be fine." She smiled tightly with the same awkward friendliness she had just given Matty, keeping me at a distance like she didn't want to involve me in the nitty-gritty. But wasn't that what family was for? To share the weight of the good, bad, and ugly?

"Mom. I'm here to help." I said the words slowly, unsure of how to break through the stress on her face. I decided to start with something more immediate. I sniffed the air, hunger growing impatient in my stomach. But my needs would have to wait. I needed to feed my mother her love language—which was always *do more, say less*. "Have all the guests eaten?"

"Not even close," Mom said as she wiped her brow with the back of her hand. "Grab a hairnet. We're shorthanded."

"I saw the hayride earlier. There weren't many guests," I said to my mom's retreating figure. She tightened her apron strings behind her waist.

"Well, the guests have dwindled to a trickle, that's true. But we have Sturgill playing tonight," she said over her shoulder as she swung the saloon doors open. "And Sturgill and his band draw a big crowd for dinner and drinks. So expect to barback too."

"Okay." I nodded slowly in compliance, still skeptical of this supposed dinner rush. I didn't see what all the fuss was about. There were only five guests on the evening hayride. There couldn't be more than five more in the dining room. I grabbed a hairnet from the dispenser on the wall. Matty reached out to grab one too.

"Omg, stop." I put a hand over Matty's, preventing him from grabbing a hairnet from the bin on the wall. "Just sit in the break room. Please? I'll bring you a plate in a bit."

My eyes widened. I was pleading with him. Seriously, if my crush saw me in a hairnet serving tourists red meat and baked beans, I might actually die. This was so embarrassing. I knew this was a bad idea, me bringing him to the ranch.

"I told you. You don't have to worry about me." He rubbed my shoulder. "I have to see this Sturgill that your mom said was gonna draw such a big crowd. Come on, please?"

"Fine," I grumbled under my breath, then pushed him toward the swinging doors.

Matty walked slightly on his tiptoes, his wiry bird-body weaving in between the wooden chairs. He found an unobtrusive table near the back of the room, one where he probably couldn't see my hairnet from all the way over there. At least I had that as a silver lining.

My dad walked in with the chalkboard, where he'd scribbled the specials for the night.

2 MEAT SPECIAL $14.99
LONESTAR ALWAYS ON TAP
STURGILL WATSON TONIGHT IN THE BIG HOUSE

As I had countless times before, I served the food alongside my family—smiling and nodding at guests, sharing my home with complete strangers. All so we could keep the lights on. It *always* felt weird. And tonight was no exception.

"Good to see y'all coming out tonight." My dad winked at some of the guests in the buffet line. He winked at me out of the corner of his eye, then turned back to the queue of folks. That was so Dad— putting the guests before family. I expected him to give me a real hug after the dinner rush. He waved his arms to the growing line of people forming in the hallway, beckoning them to come closer to the cash register. "We got a special lineup for y'all. And there's room up here close for dancing. So don't be shy."

"Hi," I said in a low voice, smiling awkwardly as I slopped a spoonful of beans onto a guest's plate. I looked down the serving line, surprised to find the line had grown even longer. I leaned over to speak into my mom's ear. "Who are all these people?"

"Locals." Mom pursed her lips, almost like it was painful to admit.

"Locals?" I whispered softly so that none of the guests could hear us talking about them. The locals I knew were the ones who would be coming to the Jubilee celebration this week. But this crowd . . . well, it wasn't the usual crowd. I didn't recognize any of the faces from church or from Uncle Pop's General Store on Main Street. And that's when I realized we were talking about the *other* locals, the ones who normally didn't rub shoulders with *us*. My breath hitched. "But they never come here."

"They do for Sturgill." My mom tilted her head up as if she smelled something foul just by saying the man's name. Then she plastered that tight smile across her face and grabbed a piece of brisket with her tongs. She put it on a customer's plate. "Hi, good to see y'all tonight!"

It was almost a convincing display of affection.

The strums of country music filled the hall. Why this was the epitome of entertainment at the ranch, I couldn't understand. We could have had native flute players, or spirit dancers from church; we could have featured the burgeoning folk music scene or rap music that was flowing into Bandera from San Antonio and Houston and Austin. But that's not what the majority of our small town wanted. They wanted to hear this dude.

Sturgill Watson waddled over to a nearby stool, dragging the mic stand behind him, his left cheek bulging with chew. He swung his guitar over his shoulder and sat. The shoulder strap was clad in an unmistakable Confederate flag pattern. I dropped my ladle into the baked beans.

"It's okay, baby. Just wipe it off with a napkin." My mom nodded to the stack of folded cloths between our trays.

"It's *not* okay," I said in a tense whisper that bordered on loud. "Look at him!"

"I've seen him. You think I ain't seen him?" My mom cocked her head to the side, tucking her bottom lip between her teeth and gnawing anxiously—her expression equal parts indignant and embarrassed. She lowered her voice so that the guests in the serving line couldn't hear us. "Listen to me. Half the guest rooms are closed to the public while we sort out the water damage. That means the business is struggling. We need local support. But they'll only support one of their own. That's not *us*. Even though we've lived here forever. That's *him*—they'll support him."

My mouth gaped open as I looked from my mom to Sturgill.

"Their money is green and deposits just fine," my mom said, as if she could sense my disbelief. "Believe me, I'm sick to my stomach, but this is just the way things are."

"We're gonna start off with a special one for y'all. Raise a glass to good ol' 'Dixie's Land.'" Sturgill raised a paper cup as if to cheers and then spit his chew into it.

> *Oh, I wish I was in the land of cotton*
> *Old times there are not forgotten*
> *Look away! Look away! Look away! Dixie Land*
>
> *I wish I was in Dixie, hooray! Hooray!*
> *In Dixie Land, I'll take my stand*
> *To live and die in Dixie*
> *Away, away, away down south in Dixie*
> *Away, away, away down south in Dixie*
> *Away, away, away down south in Dixie*

What the actual fuck.

My stomach soured as he continued singing about the way of life in the forgotten South, about the lost cause war and about his fallen brothers. Sturgill was straight up singing about the good ol' days of the Confederacy when Blacks were enslaved.

Matty jumped up from his table and trained his phone on the band. He swayed his hips side to side as he filmed Sturgill singing along to the slow ballad. I blinked rapidly, having difficulty understanding what I was seeing. He'd said he was a total ally. He'd said I didn't have to worry about him. But now Matty was streaming on social media, spreading this fool's performance so that even more people could get warped ideas.

I glowered at him, at the crowd, at the disgusting display of it all. I couldn't believe the audience was bobbing their heads along to a Confederate song.

My dad pursed his lips before lifting a tray of beans out of the server. He rushed back into the kitchen before Sturgill could sing the refrain again. Where was my dad, the history buff who was ready to refute the lost-cause movement at any chance? This was his chance.

It suddenly struck me that my parents weren't going to stop Sturgill, because they wanted to save the ranch. That meant they were willing to do whatever it took. I understood that now.

But did they have to bring Sturgill on Juneteenth weekend?

Matty swung his head over his shoulder and locked eyes with me. His eyebrows carved trenches into his forehead when he saw my lip curled in disgust. All of a sudden, he stopped dancing. He wove his way through the crowd. Not as graceful as he had earlier. He sidled up behind me.

"What's wrong?"

"What's wrong is that you're dancing to a hymn of the Confederacy." I ripped my hairnet off my head and wrapped my hands behind my back, hastily trying to undo the knot in my apron strings.

"I—I didn't know." Matty blinked innocently, shaking his head slowly. "I thought this was just a southern song."

"That does not represent people who look like us." I prodded my brown skin. Narrowing my eyes, I let out a huff. All those doubts I had about Matty swirled in my head, blooming and spreading like the mold in my family's house. "God, I thought you were more awake than this." I drew in a deep breath before turning to my mom. "This is how you're going to save the ranch?"

"Let's just step outside." Matty tugged on my elbow, but I ripped my hand away.

"Don't," I said, throwing my hairnet onto the buffet table. I stormed out of the dining room, hearing Matty's footsteps following closely behind. I whipped around to face him. "I need a break. From all of this."

"I didn't see the Confederate flags," Matty called after me. "I didn't even register them!"

"Don't follow me." I stepped away from him and ran out into the night, tears stinging in my eyes.

The next morning, I stepped onto the deck of one of the guest cottages. I'd crashed there for the night, wanting to be alone. My head pounded, a sort of hangover from family dysfunction and friend betrayal. I was in no rush to get back to them, so I ventured out to the wilds of the trees, walking in the opposite direction of people. The early morning dew soaked into my shoes as I trudged down the ridge to the Medina River, where I used to collect specimens when I was a kid.

The ranch had always seemed so invincible back then—full of the family pride that bound us all to this place. Now, everything was backward. Our house was ruined, my parents were catering to Confederate sympathizers, my lab partner didn't have a clue, and my sister hated me for leaving.

The only home I had left was on the banks of the Medina.

The flood had ripped out chunks of dirt from the shoreline, gouging out trees from their waterfront perches. I zigzagged along the side of the water, which flowed peacefully now. It rippled over the exposed shale rocks. Something strange caught my eye.

Bending down, I picked up an odd-looking stone. It had a swirl in the middle, almost like the imprint of a shell. There were no fragments inside it, but the cast was quite detailed—all the little ridges and swirls perfectly preserved. I traced my finger against its spiral, wondering what period it was from. I couldn't remember ever seeing a bug this shape before, and I'd seen lots of small fossils here.

This part of Texas was mostly Cretaceous period, which was of particular interest to my biological anthropology professor. I took out my phone and turned it on for the first time since last night. I had a dozen missed calls from my mom and Matty. Even Edith had put in a call. But I wasn't in the mood to sift through the wreckage of my family and personal life. I snapped a picture of the ammonite and emailed it to my professor, who would be thrilled to see a raw find.

I wandered for a while, feeling like a loner kid again, on the hunt for fossils and treasures and keepsakes. Out here, where only the cicadas strummed and the water babbled, this was where I found peace. The outdoor music was like a soothing soundtrack for meditation. I let the hum of the hill country wash over me as I hopped over fallen logs, skirted large boulders. Head hanging low, I walked the newly uncovered shoreline, picking up interesting shells and rocks. I wanted to look at them underneath a microscope.

My footsteps slowed as I reached a gouged-out portion of the riverbank. The soles of my shoes tapped against hard, smooth rock that almost looked like concrete floor except for a few bumps here and there, a few low spots collecting rain.

I pressed my hand against the smooth stone ground, surveying the expanse of exposed earth I'd never seen before. In the destruction of the storm, the soil had been stripped away, leaving this shale exposed. My heartbeat ticked up. Rustling above me snapped my attention upward.

A lone figure leaned against the tree with the old tire swing. My mom stood with her early morning coffee. Its steam wafted around her while she looked out to the neighbor's yard on the opposite bank. I slowly stood, hoping to disappear up the riverbank before she saw me. But I stepped on a stick. The sound of crunching woods snapped her attention in my direction.

"What are you doing down there?" My mom slapped a hand on her hip, clearly exasperated. "It's not safe. This wall could crumble at any time."

"Look." I shoved the rock with the swirl fossil upward in her direction.

"Okay?" Her voice hitched up as she looked at my rock. She couldn't make out the fossilized swirl from her vantage point.

"This is an ammonite. And this," I said, gesturing to the slab of smooth stone surrounding my feet. "This is shale."

"Yes, Edith said we needed to come out with some caution tape and block it off for the guests." My mom scrunched up her eyebrows. Her curly coils whipped in the wild, blowing over her face. "Please don't make me yell down at you. Could you come up here?"

"I'll try." I shoved the stone into my pocket and clawed my way up the steep hill, slick with fresh mud.

"Careful." Mom brought her hand up to her mouth. "There's a tree root just over there. Oh, be careful."

"Mom, I'm fine," I grumbled under my breath as I gripped a protruding root and heaved myself over the edge. She grabbed my arm to steady me, but I shrank out of her embrace. I was still angry with her. With everyone. And she'd intruded on me in my wilderness church.

"You always had me worried. Wandering off as a kid. Bringing

148

home all sorts of rocks. Couldn't make heads or tails of it." She tucked my hair behind my ear. "But I am proud of you."

"Mom . . ." I groaned, and backed away from her. I wasn't ready to have a tender moment. Not after last night.

"Your young man from New York is looking for you. He must have called you ten times. So did we."

"I turned my phone off." I clenched my jaw, then looked away from her too. "Where is he?"

"He's fine. Probably still asleep in the cottage. He was up late waiting for you to join us." She took a long sip of her coffee, and I could almost hear the wheels in her head turning. "Honey, I think he feels awful."

"Good." I nodded curtly. "But I'm not sorry."

"I don't blame you." Mom took another sip of her coffee, then sighed heavily. "Sometimes you have to give people a chance to make good. You can't expect him to be perfect. What's important is that he is sorry and he wants to learn from it."

"How could he not see the flag on Sturgill's guitar strap?"

"Sometimes white folks aren't looking for the signs we see." She pursed her lips and tilted her head while she considered this. Then she added, "Sometimes they don't want to see it."

"But we don't have that privilege, Mom." I slapped my hands at my sides. Just like my mother, I was exhausted. "What was that last night?"

"I should have told you about Sturgill's set list."

"There's a lot you haven't told me." There was an accusatory edge to my voice, laced with rage and hurt. I was sure my mother could feel the heat rippling off my shoulders. The hurt and betrayal had simmered in me from the moment I saw our flood-damaged house.

And then it hit a fever pitch when I saw Sturgill singing on our stage during what was supposed to be a weekend of celebration.

"Maybe I should have told you just how deep things had gotten here, but I didn't want to worry you."

She was quiet for a while, letting the cicadas and grackle caws fill the silence.

"We didn't think you were coming," she said in a low voice. She looked to the ground, as if she was scared to look me in the eyes. "You didn't come back for Christmas or Easter. And then a few days ago, you said you was coming for Juneteenth. And I guess I just froze up. I thought you'd skip this too."

"I didn't want to spend the money. I know things have been tight."

"That's not for you to worry about. You just keep studying, okay? What do you have there?" My mom twiddled her fingers in the space between us, beckoning me toward her. I stepped forward, crunching branches and fallen leaves until I was right in front of her. She took the stone and squinted at its imprint.

"It's a fossil of an old seashell. They're all over the place." I spread my arms wide, trying to capture the enormity of the new soil layer the storm had uncovered. From this height, I could see just how far the shale ran along the river. And speckled across the surface were puddles, almost forming a pattern. Left, then right, then left again. My breath got stuck in my throat.

"Hmm?" my mom asked, rubbing my back between my shoulder blades.

"See those puddles? They're every few yards." I followed the pattern farther down the rocks, hearing the thud of a large animal, the boom and the cracks it must have made while trudging through this area. They were similar to pictures I'd seen of Dinosaur Valley—a veritable highway of prehistoric traffic. But this . . . this was right in our backyard. My voice came in a breathy rush: "Mom, I think those are dinosaur tracks."

"Those are footprints?" My mom squinted over the rim of her mug, trying to see what I saw.

"I think so." I leaned over the edge of the bank, following the imprints until I couldn't see any more. "They disappear into the cliff. I bet they go on."

"I wonder how far they go."

"I know, right?" I sighed as I looked at the footprints filled with water, thinking of the photos of dig sites on my professor's wall. Our summer fellowship program was happening in Dinosaur Valley in North Texas—delayed because there was no room for our small program in the midst of the flurry of activity fawning over a new discovery. I thought of the photo I'd just sent her of the ammonite. If I thought she'd be thrilled to see that, I knew she would be happy to see possible tracks preserved in shale. "I think it's time you talked to my professor."

"Yes." Mom nodded while she spoke to Dr. Riley on the phone. She paced the living room in front of Edith, Dad, and me sitting on the couch. "Mm-hmm, yes, she found it just on the surface."

"Tell her about the tracks near the cliffs." I bobbed my legs excitedly, jostling Edith's legs. She swatted them away.

"And the large bone fragments," Edith shouted so that my mom could hear her.

"What bones?" I sat up straighter, frowning at Edith. "You didn't tell me about any bones."

"Okay, *okay*," Mom said, covering the microphone with her hand. I could hear my professor prattling on the other end of the line, likely gushing about her Cretaceous research, about her desire to find more intact fossils. Mom nodded her head. "Yes, she can send you more pictures."

When she hung up the phone, my family leaned forward in their seats. Three pairs of beady eyes looked at my mom.

"Well?" my dad said in a strained whisper. "What'd she say?"

"She thinks we could qualify for a sizable grant." She let out a breathy sigh, hugging the phone to her chest. "And she wants to pay for research access to the property."

"Is it enough?" My eyes darted from my mom to my dad and then back to her again.

"It's definitely enough to keep us afloat for a couple years." Her nostrils flared as she sucked in a deep breath. "And she wants you to work on the research team."

"So." Edith nudged me with her foot. "I guess we'll see more of you next year."

"We have a lot to discuss." My dad looked at my mom. "Maybe after we serve dinner tonight."

"What is there to discuss?" My mom waved her hands in the air, shaking her head. "Our girl is going to come home more often and she's found funding for the property. John, this is *great* news."

"Shoot." Edith shot up from her chair, beaming with a genuine smile. "I think we should celebrate. Come on."

She grabbed my hand and yanked me toward the door. Then she ran down the gravel road, throwing her head back with a howl. We used to do this when we were kids—run full tilt down the hills until we made ourselves dizzy and giddy. I threw my head back and screamed at the sky, and my legs picked up faster and faster until I nearly collided into my sister at the base of the hill. I careened into the side of the big house, laughing between gasps.

The poster for Sturgill Watson was taped to the front door. I groaned and rolled my eyes. "I almost forgot about him."

"I didn't," Edith said, her eyes wild with mischief. She reached over my shoulder and ripped the flyer off the door. She crumpled it into a tiny ball and shoved it into her pocket. Then she kicked the corner of the A-frame chalkboard, making it clatter to the ground. She snatched a piece of chalk from the windowsill and shoved it into my hands. "You do the honors while I hunt down the rest of these flyers."

"With pleasure."

I knelt over the chalkboard and drew a thick line through Sturgill's name. Then another and then another, until he was gone without a trace. Soft footsteps stopped on the edge of the chalkboard. I looked up to find Matty. His flushed cheeks turned an even deeper shade of red. I wasn't sure where to go with him, but I knew I didn't want to deal with *us* now. I held my finger up. "Hold on. I'm almost done. Then we can talk."

I scrawled out my addition to the sign, then knelt back to look at my handiwork.

2 MEAT SPECIAL $14.99
LONESTAR ALWAYS ON TAP
~~STURGILL WATSON TONIGHT IN THE BIG HOUSE~~
JUNETEENTH CELEBRATION TONIGHT

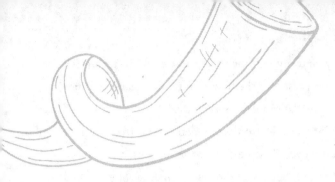

Making Up
Is Hard to Do

BY DAHLIA ADLER

You could promise me forgiveness for every one of my sins until the end of time, and still I would not touch a fish head with a ten-foot pole.

"More eyeball for me!" my dad says gleefully, and if I weren't waiting for exactly that sentence, I probably would've retched onto my honey-streaked plate. Instead, I just shudder and spoon up a pile of pomegranate seeds.

"I'm covered, thank you," I tell him, gesturing at the dish full of Rosh HaShanah symbols in front of me. My sweet year–guaranteeing apple and honey are long gone, but according to the laminated card my family and I keep passing around our dining room table with all the different little Yehi Ratzon blessings on it, the twelve months ahead of me should be filled with merits (thanks to the ruby-red seeds) and the destruction of both our enemies and any evil decrees (thank you leeks, beets, and dates). If I have to pass on being like the "head" of the year rather than the tail by turning up my nose at salmon brains, that seems like a small price to pay.

Then again, I'm going into the Jewish New Year feeling very much like a tail, so maybe there's something to sucking it up and chowing down on fish-face after all. Fenugreek, whatever that is, may be a good omen, but I'm pretty sure starting off the new year fighting with your best friend isn't.

I hold out my hand for the card so I can look up the prayer over pomegranate seeds, but I can't help scanning for an idea of which symbol on the table might help with our feud. Not that I'm not still mad—Shani Roth didn't just switch schools for our *senior year*, but she did it without even *telling* me until the night before—but for a holiday about repentance, the vibes are just *off*. All I'm thinking about is how much work I've put into avoiding her since school began, going away every Shabbos so I won't bump into her at shul, and now Rosh HaShanah's going to ruin it.

I make my way through the seeds, a carrot, and another apple with honey—a little extra sweetness can only help—and push all thoughts of Shani out of my head. Maybe she'll be sitting at a different minyan this year; with so many people not just coming to shul for Rosh HaShanah but having guests, we spill into every possible room of Sha'arei Shamayim synagogue. Usually, my family and the Roths sit in the social hall, but I can only pray (heh) that Shani asked her parents to switch it up this year (and had more success than I did with the same request, which was met with a mom eye roll for the ages).

It's not hard to forget about her once the food comes out; both my mom and Bubbe Basha outdid themselves, as usual, and even my sister Michal contributed her apple kugel, which is literally just cake by a different name. The round, raisin-studded challahs drizzled with honey are perfection, and the chicken soup is hot and soothing going down, filled with everything from my grandfather's fluffy matzoh balls (I may know that the secret is seltzer, but that doesn't mean I can replicate it when I try) to meltingly soft parsnips and carrots. And then the main course: brisket glistening with sweet-and-sour sauce that drips into the crispy potatoes around it, garlicky brussels sprouts I can smell from across the table, the aforementioned apple kugel, a colorful salad spotted with yet more pomegranate seeds, and my favorite chicken with roasted apples and cabbage.

We take our Rosh HaShanah menu extremely seriously in this house. We haven't even gotten to dessert yet, but I know for sure honey cake, apple cake, *and* sticky toffee pudding (my British cousin Ahuva's recipe, naturally) will all be passed around the table along with ice cream made from whatever nondairy milk is big this season. Everyone will ooh and ahh and insist there's waaaay too much, but it'll all be gone by the end of the two-day holiday.

"So, Eliora, have you decided where you'll be going to college yet?" Bubbe Basha asks, her eyes focused on me even as she taps frantically on Zaydie Anshel's arm to stop him from taking a third slice of brisket.

"Well, I've decided where I'm *applying*," I answer, confident I sound polite until a pinch on my thigh from my mom suggests I am not. "But applications aren't due yet, so we have to wait and see where I get in."

"You'll get in everywhere," Bubbe says confidently. "You're a genius. All my grandchildren are geniuses."

My smile at that is genuine—it's Bubbe's favorite refrain, and my cousins, siblings, and I repeat it constantly, especially when we do incredibly stupid things. But applying for college, deciding where we'd go together to be roommates, was another me-and-Shani thing. I don't even know if she's still applying everywhere we discussed. For all I know, she could be planning to go to school across the country.

"And what about that friend of yours?" Bubbe continues, as if reading my mind. "Does she know where she's going?"

The sweet chicken turns to ash in my mouth. "I wouldn't know."

It's a tradition for my mom to buy each of us a new article of clothing for the new year, and almost as traditional for us all to secretly hate her choices. (Except my brother, Eyal, who always gets something totally innocuous, like a plain leather belt.) However, unlike my sister Aderet, who graciously accepts whatever it is and then shoves it in the back of her closet, never to be seen again, I always try to make it work.

This year it's a new shawl, and it's been . . . a challenge.

I always take my time getting ready for shul on Rosh HaShanah, because I do not have the capacity to sit for five hours of davening, but between the grandmotherly shawl and the idea of seeing Shani again for the first time in months, I'm dragging my feet extra slowly.

"Are you coming or what?" Michal asks, swinging open my door and sticking her head inside, her perfect curls swaying like a curtain in the breeze. "You're gonna be late for Mussaf."

"I will not. Yonah Marcus takes forever. I probably still have half an hour."

"Ugh, I forgot he was leading davening. He's the worst." I love how on Rosh HaShanah, we all commit to things like not saying unkind things about other people, but trashing the chazan for being too slow is always acceptable lashon hara, even on the High Holidays. "But still. Hurry up, or Adi and I are leaving without you."

"So leave. I'll go with Mom."

Michal snorts. "Mom's been gone for, like, half an hour. You think Bubbe was gonna wait around?"

Fair point. "Just give me five minutes."

Michal twirls out, and I give myself a final look in the mirror. I'm dressed, but am I "see my former best friend for the first time in months and make absolutely clear I'm even better off without her" dressed? It's hard to find the perfect armor for that occasion. A killer pair of heels would be the obvious choice, except that Rosh HaShanah davening lasts at least two hours longer than regular Shabbos davening (minimum three when Yonah Marcus is leading it), and I am simply not that resilient.

Finally, I throw on a necklace—in this house, we add an accessory before leaving to spite Coco Chanel—and stomp out after Michal.

"What are you so cranky about?" she asks as Aderet steps outside and determines that the September sunshine in our New York City suburb is strong enough that we don't need coats. "The shawl isn't that bad."

"It is that bad," says Aderet as we head out and she locks the door behind us, "but it's not the shawl. Eli's in a fight with Shani and doesn't want to see her."

"Shut up, Adi," I say warningly. It should be a nice thing, having your sisters home from college for the holidays, but it always goes downhill fast.

"Oh, grow up." We're walking side by side, so I can't say for sure, but I can feel Aderet rolling her big brown eyes. "Yeah, it sucks that she didn't tell you she was switching schools, but if she switched for senior year, she had to have a good reason, right? It's Rosh HaShanah. You're supposed to be forgiving and forgetting."

"Actually, you're supposed to be apologizing, which is something she hasn't done," I point out. "And shouldn't she be telling me that reason, if it's such a big deal?"

"Maybe you should be giving her the benefit of the doubt that if she could tell you, she would," Michal says, ever the angelic peacemaker. "But anyway, people are allowed to have secrets, even from their best friends."

No, they're not, I want to yell back childishly. Instead, I just pull my hideous new shawl around me tightly to ward off the early autumn breeze.

As soon as we get to shul, Michal takes a quick glance at the seating chart and strides inside, Aderet goes to the coatroom to change from the sneakers she wore for the walk into her ridiculous heels, and I sail straight over to the Cohen twins, Nili and Neima, who arrived just before we did and are instructing their little brother, Natanel, on where to find their father in the men's section.

"Your mom gave you that shawl for Rosh HaShanah, didn't she?" Nili asks immediately, her bright blue eyes dancing with laughter.

"She sure did. But I'll be the one laughing when we get in a time machine to 1880s Poland, and *I'm* the one in style."

159

The three of us head over to the seating chart, a feat of organization necessary only during the High Holidays, and I find our seats easily—our five Goldin seats are always located five rows from the back, with the Cohens two rows behind us. But I can't help scanning the chart for the two Roth seats that are usually in the row in front of us and noticing that they've been replaced by a pair of Sterns.

She did it. Shani actually moved seats to get away from me on Rosh HaShanah. I can't believe she did that. And despite the fact that it's what I was hoping for, I didn't actually think whoever organizes the seating would *go* for it.

Now I'm kinda pissed.

"If you're looking for Shani and her mom, they're at her aunt's for yuntif," Neima says, making me jump a foot in the air; I'd forgotten she and Nili were even there.

Nili looks over my shoulder. "Who are the Sterns?"

I have no idea, but somehow Neima does. Still, I don't hear what she answers her sister. I don't hear anything other than a voice in my head telling me that on this holiday of renewal and forgiveness, my best friend and I are further apart than ever.

Shani and her mom must've really loved their Rosh HaShanah at her aunt's, because they go back for Yom Kippur, and I manage to go the entire High Holidays without seeing her once. My mom is probably glad about it—she hated how I used to slip into the seat next to Shani's whenever it was vacant, and Shani's mom would do silly things like play foot puppets with us during long stretches of davening or Torah reading—but all it does is make it harder for me to feel sorry about anything. When I thump my fist against my chest for the Viduy prayers, I focus hard on how all the language is "we"—

a communal confession—and think about how many of these Shani and I have committed together.

Sins of disrespect—definitely both guilty in Rabbi Diamond's class.

Sins of slander—we're not *not* huge gossips, especially on the bus.

Sins of rebellion—I mean, *rebellion* is a strong word, but if I've done any of it, Shani has been at my side.

She's always been at my side.

So why isn't she there now? Why wasn't she next to me to complain about how much she hates wearing white and to daydream about everything we're going to eat and drink when the twenty-five-hour fast is done? Adi and Michal stayed at school, not deeming it worth it to come home yet again for a one-day holiday (especially when they'll be back in a few days for Sukkot), which left me standing alone to count down the final prayers of Neilah, to close my eyes at the sound of the shofar and wait for the feeling of being cleansed, forgiven, and sealed in the Book of Life to sink in.

But how am I supposed to get a fresh start in the new year when my mind is still stuck in the last one?

The four days between the end of Yom Kippur and the beginning of Sukkot are, as always, a nonstop whirlwind. As soon as we've eaten our post-fast meal, Eyal and I get to helping my dad build the biggest sukkah our deck will hold, complete with fabric walls and window shades, a roof of bamboo poles and mats for s'chach, and enough folding tables to seat the million guests my mom always manages to wrangle. Sukkot is her favorite holiday to host—a combination of liking to cook autumnal food and loving the fact that no one comes in the house except to wash hands or use the bathroom. Truly, it's always been my favorite holiday, too. There's just something really fun about eating every meal outdoors, and Adi always does an amazing job with the decorations. It feels festive and magical and joyous in a way the High Holidays don't quite land for me.

Plus, my friends' and my favorite silly tradition is on Sukkot, and as an absolute candy fiend, nothing satisfies like the sukkah hop, even if we're about ten years too old to be doing it. Because, of course, when little kids go from sukkah to sukkah in groups, stuffing their mouths with treats and oohing and ahhing at new sets of decorations at every house, it's cute and expected and organized by the shul, but when *my* friends do it, it's "Uhhh, aren't you guys a little old for that?" (Michal) and "No, really, it's weird—even Eyal knows he's too old to sukkah hop, and he's barely bar mitzvahed" (Aderet).

Honestly, jealousy looks even uglier on them than our new shawls.

It's something I always look forward to, or at least I did; like all traditions with friends, it involves Shani, and no, thank you, I will not be dealing with her just yet.

EDEN: You've gotta be kidding. You're really bailing on the sukkah hop?

I'm not *bailing,* I lie to the group chat, feeling a wave of guilt as I do it. The Carmels just moved here a couple of years ago, so Eden's the newest to the tradition and perhaps the most attached. Well, except me; I wouldn't be canceling the stop at my house if I didn't have a really good reason, obviously. But it's awkward to confess it to Eden,

Neima, Nili, and especially Caleb and Rami, who will one thousand percent dismiss it as "girl drama" with annoying rolls of their eyes. I'm sick. You don't want me getting you all sick, do you?

NILI: It's outside. Sit across the sukkah. We'll be fine.

NEIMA: Unless there's maybe another reason you're "sick."

RAMI: OooOhhh.

ELIORA: Shut up, Rami.

A text comes in from Neima direct to me. You can't avoid her forever. And you shouldn't.

Can't I, though? She went away for Rosh HaShanah and Yom Kippur. As long as I help out with the house and lunches, my mom won't make me go to shul. And next week, for Simchat Torah, I'll be the one out of town—my camp BFFs and I are all going to a friend's house in Fair Lawn for the holiday, where I won't even have to think of Shani's name.

But I don't say this to Neima. In fact, I don't say anything to Neima; I'll deal with that later. All I want to do now is take a shower and think about what I'm going to pack for next week. Simchat Torah may technically be about celebrating the end and re-beginning of the cycle of reading from the Torah each week, but it's also *the* social holiday, and you never know who you'll meet or how tall, dark, and handsome they may be. (Though I would easily trade in the first two for a guy who looks hot in glasses. What can I say? I like what I like.)

For the rest of the week, I push Shani and the sukkah hop out of my mind, opting instead to be the world's best helper, digging the shiny decorations out of the garage, roasting corn for soup, lopping the tops off acorn squashes and scooping out the insides so we can turn them into the perfect on-theme bowls for a dramatic autumnal presentation. (Have I mentioned my mom loves Sukkot? My mom *loves* Sukkot. Perhaps more than is healthy.)

But when the holiday actually hits, even the sight of our beautiful sukkah, strung through with blinking grape-cluster lights and shiny Mylar pomegranates, can't bring me out of my funk. It's *senior year*. Next year, we'll be spread across seminaries and colleges, leaving the sukkah hop tradition in the dust. And I'm going to miss our very last one?

I may have made a mistake.

But it's too late to change that now. The group will be circulating tomorrow after lunch, and unless I want to go to shul in the morning (and I do not), there's no way to tell them I've maybe reconsidered—the downside of not using phones or computers (or any electronics) on holidays. So I plaster a smile on my face while Aunt Kaye shares all the Five Towns gossip no one asked for and stuff my face full of Uncle Avi's dirty rice, which is my second favorite Goldin family tradition.

And in the morning, I sleep in and help prepare lunch, then borrow my father's lulav and etrog to make the blessing and shake the former in all directions. The sukkah hop weighs heavy on my mind through potato-leek soup and kale salad with roasted butternut squash and teriyaki salmon and Aunt Kaye freaking out about bees until finally she flounces inside. (I'm not saying I would've *thrived* during the Jews' forty years of wandering in the desert, but Kaye would've checked out by lunchtime on day one.)

"Hey, Eli, are your friends coming today?" my little cousin Yakir asks, the gaps in his teeth making a slight lisp.

Et tu, Yakir? I think, but then I remember last year, when he not so subtly stared at Eden for the entire hour my friends were at our stop, and my heart sinks at the thought that he's probably been looking forward to seeing her again all year, only for me to stamp out those hearts in his eyes.

"Not this time," I say, trying to keep my voice upbeat, but it doesn't stop everyone from looking at me anyway.

"Really?" Even Uncle Avi somehow looks disappointed. "I always thought that was a nice tradition you and your friends had."

"Things change." I stab my sesame noodles a little harder than necessary, stuffing my mouth so no one will ask me any more questions.

"Guess you had to get too old for it eventually," Dad says, sounding a little wistful, and somehow that hurts the most of all, because against all odds, we didn't, and somehow things just changed too much anyway.

After the awkwardness of the first three fall holidays, nothing could feel better than one of Kassia Rosen's bone-crushing hugs. We've been camp friends for literally half our lives, and spending Simchat Torah with her, Liat Farber, and Tzippi Moscovich has been my favorite tradition that never involved Shani Roth in the first place.

We all get settled in and then immediately take to catching up, straightening our hair, and doing our nails. We talk about who's here, who's broken up since camp ended, and who's planning to return to camp as staff, and in this space where there's no talk (at least not yet) of home life or friends or college applications, I am the happiest I've been all month.

165

The good mood continues as I pull on my new black leather skirt and red sweater, borrow one of Kassia's lip glosses, and let Liat do my eye makeup with her talented hands.

It holds through the walk to shul in the evening breeze that's the perfect level of chilly to stir up my hair and put some pink in my cheeks. We utter a "Chag sameach" or "Good yuntif" to everyone we pass on the street, and they do the same.

It continues when we let ourselves into shul and actually manage to find four empty hangers in the chaotic coatroom, and picks up when I see two cute boys who look to be our age or a little older talking and laughing across the lobby.

And then we turn to head toward the sanctuary, and I find myself face-to-face with none other than Shani Roth.

"What are you doing here?"

I'm not sure which one of us says it first. We both blurt it, and then I know her face mirrors mine in regret that either of us said anything at all. "It's Simchat Torah," I say flatly. "I'm at Kassia's." She may not have known exactly which of the four of us was hosting this year, but it was a twenty-five percent chance I'd be here; *she's* the one who has to explain herself. Who could she possibly be staying with? She doesn't even go to sleepaway camp, opting instead to work at a local day camp.

"I'm at my friend Olivia's. From school."

School. Right. The place I know nothing about but that apparently is sooo great that it draws girls from as far away as Fair Lawn.

"Cool." Next to me, Kassia, Liat, and Tzippi are waiting expectantly, and I make introductions. There's a lot of "I've heard so much about you," which is true; the one thing they *haven't* heard is that we're not friends anymore, which they can clearly tell.

I wonder what Olivia's heard about me.

I wonder if Olivia's her new best friend.

I don't care if Olivia's her new best friend.

"Well, we should get inside," I say, already walking away. "Hopefully, we'll see you later."

I'll make up for lying about that "hopefully" next Yom Kippur.

No one grills me about the weird interaction during davening, and we spend the walk home talking to some of Kassia's school friends, parting with an assurance we'll see them at a party at some guy's house later. And we don't talk about it during dinner, which is mostly just us shoveling food into our mouths in between answering Mrs. Rosen's questions about school and applications and whether we saw any cute boys at shul. (I give Tzippi's hand a quick squeeze under the table. We're not all looking for boys, but clearly Mrs. Rosen doesn't know that.)

Finally, after a slice of Oreo pie and the quickest-possible round of bentching we could utter with even a chance God heard us thanking Him for our food, we're back out in the now downright chilly night, making our way to the house of some boy named Adir while Kassia explains that he always hosts the parties because his basement is amazing, and because he has so many siblings that his parents never care what he does.

"That seems kinda sad, no?" I ask, jamming my hands deeper into my pockets as if that'll warm them up even more.

"You know what seems sad?" Liat gives me a side-eye. "You and Shani. Are you guys in a fight or something? I thought you'd be so excited we finally met, especially since she had Covid the year we all came to you. But you had a serious 'she killed my puppy' vibe when you saw her."

"I was just surprised to see her." The lie feels fizzy on my tongue, especially so close to Yom Kippur, and not in a good way. "We're not really friends anymore. She's at a new school. Whatever, it's fine." That doesn't even count as a lie, given how obvious it is.

"Well, she's definitely going to be at Adir's; Olivia and his brother Hallel have been going out for, like, ever."

I stop in my tracks. "Any chance we can go home? I'm suddenly not at all in the mood for this."

"Oh, yes, you are," says Liat. "I saw you and Glasses Boy smiling at each other earlier. Tell me you haven't been hoping he'll be there."

Ugh. Liat is annoyingly perceptive.

"Glasses Boy?" Kassia waggles her eyebrows. "Tell me more. I wanna figure out who he is."

Reluctantly, I get walking again as I spill whatever details I can remember—brown hair, black kippah, gray suit—while Kassia spits out possible names, as if somehow hearing the right one will trigger a realization, even though I don't know any of them. Still, it works, and we're at Adir's house before we know it, the noise from the crowds inside spilling out onto the street.

Every single yeshiva high school student in Fair Lawn must be inside this house right now, and it takes a solid five minutes to squeeze our way to the kitchen for drinks. "Do you see him?" Kassia asks as we finally come up for air next to a half-empty bottle of vodka the size of a small child.

I reach around it for the Fresca and pour myself a cup while I scan the crowd. "Nope."

"Well, there are a million people here." She pours herself a cup of vodka and cranberry juice, heavy on the juice, and Tzippi does the same, while Liat just cracks open a can of seltzer. "I'm sure you'll see him eventually."

I scour the alcohol selection and pick the fruitiest one I can find, a small clear bottle of raspberry Bacardi. Pouring the tiniest bit into my Fresca, I imagine running into Shani again and pour a little more before capping it and putting it back. Then we take our drinks and start the process of gingerly pushing our way back into the masses when— "There!" My face flushes as I realize I've practically yelled it. "I mean, I see him. He's that guy talking to . . ." *No.*

"Shani?" Liat guesses.

"Of course." I take a drink, hoping the sweetness will drown out the bitterness of my voice. "Of course he's talking to her. Someone tell me he looks miserable."

"Like he wishes he could run screaming into the night," Tzippi confirms.

Kass, the shortest of us, stands on her toes and cranes her neck to see. "Oh! Yoav Abrams! I didn't even think of him! That's my friend Nava's older brother. He's really nice."

"A little *too* nice," I grumble, shooting one last glare in their direction. Unfortunately, it's at the exact moment that Shani glances my way, catching the full death laser effect. I quickly look away, staring down into the clear, bubbling liquid in my plastic cup instead.

Liquid that splashes all over my hand thirty seconds later when someone yanks my other wrist and drags me toward the door. One of my friends snatches the cup from my hand as I helplessly follow Shani out into the cold.

"What the hell is wrong with you?" she demands once we're outside.

I start shivering immediately, wishing we'd at least paused in the den where everyone chucked their coats on the couch. "What's wrong with *me*? You just pulled me out into the freezing cold at a stranger's house and, oh yeah, *completely abandoned me* this year without a word. Then you show up where *I* am for Simchat Torah, flirt with the guy *I* was flirting with . . . Haven't you had enough of ruining my year?"

"God, Eli, not everything is about you! I didn't know you were gonna be here, I obviously had no idea you were interested in Yoav, and I didn't freaking *abandon* you! You're not the one whose year was ruined, in fact! Have you even thought for one second about what it's like for *me*, going to a new school my senior year? Not having you or Nili or Neima or anyone else? You think I *wanted* to uproot my whole life? For *what*?"

"I don't know! To get away from me?"

She barks out a ridiculous laugh. "Wow, you're even more self-centered than I thought possible."

"Okay, yes, it's a self-centered response, but what else am I supposed to think? You stopped answering my texts and calls. You bailed on our sleepover. You didn't even tell me you were leaving. And then you even disappear for Rosh HaShanah and Yom Kippur?"

"Would you have talked to me on Rosh HaShanah and Yom Kippur?"

"They're forgiveness days," I say meekly, even though we both know the answer. "The spirit would've moved me, maybe."

She rolls her eyes in a most Shani fashion, and okay, yes, I deserve that.

"Fine, I'm being a jerk. But what was I supposed to think? You and I had planned this whole college future together, and it felt like . . . like maybe you were sending me a message that you were leaving me behind. I got scared, and I spiraled, and I revisited every stupid argument we've had in the last year to figure out which one was the straw that broke the camel's back."

"None of it was about you, Eli. My parents"—she takes a breath—"My parents are getting divorced. My dad moved to the city. Switching to Riverdale Jewish Academy made it easier to share custody, and they have much better scholarships than Dror; divorce is expensive, as they both keep telling me."

"Oh, Shan—"

She holds up a hand to shut me up. "We went to my aunt's for Rosh HaShanah and Yom Kippur because my mom wanted to be with her sister for her first holidays without my dad. And I didn't tell you because I didn't want to tell *anyone*. But I was planning on it, at the sukkah hop."

"Which I skipped," I mumble, my stomach sinking down into somewhere around my knee area. Perhaps lower. I feel like a giant worm, so maybe my stomach is actually on the floor already.

"The reason I was able to stay in touch with everyone else is because I was okay temporarily lying to them about why I was switching. But you . . . I knew if we hung out, or even just texted, it would all come spilling out. And I wasn't ready for that. So when I say it's not about you, Eliora Goldin, I mean that it was a little bit about you, but not how you think."

This time I do hug her, and she lets me, warming me up as much as possible in the cold night air. "I'm so sorry" is all I can manage. "Michal—Michal said that if you could tell me what was wrong, you would, and I should've listened to that."

"Listening to Michal is always both a good idea and easier said than done," Shani says with a little smile playing on her lips, and my heart flips a little at how well she knows me and my family, how

171

lucky I am to have a friend who does. And while I missed the perfect opportunity to make amends during the days leading up to Yom Kippur, on Simchat Torah (and anytime we finish reading a book of the Torah) we say, "Chazak, chazak v'nitchazek"—"Be strong, be strong, and we'll be strengthened together."

Shani's been so strong. I should've been there to be strong with her. But hopefully, it's not too late for a new beginning.

"I should've known something was wrong. I should've guessed. And I certainly should've asked instead of assuming the worst. I was just so stunned, I didn't know what to do with myself." I swallow hard, willing myself not to let any tears out. I've been known to be a crier, and the cold air pricking my eyeballs isn't helping. "But you deserve better than that."

"I do," she agrees, but she's smiling as she wraps an arm around my shoulders and steers me back toward the house. "Speaking of which, you can have Yoav—he puts sour cream on his latkes. Total lost cause."

"Oh, ew. Hard pass. Let me introduce you to my friends for real, and meet Olivia, and then we can start the search again."

And then my best friend and I head back into the party, ready to embrace some joy.

The Return

BY ADITI KHORANA

The reason Lakshmi was on the Amtrak Vermonter, the rust of autumn foliage blurring in her peripheral vision, was because she was suspended for a week from boarding school. The reason she was suspended was because she told a truth. The reason she was attending boarding school in the first place was . . . well, that was something she didn't want to think about.

In all honesty, she was glad to be on a train and away from the manicured greens, pruned hedges, and stone cathedrals of Spence. Once upon a time, that entire forty-acre campus was just forest, and then of course the forest was cut down to construct buildings and chapels and tracks and a football field: an institution that shaped and molded the "future leaders of tomorrow." Or at least that's what the school's pamphlet proclaimed in bold maroon-and-gold letters.

It went without saying that Lakshmi resented the shaping and molding, and she'd be appalled if any of her classmates were the future leaders of tomorrow. Well, maybe it needed to be said. Apparently, it needed to be expressed, and it was, from some deep place within that consistently rose up in rebellion. Still, most of her rebellions were silent, internal, or, at the very least, contained. An eye roll when Trevor Trellis III, son of a wealthy arms dealer, raised his hand in Western Civ to declare that America was a "liberator" and "a beacon for freedom across the world."

The prickle in her stomach when she watched two girls in her dorm—Hadley Sloane and Caroline Tinsey—laugh as they bullied another classmate—Mari Nozawa—online every day for weeks, adding mean-girl comments in response to each one of her posts. She could hear their cackling in the dorms late at night, their imitations of her Japanese accent.

Mari had a fashion and cosmetics TikTok, and since sartorial expression at Spence consisted of polar fleece and duck shoes, Mari was the protagonist of her own account, showcasing herself in daring outfits, many of which she sewed herself. She was a true artist, and from a distance, Lakshmi admired her. She stood out in a sea of poplin and gray. How did she do it, continue to endure in a place that was so deadening?

Lakshmi didn't say anything when she saw the mean posts or heard Caroline and Hadley whispering and giggling whenever Mari walked into a room, even though she should have—she wanted to—but she found that the best way to navigate this war zone of "liberators" or "future leaders of tomorrow" was by keeping her head down and slipping through unnoticed. It was much easier to place a wad of chewed-up gum in the hair of a sleeping Hadley, so that as she tossed and turned, the gum elongated into sticky threads engulfing an entire side of her scalp, ultimately leading to a head shaved through heaving sobs; or to steal Caroline's running shoes and throw them into the lake early in the morning, as the mist was rising over the surface of the water, the birds and the trees the only witnesses.

Poetic justice, since Hadley was a villain and Caroline merely a supporting character to villainy. Trevor was the worst, though. He shoved their peers in hallways, called people names, snickered whenever Mari walked into the classroom, called her a "weirdo" behind her back. When it came to Lakshmi, he merely sent glares in her direction, which she always returned. And yet he was untouchable, a part of the fabric of the institution and seemingly immune to any form of justice. And even though Lakshmi didn't like admitting it to herself, she was scared of bullies. It was easy to settle the score (albeit secretly) with the mean girls. But bullies—real tyrants and oppressors—were a much more dangerous sort. They knew how to cause damage.

Lakshmi noticed that cruelty had a way of begetting cruelty. This was why she admired Mari—she didn't allow the poison all around her to infect her. She kept her head high and endured it, all while looking really fashionable in her red pumps and asymmetrical shirts reminiscent of Mondrian paintings, her hair in two thick, wild braids. She was cool, which was probably one of the reasons Hadley and Caroline hated her. She had a beautiful weirdness, which was basically the capacity to be unique and striking, the best quality a person could have, at least in Lakshmi's eyes.

Whenever Lakshmi saw Mari, she made eye contact with her and smiled, and Lakshmi didn't smile at anyone. Mari always smiled back. It was as though there were an unspoken pact between them that they wouldn't allow Spence—neither the institution nor the people within it—to steal their power. Or their humanity.

After all, Lakshmi did feel bad about Hadley's hair. And she sort of felt bad about Caroline's shoes. She didn't feel *that* bad, though, to be entirely honest. Hair grew back. Shoes could be replaced. She wondered if Mari would be the same after being terrorized by her bigoted schoolmates for months.

Lakshmi asked herself if it was better to confront and fight back or to stay above the fray, instead of what she chose to do: a kind of subversion. She wondered about the real education she was getting at Spence, which had nothing to do with calculus or chemistry and more to do with how to survive in a sea of assholes. Was there an ideal way of navigating the land mines of cruelty? How could she balance her need for justice with her need to be herself and not become one of them? These were questions she wanted to ask her dad, but she couldn't. She knew he would have had good answers. She wished she had asked him all these questions when they still had time.

Things had been going well for her, or as well as they could go at a place like Spence. Lakshmi had been cruising along relatively unnoticed, getting decent grades. But today, while she was listening to music as she ran the track, Mrs. Norregard gestured to her, stopping her and telling her to come visit her office during lunch.

Mrs. Norregard was her Western Civ teacher, and Lakshmi sometimes wondered if every school had a teacher like her. Well-intentioned, but also clueless. When Lakshmi arrived, Mrs. Norregard was sitting at her desk, grading papers as she ate a ham-and-cheese sandwich.

"Lakshmi! I've been wanting to talk to you. I see on my calendar that Diwali is coming up, and I was wondering if you'd like to do a presentation in class about it?"

Lakshmi's first thought was, Why?

Her second thought was the one she expressed aloud. "I don't know how Diwali ties into Western Civ. I guess . . . it doesn't?"

"Truthfully, it doesn't. But given that we live in a multicultural society, I think it's important for us to learn about different cultures in order to understand our own history," Mrs. Norregard told her. Lakshmi was quiet for a moment. Spence was the opposite of a "multicultural society." She and Mari were the only two students of color. And perhaps Trevor, if one counted the offspring of war criminals as contributing to a diverse culture.

"There are books for that, you know? I could recommend a books list, specifically about the partition of India, or the nearly three hundred years of colonialism, or the Quit India Movement, and I think that might be more intellectually . . . nourishing than . . . Diwali. I also think everyone should learn about colonialism and its brutalities, but you don't really teach that here."

"But I think Diwali would be a great opportunity for us to discuss world cultures. We could order in Indian food and perhaps even dress up to understand the experiences of people living across the world in India."

"Indians are actually living diasporically all over the world."

Lakshmi understood what Norregard was trying to do. She wanted to soft-launch a new culture into the Spence sea of whiteness. You did this through benign things like food or festivals, instead of delving into the heavy stuff right away, which they would never do here anyway. They would light diyas and eat samosas and dress up in saris and maybe do a garba raas and all pretend to be friends.

"I'd rather talk about colonialism, if I have to talk about anything. Did you know that fifteen million people were displaced in the partition and that it was the largest exodus in human history?"

"Hmm . . ." Norregard smiled, waving away colonial atrocities as one does. "But the story of Diwali is a beautiful one! Isn't it?" She smiled a wide smile. "The story of light overcoming darkness. The story of returning home to the kingdom."

She didn't mention what kingdom or who was returning home, which she might have learned if she had actually clicked on any of the hyperlinks on Wikipedia. Ram, his wife, Sita, and his brother Lakshman were the ones returning home to Ayodhya after years of exile, after defeating the demon Ravan.

"I think it would be good for you to open up to some of us, especially after what happened last year around this time. Your mother called Mr. Lovett and wanted to make sure you were doing okay."

Ah! So that's what this whole thing was about. Her mother had called her guidance counselor to check on her, because Lakshmi hadn't been returning her mother's calls. She was still angry her mother had enrolled her at Spence, breaking up what was left of their family, shipping her to this terrible place because she couldn't handle what had happened.

Lakshmi considered telling the truth, which was: *I don't want to celebrate Diwali with all of you, with any of you, actually. I want to spend Diwali eating mitthai from Gole Market in Delhi with my dad. I want to light diyas and wear a new outfit that my parents bought for me. I want to go back to the past, to a time when I was happy.*

But instead, she was going to be coerced into being the spokesperson for her culture for her peers, who she hated. The central conflict of her life was whether to be fierce or in good taste. And she didn't mean fierce™ in *that* way, the way that had been sold to her generation by a bunch of rich people colonizing the minds of the young with their branded T-shirts, but that she wanted to be bold. And yet she wasn't bold. Lakshmi was not Durga, the warrior goddess, after all. Lakshmi was *expected* to always be in good taste, expected to perform, to walk the tightrope of others' expectations, and now Norregard was sitting before her with an expectant smile, leaning toward her.

"So you'll do it? You'll curate a Diwali celebration for us?" Norregard asked, and because of who she was, Lakshmi knew she didn't have a choice.

As she left the classroom, she saw Mari lingering in the hall. "Is she going to make you read the *Ramayan* to the arms dealer's kid?" Mari asked. They had never really spoken, and Lakshmi wondered if Mari knew she was responsible for hair-gate or shoe-gate, which were certainly dramatic events this past semester.

"You know it's not entirely confirmed that his family is responsible for every genocide in the Global South, okay?" she said, straight-faced. They looked at each other silently for a moment before they burst out laughing, then stopped themselves from laughing at a joke that was kind of not funny but was also about someone they hated for good reason.

They started to walk toward the mess hall together, and Lakshmi turned to her. "Honestly, it would be nice to have a samosa. I haven't had one in months."

"Norregard just wants an excuse to wear a sari."

"You should post a picture of her in a sari on your social media and accuse her of co-opting a culture that isn't hers."

"So they can tell the girl who looks like she 'fell asleep with a mouthful of Skittles,' 'Sari, but this is stupid'?"

Lakshmi groaned. "They're not even particularly clever."

"To be honest, I kind of understand what they mean there," Mari offered, pointing to her multicolored lipstick, and then they both laughed again. "Are you having lunch?"

"I usually just grab lunch and—"

"Head to the library? I know, I've seen you."

She remembered that Mari often sat alone in the mess hall with a book. She was a little intimidating, in that she dressed cool and read a lot and just seemed way more interesting than everyone else here. They were both loners, and now Lakshmi wondered why she had never spoken to Mari, why she hadn't ever joined her.

They existed on a sea of emptiness. Like Ram and Sita in the *Ramayan*, they were exiles, separated from those they loved, banished to a place they didn't want to be, but at least for Lakshmi, she felt separated from her own value system here, too, the beliefs her father had instilled in her: to be kind, to be open, to try to connect deeply. But how was one to do that in a place where most people were neither kind nor open and most definitely did not have depth?

Spence was full of kids from wealthy white families who lived in gated communities, and wealth and whiteness could be a particularly pitiful silo, in that it made one parochial, locked in a small world with their own small minds. It didn't have to be a terrible thing in and of itself, but here, in this space, it was, because no one questioned it.

No one questioned *anything* at a place like Spence, because everyone was kind of the same here. It was a monoculture of humans. And anyone who was different was excluded or bullied, despite the administration's annual talk on "diversity" during orientation week.

But racial diversity wasn't the only kind of difference. Lakshmi sought differences in opinion and tastes, in experiences and ways of expression, in desires and stories, and that wasn't a thing at all on the Spence campus. They were urged to speak the same, think the same, dress the same. It was why she had always admired Mari from a distance, in her platform boots and vintage shawls and hand-sewn dresses and green eyeliner.

"I really love your dress." Lakshmi nodded at the yellow silk kimono-turned-miniskirt.

"I can make one for you, if you want."

"I can't believe you made that. You're really talented."

"Hey, you should tell them it's your birthday," Mari said to her as they walked to the salad bar. "After all, Diwali *is* your birthday, right?"

Lakshmi smiled, impressed that Mari knew this—that the goddess Lakshmi was born of the ocean on Dhanteras, the first day of Diwali. This was the oldest story about Diwali, and the oldest story of her namesake, who was the goddess of wealth, fertility, beauty, power, and good fortune.

"But they'll want to hear about the *Ramayan*," Lakshmi groaned as she pulled a slice of toast from the toaster and filled her plate with lettuce and roasted vegetables.

"You can tell a modern version of it; it doesn't have to be the basic one," Mari told her, spooning tofu into a bowl.

"How do you know so much about the *Ramayan*?"

"I read," Mari told her. "Also I've traveled to India." She looked around the room. "I heard Trevor telling someone he doesn't have a passport because 'why would anyone want to leave America, the best place on earth?'"

"He's an idiot drip."

"He's a dangerous drip. Like . . . the things he says, the way he acts."

"Apple doesn't fall far from the tree. I didn't even realize people like that existed before I came here. A total lack of—"

"Humanity, worldliness, internationalism, solidarity . . . I know." They sat down at a table and Mari took a sip of her Coke. "How can someone have any curiosity about the world when that same someone's country is supported by their dad's role in bombing it?"

"We shouldn't conflate him with his dad, though, right?"

Mari shrugged. "We should bully the children of global bullies relentlessly. Not give them a moment of peace. Unless and until he becomes a vocal peace activist and turns on his dad."

"I really don't see him as a Luke Skywalker archetype."

"No, he's more Ravan." Mari glanced at Trevor, who was grandstanding at a particularly packed lunch spot, three tables down.

"Oh, demons are *way* more interesting than Trevor." Lakshmi grinned before she took a sip of her lemonade. "Dussehra is a much more compelling holiday IMO. And we burn effigies of Ravan. We could use some pyrotechnics at Spence. Diwali feels much more basic, like it was written by someone who cribbed it on a deadline, you know? Heroic King Ram is shunned and exiled by his—"

"Evil stepmother, of course."

"So he goes into exile for fourteen years with his brother Lakshman and his wife, Sita—"

"Who is dutiful, kind, and devoted to him, and why wouldn't she be? He is, after all—"

"The ideal man. But I've always wondered . . . what makes him the ideal man? That he's supposedly unwavering in his principles as a husband, son, prince, brother, human being, but then after Sita is kidnapped by Ravan and he manages to rescue her, he accuses her of infidelity and then puts her through a purity test to prove her devotion."

"Ick," Mari said.

"I know," Lakshmi responded. What she found frustrating about the story was that it told you who the good guy was, and the good guy was exactly who you expected him to be.

In Lakshmi's own life, she wanted to discover who was good and what was good over time and through her own experiences. But even more than this, she didn't want to divide the world into good and bad. She wanted to allow for a certain complexity, to acknowledge that everything and anything coexisted within each one of us. But Spence made that hard, because it was ultimately an institution that manufactured consent, like all schools. She wished more people her age knew this. It seemed like Mari did, just because of how she acted. But there weren't a lot of people like Mari at Spence. She hoped that kind of multiplicity existed out in the world that she couldn't wait to be a part of, but here, she felt separate from almost everything around her.

"The thing is, I *love* Diwali," Lakshmi said. "I love cleaning the house and lighting all the lights and getting new clothes and eating sweets, but the story doesn't mean anything to me. I love celebrating Diwali because it makes me feel part of an ancient tradition, because it connects me to the past." She paused but didn't say anything else. She remembered her last Diwali, her father feeding her mitthai, and she didn't want to think about that right now. "And I like the idea of diyas as a symbol, you know. This tiny light that guides a person through darkness. And that people lit these diyas all over Ayodhya in order for Ram and Sita to return home. Like, that's a beautiful idea. I like everything in the story except the main characters."

"Sometimes that's how I feel about this place," Mari said.

Lakshmi laughed before she looked around. "You like the setting, too?"

"The setting really isn't bad. Architecture's stuffy, but aesthetically okay. That lake is gorgeous. The old trees, the mist in the morning, the sunrises . . . didn't you notice all that when you dumped Caroline's shoes in there?"

Lakshmi grinned but didn't say anything.

"I wake up early, like you. Saw you swipe them and then I followed you." She waved her hand. "Don't worry, no one else saw. I guessed you had something to do with the gum, too." Lakshmi didn't respond, but she couldn't help the small giggle escaping her lips.

"Thank you." Mari gave her a look. "Anyway, I think the people in our grade aren't super complex, intellectually or psychologically. They're basic, so they might vibe with the story of Diwali," Mari offered. "Think of it as community service."

"Do I just tell them a story?"

"No! You have to make it theatrical," Mari mused. "Tell a modern version. I'll costume you."

"A modern version?" Lakshmi laughed.

"Yeah, you're a good writer. Lessing read your essay about Greek tragedy to the entire class."

"The one where I talked about how we never left the era of Greek tragedy and that the story of civilization, and especially civilizational decline, *is* a Greek tragedy in and of itself?" She paused. "But I'm not in a position to write a modern version of Ram and Sita's return to Ayodhya," Lakshmi offered.

"All the materials you need are here," Mari said, glancing around the room. "There's your Ravan." She nodded at Trevor.

"Who are you?"

"Sita, maybe. I guess you're Ram. Why must we live in their world, when we can always make our own?" Mari asked.

She looked at Mari for a moment. It was the strangest thing anyone had ever said to her. But it made her heart soar. She had kept her head down for so long, but she was always still living in someone else's world, not her own. Lakshmi glanced around the room, and as she did, she began to smile.

Over the course of the next two weeks, Spence became Ayodhya, the mythical kingdom of Ram, Sita, and Lakshman, at least in the minds of Lakshmi and Mari. Lakshmi began to write a new version of the ancient story, and Mari spent late nights in the art lab, sewing costumes on the school sewing machine. Lakshmi joined her, getting special permission to stay up late. They ate popcorn in their pajamas and talked as Mari sewed.

"This is the first time in months I don't miss Tokyo," Mari told her.

"What do you miss most?" Lakshmi asked.

"I mean, the food. But also, my parents, my dog, Willis. My old friends." She stopped sewing for a minute. "Do you miss home?"

Lakshmi hesitated. "I miss my mom, who I'm mad at for sending me here. But mostly, I miss my dad," she said.

Mari nodded. "I heard Norregard mentioning your dad once."

"After he died, my mom just couldn't . . . handle anything, I guess. Handle . . . me. So she sent me here."

"How are you . . . handling things?" Mari asked.

"I just . . . am." She shrugged. "But I . . . like . . . want to go home. Like on a weekend sometime. I can't because my pride prevents me from talking to my mom and telling her that, and also . . . now I'm here, I've gotten used to a certain level of freedom."

"Is that what you call it?"

"Solitude is a kind of freedom."

"I love solitude," Mari said, sighing. "It's so much better than hanging out with people who don't understand you." She gestured to the hall. "All they talk about is their crushes and what colleges they want to get into. They don't care about the world. They don't care about art or social justice. I'm here because it's a good education, my parents wanted me to go here, but I can't help but think *they're* lucky to have me."

"That's a bold statement. And admirable." Lakshmi laughed.

"Years from now, they'll forget the way they acted toward me. I know this. They'll go around telling people they once knew me," Mari said as she pulled the green fabric from under the sewing machine. Lakshmi looked at what Mari was making. It was a beautiful dress constructed of pleated green and gold silk.

Lakshmi had never met someone with so much confidence. When she drowned the sneakers and experimented with gum and her classmate's hair, she didn't realize that Mari didn't need her help; she was doing just fine. And then she realized she didn't do what she did for Mari. She did it for herself. Her subversion was an expression of the rage she felt. Toward this place and these entitled, cruel people, all the time.

"That's the part that's been hard about Spence. I can't talk to anyone about anything that I actually care about. Wars are waging all over the world—"

"Yeah, because of Trevor's dad."

"I mean . . . that's definitely true. But also, there's a Frida Kahlo exhibit in downtown Montpelier. I just watched *The Constant Gardener*, have you seen that film? I can't talk to anyone about anything here."

"Yeah," Mari offered, "because . . . we're exiles."

Lakshmi laughed at first, but the more she thought about it, the more she realized Mari was right. "We really are Ram and Sita," she said.

"I think you should talk to your mom," Mari said without taking her eyes off what she was sewing.

They were inseparable as the next two weeks went by, telling stories, doing assignments together, hanging out in the dorms, staying up late at night. The days were getting shorter and there was a chill in the air. Diwali came at a time when the darkness was beginning to overtake everything. It was a time when, technically, one could drown in darkness. But then, when you least expected it, a spark of light.

This was the time of year her ancestors knew to look for light, to find it, and to honor it within the world, within themselves. It was the time when they returned from exile, from the faraway places that had kept them separate and lost for so long, they might have forgotten themselves entirely.

Light could lead one in a new direction. It made the journey easier than the opaque fog that came before it. For the first time in a long time, Lakshmi felt guided by light. Good conversation was light. To feel a sense of belonging was light. Friendship was light. And she had denied herself all these things for so long, believing she could go without them. And she had.

She was in mourning for so long, she could no longer sense the contours of her own grief. She had become *mourning*, a dark cloud, and maybe that's why they all left her alone. Why she couldn't be herself, why she endured day after day, why so many small things pierced her in the dark.

She reimagined Ram and Sita's story, to be away from home fourteen years, to be looking for light that entire time, to carry the hope of return to a land they were no longer welcome within, to reunite with family, to have the ease and comforts of their old lives again. She understood some of this in a different way now. They were no longer characters to her, but people who had struggled in darkness.

But she understood that perhaps people needed to be characters before they revealed themselves as whole. This process didn't come easily, and it arrived through challenging oneself and challenging the world. Through introspection and confrontation. It came through joy and anger and despair. And she wanted to honor all those intensities swirling within her.

Mari finished her new dress the day of the Diwali presentation. It fit Lakshmi perfectly. It was deep green, the color of the woods, her dad's favorite color and hers, too.

"I threw away my script. I don't know what I'm going to end up saying," she said to Mari as she looked at herself in the mirror. "But at least I'll look good." If this was that time of light in the calendar of her ancestors, she could find her light, too.

Norregard ordered samosas and butter chicken and saag paneer and chole and naan from a place in Montpelier, and Lakshmi's classmates lit diyas and placed them on the windowsills. She was surprised at how deeply moved she was by the gesture. Then, dressed in her new outfit made from a vintage sari that Mari had sourced off Etsy, Lakshmi stood before the class and began to speak.

"The story of Diwali is a story of a return after a fourteen-year exile. The story centers on Ram, a prince, and Sita, his wife, who were cast out because Ram's stepmother didn't like him. So Ram, Sita, and Ram's brother Lakshman endured the loneliness of the woods for fourteen years. During this time, Ravan, the king of Lanka, kidnapped Sita, hoping to make her his queen. Ram was able to rescue her, and they were ultimately able to return to Ayodhya, but in modern times, we don't need archetypes of princes and stepmothers to understand this story."

Lakshmi looked around at her classmates, eating samosas, and she was irked at the tableau before her. Here she was, expected to perform her culture, to make the world that was foreign to them palatable. But dumbing things down made the entire enterprise insipid, dull, weak. The only real beauty, the only real light, was allowing a thing or a person to be exactly who they were. And she knew exactly who she was, even if the people around her didn't.

Lakshmi took a deep breath and went on. "My family—my grandparents and great-grandparents—had to leave their homes in Pakistan in 1947 following the partition of India, which happened because when the British left my country after nearly three hundred years of colonialism, they decided to carve borders into the land, displacing fifteen million people. It was the largest exodus in human history. But colonial enterprises have had an effect on the entirety of the Global South. The world is full of displaced people, people who have lost their homes, who are suffering in war zones, enduring all kinds of atrocities. People who have had to flee their homes because their homes were no longer safe."

"That's why we need to bring American values of democracy to them," Trevor said out loud between bites of his samosa.

Lakshmi glared at him. "This isn't about American values," she said to him.

"A lot of people are displaced because they elected the wrong leaders," he insisted.

"Or because America overthrew their democratically elected governments," she said. Then she took a deep breath. "Or because of people who profit off pain, like your dad, who is an arms dealer, and a global villain," she said to the rest of the class. "It's an open secret. I don't understand how much money Trevor's dad had to give to this institution to get him admitted here, blood money to get his idiot son into this institution so he can probably carry on the legacy of supplying arms to entities that blow up hospitals and snipe old ladies and doctors and aid workers and poets and maim children."

Norregard's face turned red. "Lakshmi, I don't think we need to—"

"But we *do* need to talk about it," Mari spoke up in support of her friend. "We need to speak about darkness, and war is darkness, and we can't stand by as our classmates and their families profit from war."

"What are you gonna do about it?" Trevor yelled.

But Lakshmi's voice was louder. "If we're going to relentlessly bully anyone at this institution, don't you think it ought to be this guy whose tuition was paid with criminal money?" She repeated Mari's thoughts. "Shouldn't he go through a process of self-interrogation?" Lakshmi shrugged. "It would be good for him and good for society. And what I don't understand is . . . why don't any one of you ever say it out loud? Why don't any of you ever ask him to his face if he supports what his dad does?"

"He sends arms to dictators who oppress their own citizens. And arms colonial enterprises across the globe. That's . . . not great," Mari added.

"Look, I get it—this POS didn't choose his dad, but shouldn't he at least exhibit some existential questioning and shame? If not now, then when? When he runs for public office? Maybe he'll always be a smug asshole, but smug assholes are the people who make the world a dark place. I'm not saying we should turn him into a social pariah . . ." Lakshmi shrugged.

"But also, like, maybe we should?" Mari put her hands up in question.

By now, everyone was whispering, a handful of them laughing. A few of her peers caught Lakshmi's eye and smiled. They agreed with her. Perhaps they had just been waiting for someone to speak the truth aloud.

"Anyway, happy Diwali, everyone." Lakshmi smiled widely. And then a few students clapped. But some of them didn't. Some of them looked at her with defiance. Perhaps they were scared. Or perhaps they felt the world was fine just the way it was. But Lakshmi knew that she didn't. That she would never share a value system with some of these people. But at least she knew her own value system. "Banish the darkness! If you want to learn more about the holiday, you can look it up on the internet. You can find information about war profiteers there, too!"

In the midst of the chaos, she grabbed a samosa and sat down. Norregard had lost control of her classroom and honestly didn't know how to handle the situation, but many of the students were giggling and talking excitedly, except for Trevor, and Hadley, who was trying to comfort him.

Lakshmi realized she didn't care. She felt an overwhelming sense of satisfaction. She glanced at Mari, who grinned at her. The classroom was no longer a dead space of silence or performance, but a space of questioning, a place of aliveness. At the end of class, Norregard sent Lakshmi to the headmaster's office, where she was interrogated about what she did. The entire time, she couldn't help but smile. Something had shifted within her. She felt free. She had become bold. She wasn't scared. Maybe Mari had inspired her.

The headmaster let her know he had no plans to expel her but felt the need to give her a slap on the wrist. A week's suspension.

She was fine with it. Lakshmi wanted to discover what she believed, and what she loved, and what she stood for, and who she was, through a process that she knew would entail mistakes.

She could stay at Spence feeling sidelined and locked within herself, a fringe character in someone else's story, or she could find her own light. What she knew for certain was that the only way to find that light was to go through darkness. To be in darkness was to not know oneself, to not be able to express oneself. And she wanted to be who she was openly and unabashedly. She could no longer perform other people's expectations for them. That was an old story, tired and not very inspiring. But old stories sometimes had to be remade, and how could they be remade without people like her, people like Mari, stepping into their aliveness, into their light?

Most days it felt like they were alive in a dead world, nursing small pilot lights within themselves. Those lights deserved to be seen, no matter how chaotic they were. They deserved to illuminate darknesses, no matter the consequences.

So she was going home for Diwali, unexpectedly. And even though her mother sounded worried when they spoke on the phone, she also sounded relieved, especially when she heard Lakshmi laughing, which she hadn't done in so long. She knew that when she got home to the apartment in New York, everything would be freshly cleaned, her mother would have a new outfit laid out on her bed for her, and there would be a box of mitthai sitting on the kitchen table and lit diyas lining the windowsills. She would be happy, or happier than she had been in a long time, and she would try to make peace with her mom and try to be herself again, a self that had gotten lost after she lost her dad.

As the forests of Vermont gave way to the city blocks of New Haven, she had a memory of herself as a child in Delhi, lighting diyas with her father outside the house in Janakpuri, the home of her grandparents, the home she was born into. She remembered her father telling her the story about Diwali that she found less than fascinating even then, clearly some trope about good and evil and indoctrinated heteronormativity, which didn't sit right with her, even if she couldn't express why.

But then she remembered her father lifting her up and showing her the rows of diyas and lights across every home in the neighborhood. She remembered how he pointed across the horizon to all the small flames of that old world that was no longer her world. And no longer her father's world either. She remembered his voice and his smell and how safe she felt in that moment. And then she understood how important this was—to feel safe, to be held and seen, and to be able to finally return home.

Honor the Dead to Honor the Living

BY SONORA REYES

Trigger warnings: death, mental illness, grief, suicide mention

I take a step back to admire the ofrenda I stayed up all night putting together for Día de los Muertos. I had to make the offering overnight to keep it a secret from my parents and Abuela so they wouldn't try to stop me. It's not that they don't respect the dead . . . or, maybe it is. But I wouldn't know either way, because the dead are off-limits as far as discussion topics go. We haven't celebrated Día de los Muertos since my abuelo died when I was eight, and since then, we've lost my Tía Perla, Tío Oscar, and my older cousin Mina.

I never knew any of them very well. All I'd been told about them were the excuses my abuela or Mina's parents would make about why they weren't available to show up to any of the family get-togethers. Tía Perla "had an internship for her dream job in California" (translation:

rehab). Tío Oscar "married a foreigner and moved out of the country" (translation: jail), and Mina "got a full-ride scholarship to UCLA" (translation: psychiatric hospital). It wasn't until a year ago, when I was diagnosed with schizoaffective disorder at fifteen, that my mom finally told me the truth, under the condition I'd never mention them to Abuela under any circumstances.

The truth was, I was like them. Did that mean I was destined to die early too? I don't really struggle with suicidal thoughts like Mina or Tío Oscar did. Then again, maybe I'd get in an accident like Tía Perla, so caught up in the psychosis that all sense of self-preservation died long before she did.

Even now that they're gone, everyone just pretends they believe the excuses. That they were all living their dreams before they died, no drugs, crime, or the way more shameful thing they—we—all have in common. Psychosis.

It feels good to acknowledge their existence today with this ofrenda. I took all the books out of the bookshelf in the living room and dedicated a shelf to each of them, with pictures and an offering specific to that person. I also decorated the entire bookshelf with bright yellowish-orange cempasúchil flowers I hand-made from tissue paper.

The top shelf is for my abuelo. The pictures are mostly from his younger days, some of them in black and white, most of them of him with my abuela at their wedding. The offering I made for him is an old cassette tape that I filled with his favorite music, most of the songs being from his idol, Vicente Fernández.

The second row is for Tía Perla. Even though she died only a couple of years ago, she never had social media or anything like that for me to find pictures of her, but I was able to find some older family photos with her in them. Most of the pictures show her with my mom and the rest of their siblings, either playing or posing for the camera. Her offering is a bunch of those retro dollar romance books she always used to read.

The next shelf is Tío Oscar's. He stopped coming around when I was ten and died a couple of years after that. The only memory I really have about him is the white elephant gift exchanges at our family's Christmas parties. The gifts he always offered were just a framed headshot of himself, so I used a few of those that we'd gotten over the years to fill his shelf. I guess that was his way of opting out of having to participate while making it into a joke. I never knew much about him other than that he didn't take himself too seriously, and that his favorite animal was a cheetah, so I put one of my cheetah stuffed animals as an offering on his shelf.

The last shelf is for Mina. She's the only one out of all of them who was active on social media, so I took some pictures from Instagram and printed them out at the library. It was actually really hard to pick which pictures to use, since she had so many to choose from. I ended up going with some that showcased her hobbies: yoga, fashion, and photography. I still need to make her offering—peanut-butter chocolate-chip cookies. Her favorite.

I had hoped to finish making the cookies before anyone woke up, but I'm still looking for the peanut butter when the door to my parents' room opens and my mom meets me in the kitchen.

"You're up early, mija. What are you making this early in the morning?"

I glance over at the clock on the oven. It's only six thirty a.m., but my parents usually tend to wake up for their morning hike way before I do.

"It's not that early." I brush her off, continuing to look through the cabinets and pantry for the peanut butter, which is nowhere to be found.

"Are you looking for something?" she asks, hovering behind me, looking into the pantry behind my shoulder.

"Yeah, do we not have any peanut butter?" I turn to look at her, and she frowns.

"Are you feeling okay, mija?" She puts a hand on my forehead, like she's worried I might have some kind of fever.

"Ay, ya, I'm fine," I say, swatting her hand away from my forehead. "Why?"

"You hate peanut butter. We haven't bought any in years. Why are you suddenly looking for it?"

Shit. I didn't want to tell her about my ofrenda until it was all finished. If I tell her before it's perfect, she might not be impressed. I had hoped everything would be set up before I showed my parents and Abuela all the work I did overnight. If they see the final product, they'll *have* to understand. They'll see how much this means to me and how much work I've put in. They'll see all the pictures and offerings for their loved ones and they'll remember how important they once were.

I have to make them remember.

"I'll show you," I finally say before walking away into the living room, where the bookshelf is standing against the wall, all the books stacked in neat piles on either side of it. She follows me slowly, leaving me waiting for several long, suspenseful seconds before she walks in and sees the almost finished ofrenda I've put together.

Her eyes slowly move from one shelf to the next, taking it all in. I fold my hands together behind my back so my mom doesn't see them shaking. Is she happy? Sad? Proud? Angry?

"Say something?" I finally get out, and she looks at me with that

198

same concern etched into her features, like she thinks I'm sick. Only, the other kind of sick this time.

"Yesenia . . . did you stay up all night doing this? Are you manic right now?"

I roll my eyes. "It's Día de los Muertos. We haven't celebrated in so long, I thought maybe—"

"No," she says firmly, which throws me off.

"But I—"

"This would give your abuela a damn heart attack! Do you want her to end up on that ofrenda with the rest of them?" she asks harshly before turning around and grabbing a blanket from off the couch.

"But *why*? Why is everyone so ashamed of talking about them? Is it because they're like me?" I return her harsh tone, but she doesn't seem to notice. Or she pretends not to.

The door to my parents' room opens again, and this time my dad walks out into the living room, already dressed in his hiking gear.

"What's all the commotion? Everything okay in here?"

Mami clucks her tongue and gestures to the ofrenda like it's some kind of shameful abomination and not a project honoring the family members she supposedly loved. Papi eyes the ofrenda and then looks from me to my mom.

"Mija . . ." he says with a soft tone. Maybe he's also worried about me being sick.

"We really don't have time to deal with this," Mami says, "but you can *not* let your abuela see this." She throws the blanket over the bookshelf to cover it up. Just like she covers up every "shameful" part of our family history. Including everyone I ever knew who could have understood me and what I'm going through.

"I'll be in the car. The sun's already coming up!" she says to my dad, but doesn't wait for an answer before rushing out the door.

199

I clench my jaw to keep my chin from quivering. I don't know what I was expecting. Of course she didn't approve of the ofrenda I put together. Of course she doesn't want to celebrate the one day dedicated to the people whose memories are tainted with lies. The one day I could have heard joyful stories about people like me instead of pretending they never existed.

I'm pulled out of my thoughts when my dad puts a comforting hand on my shoulder.

"Mija, your mami isn't trying to be mean, but you have to understand that these memories are painful for her and your abuela."

"But it doesn't have to be painful! Today is supposed to be happy. A celebration of all the good things these people have brought to our lives! No one ever gives them any respect. You all just act like they never even existed in the first place! All I wanted to do was give them something. But I can't even make Mina's favorite cookies because we're out of goddamn peanut butter!" I don't realize I'm crying until my dad holds both my shoulders and squeezes.

"You know what, mija? It's okay if you want to honor your prima and tíos. It's just that your mami and abuela aren't ready for that yet. Just . . . don't let your abuela see it, okay? But here . . ." He pulls a ten-dollar bill out of his wallet. "They should have peanut butter at the Circle K down the street. Why don't you go for a little walk?" Then he winks, putting the bill in my hand before walking toward the door to follow my mom to the car.

I blink away my surprise before smiling wide and rushing after my dad, giving him a firm hug from behind.

"Thank you, Papi," I say, blinking back tears.

"Don't mention it," he says, turning around and returning the hug. "Seriously, don't tell your mami about this."

I laugh, then wait for their car to drive off before I head out the door and start walking. If I can make it back home and put the cookies in the oven before Abuela wakes up, then no one will be able to stop me from having my own personal Día de los Muertos celebration.

I picture Mina, Tío Oscar, Tía Perla, and my abuelo walking alongside me. I almost wish they were hallucinations and not just my imagination, so they could tell me something coherent about themselves. But my imagination refuses to let them tell me their own stories because I hardly know anything about them. It just feels wrong to make up stuff about them that might not be true. If only my mom or my abuela would open up for one day to tell me something meaningful.

It doesn't take long before I'm back home with the peanut butter, and I'm relieved to hear my abuela still snoring loudly in her room. I quickly whip up the ingredients into some cookie dough and scoop a few lumps onto a tray to stick in the oven. Now all there is to do is wait.

The cookies are halfway done by the time the door to my abuela's room opens and she comes out into the living room. I go to meet her, hoping to get her in a good mood so I don't get in trouble for making Mina's favorite cookies.

"Buenos días," I say, leaning down to kiss her on the cheek. "How did you sleep? Do you need help with anything today?"

Her eyes crinkle at the corners with her warm smile, and she closes them as she breathes in deeply through her nose. "Are you using my favorite cookie recipe?"

I'm about to answer on a reflex, saying I'm making them for Mina, when it hits me what she just said. "Wait, isn't this Mina's recipe?" I ask, regretting my words the second they come out of my mouth. But for once, Abuela doesn't seem upset to hear my cousin's name.

"And where do you think she learned how to make them?" she scoffs, as if offended that I never gave her the credit.

I let a smile crack, and a sliver of hope seeps through in my voice. "You taught her?"

"Of course I did. These were my favorite cookies before they were ever . . . hers . . ." She trails off as if deep in thought before shaking her head and coming back to the conversation. "What made you want to make these cookies today, mija?"

It takes me a moment to gather up the courage to answer the question. "It's Día de los Muertos, right? I . . . I've been thinking about Mina, and the others, too . . ." I pause, trying to figure out how to say what I want to say. "Can you . . . tell me about them?"

That's when Abuela's face changes from one of fondness into a blank expression. She shakes her head. "Why do you always want to talk about sad things, mija? Let's not burden ourselves with such thoughts, hmm?"

And that just feels like a slap to the face. Is it really a burden to think about the people we once loved? To acknowledge the lives they lived? The space we once shared together?

"I wasn't trying to make it sad," I say, barely over a whisper.

"How can it be anything else?" she asks.

I don't know what it is about that question, but it makes the previously simmering annoyance boil over into anger.

"You say that, but are you even sad? Because I wouldn't know! You act like she never existed! Like none of them did! How can you mourn someone you refuse to think about? How can you be sad about someone whose memory you won't even acknowledge!" I have to stop myself from continuing, because I know I'll say something I can't take back if I do. I just ball my hands into fists and clench my jaw. But one look at Abuela's face has me immediately regretting everything I said.

I've never seen my abuela cry before, but her eyes are misty now and her chin is trembling.

"Abuela, I . . . I'm sorry, I shouldn't have said that . . ."

She sniffles and wipes her eyes with shaky hands. "Mija, some things are just too painful to talk about."

"But why does it have to be painful? Can't we just make Mina's favorite cookies, and listen to Abuelo's favorite music, and tell funny stories about Oscar and Perla? Why do their memories always have to be associated with the tragedy of how they died? They lived entire lives before that! Can't we honor the good things, too?"

Abuela just shakes her head, but before she can respond, the fire alarm goes off.

"No!" I shout as I rush back into the kitchen. When I turn the corner, I'm hit with a wall of smoke. I race to the oven, coughing, and turn it off, opening it and letting the smell of smoke and ash fill my lungs. "No, no, no, no!" I sob, choking.

I put on oven mitts and desperately pull out the cookie tray, not daring to accept the fact that the cookies are long gone. I drop the tray onto the comal on the stove to assess the damage. They're almost completely black, burned to a crisp.

My knees give out, and I sink to the floor, letting out a strangled cry.

It's only a moment later that my abuela is in the kitchen, opening the side door to let out the smoke. She doesn't notice I'm sobbing on my knees until after she turns back around. When she finally looks at me, her expression is perplexed.

"Mija, it's only cookies. You can make another batch, right?" She puts a hesitant hand on my shoulder, like she's afraid I might explode at any moment.

Just then, the front door opens and both my parents come rushing inside, probably worried from the sound of the smoke alarm.

"What happened? Is everyone okay? Is there a fire?" Mami asks frantically as Papi turns off the smoke alarm. They're both by my side within moments, worried expressions on their faces.

"We're fine," Abuela reassures them. "It's just some burnt cookies, that's all."

"*That's all?*" I find myself yelling. "Is this what's going to happen when I die, too? You'll all just pretend I never existed and do your best to forget me?" I cry out through ragged breaths.

"Mija, what's gotten into you all of a sudden?" Mami says as she crouches down next to me.

"It's not all of a sudden! You've all been pretending I'm alone in all of this! That I'm the only one we've ever known with this illness, but I'm not! It's just that you're all too ashamed to talk about anyone who could have possibly understood what I'm going through! Are you that ashamed of all of them? Are you that ashamed of *me*?"

They're all silent, the only sounds in the kitchen being my hyperventilating. Finally, my dad takes a step toward me. He offers his hand to help me back up, and I reluctantly let him.

"We're not ashamed of you, mija. And you're *never* alone, okay? We're here for you, always."

"Then why can't you tell me a single thing about *anyone* we knew who was like me? Why can't we just talk about them like they're *people*? I'm a person! I exist! If I go like they did, I don't want to just be erased from existence like I never meant anything to you! Didn't they mean *something* to you?" I ask desperately. "Please, tell me they mean something. Their lives meant something!"

Instead of answering, my abuela walks right over to me. I tense up, preparing myself for a chancla to the side of the head, but instead she pulls me in for the tightest hug I've ever gotten. I freeze for a moment before trusting the embrace enough to lean into it.

"They meant . . . everything," she finally says, her voice shaky. "Every single one of them, including you. But they're gone now, mija . . . Please don't let us lose you, too."

It isn't until I hear the confirmation from her mouth that it finally makes sense. If I lost my *everything*, maybe I wouldn't want to talk about it, either. Especially if it couldn't seem to stop happening.

"They're not here, but they're not lost, either." I step away from my abuela, gesturing to the burnt cookies on the stove. My attempt at re-creating Mina's favorite dessert might have been a failure, but I could practically feel her cheering me on the entire time. "We can't bring anyone back from the dead, but whether we lose them or not is up to us. They were *everything*, right? How can they be lost when the music, the books, the food, everything they loved is still here? Can't you *feel* them?"

My mom takes my hand in hers and squeezes. "I'm so sorry, mija. You're right. I feel them with me all the time. Maybe ignoring them makes it easier to pretend we aren't hurting, but I never thought we were hurting you by sheltering ourselves from the grief." She pauses, putting a hand on my cheek and wiping a stray tear away with her thumb. "You are not doomed to have a tragic ending, okay? You are still alive. How could I not have seen that by not honoring our dead, we were also refusing to honor our living daughter?" She wipes her own tear away now, then looks up at Abuela. "Mami, maybe it's time we revisited old traditions."

We all stare at Abuela, waiting for her response, anticipating the grief to hit her all at once after years of pushing it down. Instead, she just looks at me with warm eyes and sighs, gesturing to the burnt cookies on the comal.

"This is my recipe. Let me show you how to make them the right way."

WINTER SOLSTICE—DECEMBER
(NORTHERN HEMISPHERE)

'Tis the Damn Season

BY A. R. CAPETTA
AND CORY MCCARTHY

YOU ARE INVITED TO
PUCK AND BIRCH'S
MIDWINTER ALL-NIGHTER
MAGIC AND ROMANCE GUARANTEED

WHERE: Puck's uncle's cabin

11 Forrest Road, Forest, Vermont

WHEN: December 21, dusk 'til dawn

WHAT: Wassailing, feasting, merriment, healing,

pageantry, karass, darkness, light

WHY: It's been a year

Bring an offering for the wishing tree! ~Puck

December 21
4:28 p.m.

Birch's phone buzzed. He looked down at a message from Puck:

> I can still call it off.

Puck's typing ellipses were dancing, had been dancing, all afternoon.

It means too much to everyone, Birch typed fast. I can do this.

Birch found the matches in the last cabinet in Puck's uncle's cabin. He slammed it and half the hinge broke.

An SUV honked and flashed its brights. Birch sent a swift message: They're arriving. Just get home safely.

In the foyer, Birch tripped over a pile of unbound garland greens. He wasn't supposed to climb ladders with his vision, so those weren't up. And the table was stacked with paper goods, still in their plastic wrappings and canvas totes. None of the food was laid out. Half of it was getting warm on the counter. He'd gone to the grocery store for the first time in two years. He was still half dissociated and turned off by the multitude of party treats made from that radioactive orange cheese.

The sound of far too many fists on the door snapped him into the moment. Not in a good way.

He knew only one pack who arrived with such bravado.

Birch whipped out his phone, ready to type, *Did you invite the sprites to an all-nighter?* But Puck had written, I didn't invite the sprites. My uncle made their coming a condition of us being there. His polycule is throwing a house party.

Birch sent, So we're babysitting.

It is their cabin. The sprites are good. Just put them in charge of the fire.

All those fists knocked again. Birch opened the door just as Kit's mom drove off. Kit, Tomie, and Buffalo slid into the room like a flame around a wick.

The friends Birch and Puck had invited would show up dressed at the height of festive queerness. The sprites, currently seventh graders, had started making their own clothes last winter, and it was touch and go at first, but now they were good at it. Six years between them, and this younger generation wore duct tape and zip ties. They didn't use any known words for their identities.

Birch felt old. When did eighteen get so outdated?

The sprites stood in a casually aggressive crescent. Too close, like when a dog *really* needs to sniff you. "Where's Puck?" Kit, the one who looked like a tiny Puck, asked.

"Puck's going to show us solstice magic," Tomie, the tall one, added.

Birch hadn't said it aloud yet. He fought to bring his voice down. "Puck's flight got canceled. He's still on standby in Boston."

"Puck's not going to make it." Buffalo's high voice sounded prophetic in the foyer. "We should go bowling."

"This night is important to Puck, and he's going to be here." Birch's face felt red. "I need your help getting the fire going."

"You didn't light the log yet?" Kit balled up. "You don't know midwinter magic. You have to light the yule log by dusk to capture the light. Which is four forty-nine p.m. today."

Tomie looked at a Lego pocket watch. "Which is in two minutes."

Someone knocked. Birch didn't know if he was relieved or

wished the ice storm that had frozen Boston could have frozen the solstice. Kept it still until Puck could be home. And have this night with their friends like he'd been dreaming about and planning all year.

Birch could start a fire in two minutes. He grabbed his coat and shook the matches at the sprites. They followed gleefully. He threw open the door and nearly bowled over Silas.

"Silas!" Birch grabbed him—the first of their actually invited guests—to keep him from toppling off the steps.

"I did knock!" Silas said. "Or maybe I didn't. Did I? I'm so sorry."

"Puck is missing!" Tomie hollered. While the sprites filled in Silas, Birch ducked back inside and grabbed a candle. Puck had taught him that the yule log was one of the most important parts of his solstice celebrations, that its flame was lit before sundown and burned all through the year's longest night. Birch wasn't messing up the solstice magic before it even started.

The five of them stood on the stoop, facing dusk. Birch scratched at the candle's coated dust, pried off the green glass lid. It took four matches. But at last, right as the midwinter sun disappeared beyond the treetops, the flame shone.

They were all entranced by the wick when Jules walked up with three towering Tupperware containers of baked goods. "What are we looking at?"

"Magic," Kit growled.

Birch handed the candle to Buffalo. "Guard this with your life. Use it to light the yule log. There. Magic captured."

Jules gaped at Birch. "That's Puck's job. Where's Puck?"

"We have no Puck." Kit's eyes had gone flinty. They were turning feral within minutes of Birch being in charge.

"Not Boston!" Jules cried. The Tupperware began to slide out of Jules's grip, like a ship going down.

Silas grabbed a container of cookies, while Birch rescued a warm pie. Tomie reached a hand under the pie's foil top and Jules shooed them. The sprites hissed and ran away. They left Birch's weak vision fast, but the candle bobbed down the dark slope of the yard toward the yule log. Snow was patched and thin on the ground, and the Vermont woods still reminded Birch of stick season. When he looked into the dark, the naked branches became needles in a full sharps bin.

Birch turned to Silas, forced himself present. "Need a favor. If you can keep the sprites from—"

"Lighting on fire?" he finished. "Sure, sure. Oh, that's why Puck invited me. To babysit. I've babysat many times. But they're not babies. They're like . . . wolf pups."

"That's not why we invited you. We like you."

"I'm sorry. I'm really glad to be here. Even to babysit." He winced. "Sorry. That sounded rude."

Birch patted his shoulder. "Thank you for watching them while I get things set up."

Silas and the sprites disappeared behind the behemoth yule log. Puck had spent *months* combing the woods for a log that would burn for more than twelve hours. This one-hundred-year-old trunk had been felled years ago by lightning. It had a thorny crown of dried roots. Silas and those seventh graders were never going to get it lit.

Jules and Birch took the desserts inside. "Birch, shouldn't we reschedule?"

"You can't reschedule the solstice."

Jules put everything down on the unlaid table and gave him a hug. "Oh, Birch. This is devastating. I love Puck parties. I've been looking forward to this for months."

"That doesn't help."

"But that means . . . *he's not here to set up the food!*" Jules went from consoling Birch to frantically working on the snack-and-treat layout. Jules was always serious about food—even when Puck hadn't specifically told her that she could be in charge of the all-important solstice feast.

"Valentine is coming," Birch called out, surprising even himself. "Maybe they can help set up."

"They don't like me!" Jules sang back. "They only like their guitar! And don't think I can't hear Puck's matchmaking coming *straight through your mouth.*" If Puck couldn't get Jules and Valentine to sync up their obvious crushes, why was Birch trying? He tripped on the garland pile again. "Why is the brie liquid?" she hollered.

His pocket buzzed. Puck had texted, The fire doesn't have to be lit by dusk. Yule is about traditions, not superstitions. Don't let anyone get too serious. We've had too much of that this year.

I love you, Birch texted.

Puck's dancing ellipses made Birch laugh. He knew what was coming next.

The GIF of Han Solo. All orange backlight. Sexy bound. Nearly in carbonite.

Birch laughed, texted, Airport that bad?

Still in line to use a power outlet. Worried my phone will die.

Birch stopped laughing. When he looked up, the driveway was ablaze with headlights.

5:21 p.m.
Valentine hit their guitar on the edge of the trunk. They swore and slammed it closed.

Birch jogged to meet them. He hugged and kissed the musician. They'd dated years ago and not for very long, but the intimacy remained. "Puck really called in a favor to get you singing tonight."

Valentine shrugged one shoulder. "I have my reason."

"Is that reason currently empress of the kitchen?"

Valentine stared at the bright square of the kitchen window. In the yard, the sprites cackled and coaxed flames out of the firepit. These were short-lived, however. Silas shouted something about them not melting their duct tape shoes.

Valentine frowned. "Puck emailed some real bad ballads from medieval times."

"Older. The solstice celebration predates the Julian calendar."

"I'm not playing lute jams."

"Please. Just for a quick video. Puck's stuck."

"In Boston?" Valentine shook their head, swore. "If Puck's not here, we don't have to do any of this midwinter stuff. We can just get drunk and go home."

"Valentine!" Jules ran down the dark path.

Jules gave them a flying hug. This crush was bonkers to have front-row seats to. They both liked each other. They both liked their art—baking and music making—more. And they both believed that paramours detracted from the pursuit of said art. Puck believed they were a click or two from becoming each other's new obsession.

Birch had his doubts. "Valentine's just going to get drunk and go home because Puck's not here." Valentine elbowed Birch, and Birch elbowed them back.

"Sounds like low blood sugar." Jules took Valentine's arm and led them inside.

Birch turned to look at the glorious full moon—and found himself face to wide-eyed face with Gregory. He looked like John Cusack right out of a nineties movie. Trench coat and all.

He held up a bottle of homemade hooch. "This batch is at least a hundred and fifty proof."

"Hello to you too, Gregory."

"Puck's not here." Gregory sniffed the night air.

"Are you . . . scenting for him?"

"Fire's not lit. You're talking to me. Puck must be missing."

"Just go set up the drinks and don't give any middle schoolers anything. Got it?"

Gregory didn't like Birch. Then again, no one was sure who or what Gregory *liked*. He usually just showed up out of the woods with drinks and smokes to offer. Puck had put him in charge of the small bar on the porch. Birch showed him the bottles and mixers with mounting concern.

He wanted to crawl in bed and forget parties. He didn't grow up like Puck with a gay uncle, music, and rainbows. To Birch, parties had been church clothes, linen napkins, and oxidizing shrimp cocktail. Standing stock-still while your mother outlined your bragging points to your meanest great-aunt.

Puck was the one who knew how to make sure so-and-so wasn't standing next to their current nemesis or what have you. He liked to conduct social events. Give people joy. Make them shout laughter so hard that whatever was wrong inside *righted*.

Birch liked to stand in the corner and watch his love work the room.

Birch left Gregory on the porch and paused at the edge of the little path that went into the woods, to the glade where Puck found his magic as a mud-covered, naked tween, about the same age as the sprites, chasing wisps and dealing with dryads. Puck joked about it, yet he had gone into the woods and come out certain of his own power.

Birch's pocket vibrated with a ring. "Puck?"

"Good news."

"You got a flight?!" Birch didn't mean to yell. Puck paused, which meant no.

"The Vermonter train is at least two hours late. The New Yorkers won't arrive until after nine. You should snag a nap."

"That's good news?"

"It's fewer people for you for a while. How's it going? My phone is only at eleven percent."

Birch was having a panic attack. He couldn't say anything.

"Love . . . ?"

"All of your New York friends are coming, and you're not here to keep them separate from the lumberqueers—or from each other! How will I—"

"I texted Marrakesh. They're going to be your point person."

Birch felt red. "Marrakesh? I thought they couldn't make it."

"They still make you blush, name alone?"

"Puck!"

"I'm sending in a hottie. Fuck, I love you. I'm so sorry about this."

"You had to go." Birch wanted to ask what the surgeon had said. That's not how Puck worked. He'd tell Birch when he was ready.

"I should hang up so I can keep texting. Two hours until my turn to use the outlet, and we only get twenty minutes. Don't let Gregory give the middle schoolers anything."

"Already on that. I love you too." Birch hung up.

Marrakesh?

The sound of jingle bells cantered over the yard.

"No Christmas music!" Birch hollered, storming back to the patio where Gregory had found the mini speaker. "This is a *solstice* celebration."

"What's the difference?"

"The winter solstice is an ancient celebration of light, harvest, and community. Christmas is a two-thousand-year-old church service. That's why it's called *mass*. Christ-*mass*." And the parts that weren't church? Well. Birch had been startled to learn how many of the things he actually liked about this season were originally yule- or solstice-based. "The Christians wanted their holiday to be that week, and the Romans wouldn't stop reveling, so they co-opted the celebratory traditions, decorations, what have you. Quite possibly Western civilization's first too-successful rebranding."

Birch stole a shot of hooch that Gregory had poured for himself. He walked it down to where the sprites were about to even lose interest in fire. Birch tossed the shot onto the yule log. It went up spectacularly. The flames exploded a little.

Birch coughed. "That's more than a hundred and fifty proof."

Silas had dived straight into a bush to avoid the conflagration. The sprites crowed and added their kindling. The fire was at least burning, although Birch wouldn't argue that the yule log had truly caught. The whole point of its girth was to have a fire that no one had to maintain. So *everyone* could party. Puck called the winter solstice an act of cathartic partying. Returning to a wild center. Facing the earth's longest night—and the darkness that grows too powerful.

Silas was apologizing to the bush for his intrusion. Birch grabbed him by the back of the shirt. "I'm so sorry. It was a reflex. Do you think I hurt Puck's uncle's bush?"

"No. Besides, for having such a nice cabin, Puck's uncle is incredibly chill about it." Puck and Birch spent most of their time living nearby with Puck's dad, and sometimes they went to New York to see Puck's mom, stepdad, and stepsiblings. But they came out here whenever they could. It was the best place Birch knew.

"That's great," Silas said. "Puck's uncle sounds really great. But if he notices the bush, please tell him I'm so sorry."

"Silas, can you stop apologizing, please? For everything? All the time?"

"Of course. Sorry!" Silas's face illuminated as the fire caught in earnest. "Sorry for the sorry. And that one too. I got to tell you, sometimes I think it's sorrys all the way down for me."

Birch's pocket buzzed. Puck could feel him faltering:

Take people breaks, love.

He waggled the phone at Silas and backed up toward the cabin. "Got to handle this. Keep up the good work with the wolf pups."

Said creatures howled, and Birch snuck back into the cabin. Jules was baking, by the smell of it. Valentine was pretending they weren't serenading her from the sofa. Birch slipped into the room he loved sharing with Puck when they were here. Although he hadn't been able to sleep a minute last night by himself.

Birch found some of Puck's discarded clothes that hadn't been washed and packed for the trip. He curled up in his boyfriend's smell and fell asleep.

9:37 p.m.

Birch woke to the robust carols of New Yorkers yelling. His eyes were extra muddy when he slept this hard. He jerked upright and stumbled out of the bedroom. The five city dwellers didn't notice him blinking like an owl in the corner.

Birch counted five new partygoers. The trio of actors from Puck's theater days had found unlikely positions on the countertops. Ryan, Will, and Nate had strict protein and muscle-sculpting routines, and Jules's yuletide feast was thus being overlooked. The other two newcomers held the room like it was court. Thaddeus wore a black suit, and Jane had smashing snow boots.

Birch glanced around. Perhaps Marrakesh hadn't gotten on the train after all.

Valentine was backed against the sink, being told a beat-by-beat rendition of the New York experience thus far this evening in the great state of Vermont.

"I told Thaddeus he'd be a fool to use Uber up here!" Jane said, shaking her head with vigor. "He's never thinking about the safety some of us have and some of us *don't*."

"I opened the app and ordered a minivan. How is that inviting a hate crime?"

"Keep thinking everyone experiences everything the way you do." Jane and Thaddeus never faced one another. They were top young queer rights fighters, yet their personalities rebounded like two positive magnets.

"Your Uber wasn't a minivan, was it?" Jules held out a plate of cookies with a threatening twitch. "Was it Troy? Pickup truck? Life preservers in the back to sit on?"

The New Yorkers shuddered. At least Jane took a cookie, thank God.

"Oh, we liked Troy," Ryan said. Nate agreed.

Will held up a finger. "As a point of character study, what happened to Troy's left eyebrow?"

"No one knows." Gregory appeared, spooking the whole room.

The New Yorkers took in Gregory's trench coat mystery—and turned to Jules's feast table. They started praising her for a job well done.

"Why didn't you call one of us to pick you up?" Valentine asked.

"We only had Puck's number. And Birch's, but he didn't pick up." Thad's voice was so loud. "That fucking freak ice storm. I was on the phone for four hours trying to get Puck a ride or train ticket while the rest of our party loudly and aggressively ran lines for tonight's pageant. Couldn't book a damn thing. The whole city is frozen shut."

Someone stepped out of the bathroom.

Not *just* someone. Marrakesh was an extremely talented musician Puck knew from his New York days. Whenever possible, Birch spent time looking at Marrakesh's tattoos. These bright cartoons were all over their body, tokens of things that made them happy. During one long night in Brooklyn that Birch and Puck and Marrakesh had spent together, Birch had felt warmed up enough to ask about each tattoo—and kiss strategically placed ones.

Birch wasn't warmed up now, though. He was cold. If Puck had seen him, he would have put Birch back in the bedroom and turned on *Owl House* for at least two episodes.

Marrakesh brought over a dark chocolate fudge bar. "Puck says you probably fell asleep, and now you're out of it." They grabbed a glass of water, too, and he drank and ate. Once he felt better, could see farther, Marrakesh held out their arms. "Hug?"

Birch gave them a hug, and it wasn't too awkward. "He's not here. I'm sorry."

"Believe it or not, I was coming up to see both of you."

Birch smiled. He took out his phone. Puck had left only a handful of messages. The first was long: Weirdest thing—my uncle's neighbors with the year-round light-up crucifix are here. They keep giving me the eye. I used to jump on their trampoline with their kids before I came out.

Birch's heart began to pound. Puck's spirits were dwindling. Birch could read it in between the words and feel it from all these mountains away. He had to get this night *right*.

Wassail around the yule at 10 PM, Puck had sent. They'll stop fighting when they're singing the same words.

10:03 p.m.

Birch held Puck's favorite wooden bowl between nervous hands. Everyone gathered around the fire with mugs, which Gregory was now filling with wassail. Puck had sent Gregory a recipe in advance— some cider, liquor, sugared fruit, it wasn't an exact science.

Wassailing was the first midwinter tradition Puck had showed Birch. When he'd left home two years ago, the holidays were still tied to his parents' competitive light displays and somber church functions. He'd tried to hibernate through the damn season, and

Vermont had been happy to oblige with snow squalls and utter darkness.

But Puck had taken Birch out into these woods, even though it was a pretty big orchestration for him at the time. They weren't even dating yet. He'd put this handmade bowl between Birch's hands, and they'd taken alternating sips of a hot brew studded with oranges and cloves. In the days leading up to their first kiss, Birch was painfully attuned to Puck's lips, and suddenly they were all that he could see, perched at the edge of this bowl, whispering that the warped capitalism festival held every December had nothing to do with where all of this started.

Puck had peeled the layers off this tradition and shown him its yule underneath.

Where the magic waited.

Now Birch was the one with the bowl, trying to explain why this holiday was so important. He cleared his throat. "Wassailing is the origin of caroling, but better because—"

"Wait, I thought we were *drinking* wassail." Jules had never met a contradiction she couldn't ferret out.

"We are. It's the drink. And the activity. And it's a greeting?" Birch had to backtrack to find what he'd meant. He remembered Puck's smirking lips, poised to kiss Birch that night . . . only to open up into song . . . with such a *voice*.

"We drink and we sing to the trees and—"

"Pardon." Nate put up a point-of-order finger. "Lifelong city mouse here, did you say *sing to the trees*?"

"Yeah, and we pour wassail on the branches so they'll have a good year." Birch's voice wavered. Puck had made this sound like magic. He made it sound like something silly.

"When I was at Juilliard," Will began, "my teachers told me never to perform without warming up, and it's too cold to properly do so, *so*."

"You went to a Juilliard summer program, babe," Ryan said. "And this fire is so hot it is melting my contours."

"Isn't there science that says singing to plants is good for them?" Silas asked.

"Yes, it's science, and it's magic, and we're doing it for Puck." Birch was starting to sound desperate.

"Puck's favorite bowl," Marrakesh said, distracting him with their hotness.

Birch looked at it. "We were supposed to drink from the wassail bowl. Before Covid. Now it's ceremonial." People booed. Even though he knew they were booing the plague, Birch winced like they were booing him personally. "Drink your . . . beverage." He twisted toward the sprites. "What do you have?"

"The blood of winters past," Tomie said, lofting a cup with sloshing crimson inside.

"Lime and cran seltzies," one of the actors stage-whispered.

Birch fumbled with his phone, trying to frame the group, fire, and bowl in his hand in the foreground. He started recording and nodded at Valentine, their cue to strum. They'd noped the lute jams, but Birch had forgotten to check in about the song selection. Valentine struck a chord. Then another. The intro sounded dour and dramatic. It sounded like . . .

"Oasis?" Birch asked.

Valentine shrugged, deeply ambivalent.

Half the group began singing "Here We Come A-Wassailing" on Marrakesh's lead. The other half followed Valentine and belted "Wonderwall." Some were vaguely singing in the direction of the

222

trees, but only the sprites were pouring drinks on them. Chucking drinks, actually, and chanting rhythmic nonsense, which devolved into howling. All three strands of sound hit a vicious crescendo. People punctuated it by spitting wassail into the snow.

"What did you put in this?" Jane asked, her face deeply puckered.

"Absinthe and crème de menthe," Gregory answered. "They're both green. Yule color."

"*Absinthe?*" Birch said, the phone wobbling in his hands.

"That is going to kill trees, not encourage them to have a good year," Will noted, taking a big swallow.

"You made me drink something *illegal* and then you said it *on camera?*" Thaddeus swiped the phone out of Birch's hand.

"What are you doing?" Birch's voice cracked.

Thaddeus punched buttons. "Killing that video. I want to go into law someday. I can't have anybody seeing that."

"But it was for—"

"Puck, we know!" Ryan said. "But we need another take anyway, don't you think?"

The actors slid from the lyrics of their respective songs into harmonizing competitions. Silas was apologizing to the trees. The sprites were covered in fake blood. Birch took a swig from the wassail bowl, but instead of finding warm, spicy goodness, he got the sense that a candy cane had died and its ghost had come back to haunt his mouth. He went to pour out the wassail bowl, but Gregory swiped it from his hands and drank the rest. All of it.

"You can't waste absinthe," he said.

There was no getting this moment back. Birch clutched the empty wassail bowl too hard and came too close to breaking one of Puck's favorite possessions.

"Stop!" he shouted. "Stop!"

223

He winced under everyone looking at him like *he* was the thing breaking. "You wanted a Puck party, but did it occur to you *he* might need this night more? He's been talking about it since last year! It was going to be incredible! Right after wassailing there was a magical Midwinter King speech, but you're not getting that speech! You're getting *this* speech." Birch felt empty.

Thaddeus handed Birch's phone back. "Once more, with legal beverages?"

"Birch, we're sooo . . ."

Birch ran before Silas could apologize on everyone's behalf. He couldn't do it. He couldn't do any of this.

10:59 p.m.

Birch took his glasses off. He fell back like a board on the bed and stared at everything he couldn't see. The dark had so many more fucking hours to go.

Could he give up?

Marrakesh knocked.

If he answered, they would make him feel better. He might rally.

If he didn't answer, Marrakesh would take over the party, and he could fall asleep.

Puck would love him no matter what he chose.

Puck.

They knocked again. "Birch?"

"Come in."

11:22 p.m.

Birch had new hope for the night.

Kissing helped with that.

Marrakesh stepped back, smiling, then traced a finger along Birch's increasingly square jaw. They placed a few more kisses at intervals, like a string of lights.

It wasn't like being with Puck. That was all eye contact and an emotional wildness. Marrakesh was lighthearted, swift-fingered. But even though Puck wasn't in the room, his presence felt undeniable. They'd even snapped a mid-kiss photo and sent it to him, a little present for whenever his phone came back online.

Marrakesh pulled back on a sweater that had gotten tossed bizarrely far away. "You'll believe me next time when I say I'm here for you too?"

"I think so."

Marrakesh looked over the mess of Puck's clothes still on the bed. "We're glad he found you. When he left the city, we lost him. He needed woods and silence after, well."

Birch needed to change the subject. "You all intimidate me a lot."

"Those assholes out by the fire are intimidated by anyone who can hold Puck's eye for more than an hour. You've had him rapt for what, two years?"

"Don't ask me how," Birch admitted.

They smelled one of Puck's shirts and made a low grunt of approval. "Was he in Boston because . . . ?"

"Medical stuff. You have to ask him." Birch swept the clothes from the bed into the hamper. "He's getting better."

"We know." Marrakesh hugged him. "There's no world where we lose our Puck."

11:57 p.m.

Birch and Marrakesh got a few cheers as they returned to the chaos of the yule log. It truly was magnificent to watch a huge trunk erupt. The roots burned down in places like horns.

He grabbed three pieces that had singed and fallen out of the ring. He handed one to each sprite. "These are magical. Use them."

"For what?" Tomie asked. "How?"

"Only you know," Birch said.

"Puck told you that?"

"He didn't have to. I live with him. I notice things."

Noticing Puck's magic was Birch's favorite pastime.

Feeling it was new.

Birch sat with them. He looked beyond the fire, surprised to find a stage. The actors had built a complete set in the last two hours. They'd rigged up a curtain out of Puck's uncle's blankets, framing one central piece: the remains of Puck's midsummer throne, which they must have dragged from the woods.

Puck had created it last June out of the wisteria creeping up from the ravine. That party had been canceled; Puck could not get Covid, and there had been another outbreak. Birch put makeup on him and took summer solstice photos to send out. Then Puck fell asleep at nine and stayed in bed for two days. He wouldn't let any one of them know that, though.

The sight of Puck's empty throne filled Birch with sudden despair.

When he hiccuped a slight sob, he was surprised to find the sprites caging him.

"There is much evil in this night." Kit wore a bandolier of holly. "The magic and the evil come hand in hand."

Tomie butted in. "We looked it up on Wikipedia."

Buffalo pointed above the throne to a huge wreath—made from all the greenery that Puck had used to decorate the cabin. The sprites had been hard at work. "The wreath symbolizes the wheel of life. It protects."

Kit grinned. Birch had never seen this one so happy. So in their element. He wanted to picture Puck at this age, with this internal fire growing ever stronger.

"Greetings, all!" Ryan yelled, dressed entirely in holly. "Who ordered pageantry?"

December 22
12:54 a.m.

Suffice it to say that the actors went too far.

The three-page script Puck emailed went on for an hour. The Holly King—Ryan—was fighting his twin, the Oak King, played by Will doing some kind of overblown Shakespearean recitation. After yet another pair of soliloquies and a quick shouting match about the difference between camp and overacting, the Holly King was defeated by the Oak King. Even with some sketchy fight choreography and a too-long run time, the truths of the solstice play remained: This battle marked the changeover of the dark to the light. From death to rebirth.

When Nate came out to name the party's Midwinter King per the script, Birch stood up and waved his arms. "We can't do this part without him. We can't. He's got to be here." He took the crown of holly and placed it on the dilapidated throne.

"How *is* Puck doing?"

Jane scoffed at Thaddeus. "Not now!"

He faced her squarely. "I was there. I can bring it up."

"You left an hour before. You were lucky."

"It doesn't feel lucky that I wasn't with him. That doesn't ever feel lucky."

227

Jane and Thaddeus locked eyes. "Agreed. Apologies. Now tell them we're dating. I know you wanted to surprise Puck, but this is getting weird." The yule log split with new flames.

"I was supposed to be there that night," Nate said. "I stood him up."

"He sent the invitation to all of us," Will clarified. "None of us went."

"Beware the evil spirits," Buffalo whispered. "They only see dark."

"Now what in the hell does that mean?" Thaddeus shouted.

Valentine stood and tossed their guitar into the fire. The sprites cheered at such sudden chaos. Everyone else appeared a bit worried. Valentine sat next to Jules, took a brownie off her plate, and devoured it. Jules looked like she was ready to kiss them right there.

The guitar made an awful sound while it burned to death. The strings snapped, the wood curled, the varnish boiled black, and everything that was solid became husk.

The New Yorkers sleepily sang a song from the show they'd been in years ago. Back when they'd first fallen in love with being together. Puck was the kind of person who had families in New York and Vermont. Who could figure out how to bring them together.

"I didn't get to know Puck from before."

Had the night amplified Birch's voice?

Everyone heard him instantly. That had never happened before. His voice was lower. More sure of itself. He followed it into unlit, uncertain territory. "I want to hear your stories. I don't think I'll ever get to meet that Puck. The Puck I know, he's different, not better or worse, but he misses his old self, and I wish I knew more about who he used to be."

"Well, do you know about the time our car broke down in Amish country and by the end of it, he had the mechanic dancing?" Marrakesh asked.

"Our very own *Footloose*," Nate reminisced.

Birch barked a laugh. "You're joking."

"Am I?" Marrakesh's fingers tangled in the back of Birch's hair. "You can imagine it."

"We'll need libations for true Puck stories." Ryan jumped up. "Where is that questionable bartender? He had strong stuff!"

"Gregory!" Kit yelled.

Gregory dropped out of a tree within feet of Thaddeus and Jane. The crowd squealed.

The party started telling Puck stories. A whole night's worth of mischief and joy.

3:57 a.m.

The yule log was a giant red heart blazing, bathing everyone with heat and light. Only Gregory was still cruising, spinning in the dark. Valentine's guitar was a skeletal husk, but they'd been cuddling with Jules nonstop since the outburst.

Birch's timer went off. He checked for anything from Puck. Nothing.

"He should have had his turn for the outlet by now," Birch muttered. He'd been curled up in Marrakesh's lap for the last two hours like a well-loved cat.

"What's next?" Jane lifted her head off Thaddeus's shoulder. "We wassailed, pageanted."

"Next, Puck wants your trust. Give your phones to Silas. Watches, too. Anything that tells time."

The grumbles at this were heard to the stars and back.

Silas went around with a tote, and to each person who dropped their tech in, he said a fervent, "I'm so sorry!" He even took Tomie's Lego pocket watch.

Birch was positive that he wasn't supposed to keep his phone either, but letting go of this tether to Puck was too hard. "I'm not doing it. When he arrives, he'll need me." He pocketed his phone. "He's got some bad pain right now. He's getting it checked out."

Birch had said too much. Puck's body was his business. Just like Birch's mind was his job. Always feed it, rest it. Soothe it. Don't let it look over the wall, into the past.

When Silas brought the phones over and intoned an apology, Birch exploded.

"Stop apologizing!" He turned to Tomie. "On the counter. Mistletoe. Go get it." Tomie ran toward the cabin.

Silas had started to cry.

Birch closed his overpressured eyes. "Silas, I'm not mad. You're triggering me. When I first moved in with Puck, I couldn't stop apologizing. To everyone, for everything." Tomie came back with the mistletoe; Birch took it. "This is my favorite bit of midwinter that Puck taught me: Mistletoe wasn't about kissing under, that's new. It was for giving as a symbol of love and reconciliation. Peace." Birch held out the mistletoe.

"Silas, we are all *so sorry* that the world made you think you had to excuse yourself for being in it. That's the world's bad. Not yours."

Silas took the mistletoe. Tears dripped from his chin.

"I am also pretty sure we had the same terrible mom, so—good news—that makes us brothers. Puck and I don't feel bad for you. We like you. We're adopting you." Silas smothered Birch in a hug. The audience cheered. Actors shouted one-word reviews.

Birch thumped Silas lovingly. "All right, time for the wishing tree."

4:31 a.m.

Birch led them down the rock-lined path to the circular glade where Puck did his magic.

He'd never been here without his love, and it felt like trespassing. The huge evergreen at the center wasn't lit up like usual. The box with the decorations sat in front of it. He'd forgotten about that, but Puck's friends knew what to do. They took everything out and finished the tree within moments.

Birch handed a long red ribbon to each of them. "Write your wish on it and tie it to the boughs. Put your offering under the tree."

The group worked peacefully, silently.

"Is it just me or is it a bit more civilized," Valentine marveled, "than chopping the tree down and watching it die in your living room?"

Birch had to agree. "Some things about this night feel more civilized, and some are wilder. Speaking of which. You feel better without your six-string ball and chain?"

"I feel stupid. But I also felt stuck. And I haven't had a date since . . . you. So maybe it's time to move on."

"It's hard to quit something that was labeled good for you. I had to leave my family. Everyone assumes they kicked me out. But I rejected them. And their way of life. If I didn't, I was never going to heal from the things they did to me."

Valentine put an arm around Birch. The tree looked incredible. At least when Puck got back, he'd see this. He'd know his friends had been here, loving him. Honoring his magic. The lights illuminated the wishes written on the ribbons.

Everyone had asked for the same thing.

They left their offerings at the foot of the tree: Gregory, a gallon-sized can of beans; Nate and Will, their lucky headshots; Ryan, his favorite concealer pencil, which they didn't make anymore, so this was a *sacrifice*. Thaddeus and Jane left the receipt from their first date. And Valentine left their guitar picks, though Jules stole two of them back.

The sprites left baby teeth torn from their heads.

"I might get a call from your parents on that one," Birch muttered, eyeing their bloody grins. Silas had left his wallet. Birch gave it back to him. "You need this."

"It's full of stuff with my dead name on it. I can't even open it."

Birch put it back under the tree. "I was wrong. You can offer it."

"Really?"

"Just say you lost it tomorrow."

"Hey, you didn't offer anything yet," Kit said to Birch.

What he had brought with him no longer felt good enough.

He placed his phone on Silas's wallet. "All right, Puck. I trust the magic."

The sprites handed around small votive candles. Everyone took turns lighting theirs off the same ancient green candle from the yule flame. The party followed the sprites uphill through the black wood, farther from the yule log and glade, holding out their candles like tiny torches. They cast an orange glow on the thin snow.

"You're freaking us out," Ryan said. "Stop it!"

"Bears," Will muttered. "I'm thinking about bears. Are there any? In these woods?"

"Tons!" Gregory shouted.

"Which are sound asleep this time of year," Kit added.

"It's the wolves you worry about," Tomie said.

Buffalo howled.

The New Yorkers began to run up the path, sensing the end of the tree line.

Birch got left behind, and he stumbled, his knee hitting a rock. Silas shot back to help him, but right away he felt the darker places in his mind. They seemed to merge with the shadows of the trees all around. Birch blinked and his tired eyes twisted everything into a post-traumatic slideshow. He saw things Puck witnessed that night. When Puck woke up screaming, he'd sometimes describe what he was reliving. Now its gory hate was in Birch's head with the ugly things that had happened in the name of his parents' church.

His mind opened up with darkness.

The shadows of miserable bigots everywhere, pointing automatic wea—

"Blow out your candles!" Gregory shouted from up ahead. "You're jumping at shadows but you're also making them!"

Birch took Marrakesh's arm and blew out their candles. Without the flames, the woods turned to a soft gray. They climbed the path in silence, to where the tree line ended. A smooth and cool rocky surface faced the black-scalloped horizon of mountains. Puck's favorite place for stargazing.

"What do we do now?" Ryan asked.

"We wait," Kit said.

"For the evil spirits to be banished by the sun," Tomie finished.

The sprites produced blankets, putting them out on the rock. Birch was reminded that Puck had given everyone instructions. Even though he hadn't been there, he'd made this all happen. For his friends. The party settled on the rock face, and Gregory passed around something that made Birch's eyes sting and the actors cough and swear. He remembered what Puck had said that first midwinter together. He did his best to capture it.

"It's not about evil spirits," Birch said to everyone, shocked by his volume, by his own changed voice. "This celebration is about the long dark that ends every year. This is the longest night, but when the dawn comes, we will have made it. It's about survival and what comes after it. The light reborn."

Birch's speech got applause. The dark movement of a hat's off from Will. It would have been the perfect moment for dawn. Alas, Birch did not have Puck's particular flair for magical appearances.

"Do we even know if we're facing the right direction?" Jane asked.

"I see light," Valentine said.

"That's the yule log," Jules corrected.

"There's light." Ryan pointed to the light-up crucifix in the neighbor's yard. "Looks like the Christian neighbors are just getting home. Party animals."

"What did you say?" Birch sat up.

"The neighbors with the light-up crucifix. They just drove up in a big van."

Dawn

Birch skidded down the rock face, toward the path into the woods.

He felt Kit next to him. "I'll get you back to the cabin the fast way."

He took the seventh grader's shoulder and closed his sore eyes. They moved so fast it was a wonder they didn't fall, but Birch dared to think that his feet wouldn't catch on anything, and Kit could see in the dark like the little bat that they were.

It was all downhill and soft, shifting leaves, and it felt like flying.

When Birch felt packed snow underfoot, he opened his eyes and skipped to a stop. He was already back by the yule log. Kit spun right around and charged into the woods, unwilling to miss the sunrise.

"Love?"

Puck sat on his throne, long shoulders and arms folded. Birch hadn't seen him in a few days and that meant he'd forgotten how skinny Puck had become. Birch knelt beside him and pressed his hand on Puck's forearm. "Hi, my love."

He didn't lift his head. "Are you alone?"

"They're up on the rock. The night had all kinds of magic, you were right."

"I saw." Puck's phone balanced on his knee. He was stiff with pain and couldn't close his fingers around it, but his thumb swiped through photos and videos from all his friends. "Kit got hold of your phone, at some point. I got five hundred and thirty-two images of the fire."

Puck laughed, winced. He doubled over. They began the wordless and beyond intimate dance of finding his shot bag and getting a holiday dose in his thigh. Birch didn't breathe as he stashed the needle in the travel dispenser and rubbed Puck's leg until it felt warm. The yule log crackled. Puck started breathing deeper. He stood.

Birch held him. "Did you really get a ride with the neighbors?"

"They rented a van. Offered me a ride. Good Samaritan programming kicked in. I am positive they think I'm a meth junkie, with all the pain sweats."

"You made it all the way here in a van with Christians and zero meds."

"Midwinter magic. Also my therapist deserves a gold medal."

"Puck. What did the surgeon say?"

"That it's good pain. Nerves reattaching. It hurts because it's healing."

"It hurts because it's healing." Birch was still fighting with this one. "My therapist says that, too. Do you need another surgery?"

"He prescribed *more time*. Apparently years of pain after a few bullets in the belly is normal." Puck touched Birch's face. "That photo from Marrakesh. Can I frame it?"

Birch pulled him down for a warm kiss. "Come up to the rock. See your friends."

"It'd take all my energy. They'll have to carry me down."

"So let them. They want to."

Puck purred in Birch's arms, his spirit lightening, his back arching. Suddenly, Birch could imagine Puck dancing. All those stories . . . now he could see it *and* believe it. And know that Puck would dance again.

Birch held him. "You're my eyes, I'm your earth. We move forward together."

"You're amazing," Puck said. "Next you're going to tell me you sorted out Valentine and Jules."

"What if I did? And helped Silas . . . I think."

Puck dropped the holly crown on Birch's head. "All hail the Midwinter King."

"Then the Midwinter King gets his wish." Birch brought Puck's lips to his. "Come up to the rock. I swear the light is waiting for you."

Merry Chrismukkah, Loser

BY KATHERINE LOCKE

The contest begins with an argument. With Noa Hotchner because, honestly, when am I *not* arguing with Noa Hotchner?

Noa has a problem with me. She's *always* had a problem with me. We've been picking fights with each other since JCC preschool, and it's only escalated. In third grade when I wanted to play Aladdin in the school play, she said, *You can't, you're not a boy*, and I was like, *Prove it*, and punched her in the nose. We've just never gotten along, and today's no exception.

We're talking about Hanukkah at religious school because it's that time of year where they like to shove all the teens into a room with some pizza and a single question written on a chalkboard and then check on us two hours later, hoping we've had some sort of theological breakthrough and the room's not trashed.

Rabbi Josh had written, "WHAT DOES CHANUKAH REALLY MEAN TO YOU?" on the board, swapping in the Hebrew letters for Chanukah, plopped down a bunch of pizza—at ten thirty in the morning, no less—and a liter of Coke, and peaced out. They've been short two teachers this year, so we Elder Teens have been on our own since early November.

So far, I'm not sure he's going to be impressed with our theological breakthroughs.

"Potatoes are not an aesthetic," I repeat, rocking one of those school chairs back and forth, trying to see how far back I can get it to balance on just two legs. I'm talking around a mouthful of cookie because while Noa Hotchner annoys me, and I make a career out of annoying her, the girl makes a *mean* sugar cookie. These are all decorated as dreidels. She gave me the one that had the Hebrew letter *nun* on the side of it. Nothing tasted so delicious.

"You can't count *peppermint* as an aesthetic and not potatoes," Noa spits out.

Of all the arguments I've had with Noa, this is probably my crowning achievement. My goal in each argument is to make Noa say the most ridiculous, inane things so the next time she says something super super smart in regular high school or boasts about her SAT scores or whatever else smart kids do, I can be like, "Remember when you argued that potatoes were *aesthetically pleasing?*"

There's also this other part where the madder Noa gets at me, the prettier she gets, and I'm sorry—not sorry I'm like this, but you'd probably get it if you were here. Something about her autumn-colored hair and how red her entire face gets and the way her brow scrunches up when she's glaring. She's one of those girls who probably looks pretty when she's crying, too, but I wouldn't know because I haven't seen Noa Hotchner cry since third grade.

I, for the record, don't look pretty when I'm crying. I don't look pretty anytime, but crying just makes me look splotchy and puffy and my nose runs like mad.

Noa hasn't seen me cry since third grade.

"Peppermint," I tell her, holding up a finger, "is red and white, and connotes a smell *and* a flavor. Potatoes are brown, smell like dirt, and taste like dirt, too."

"Peppermint isn't a *color*," Noa replies with a sniff. "That's a *candy cane*."

I shrug. "Just admit it. Christmas nailed the aesthetic. Hanukkah falls short. Christmas has music, flavors, food, colors, textures . . . Hanukkah's like *We fried some shit and there are candles*."

"You're literally eating one of my cookies right now. You've just been doing Hanukkah *all wrong*." Noa sits back, crossing her arms.

"These are delicious," I say, waving the last bite of cookie at her. "But really, you think Hanukkah's superior because you've never done Christmas."

"That's because I'm Jewish," Noa says sharply, and just after the words escape her mouth, she realizes her mistake.

I let the chair legs slam back onto the floor. "So am I."

There's a long pause.

Even though Reform Judaism recognized patrilineal descent when my parents were *children*, there are a lot of Jews who still don't think that I'm Jewish because my dad's Jewish and my mom's not. People follow this up with, *Oh, but she converted?* And no, she didn't, and she doesn't need to. Why would she need to? My branch of Judaism says I'm Jewish with just one Jewish parent, regardless of which parent that is.

And yet there are always people who try to deny my Judaism.

"I can prove that Christmas has a better aesthetic," I hear myself say.

I shouldn't have let her off the hook. I should have made her sit there in her discomfort with my Jewishness. But I like to win, and the argument isn't that I'm Jewish, but that Christmas wins at the holiday aesthetic. I'm sorry, but it just does.

Noa's smile could cut a diamond. "I can prove that Chanukah does."

This time, she says it "Chanukah," with the hard Hebrew *ch* sound at the beginning. It's a slight, I think, against the way I say Hanukkah, all anglicized with a plain ol' *h* sound.

We establish ground rules. We make up a scoring rubric, rating each holiday's aesthetic in the categories of decor, food, music, and story. One to five. Best score wins. Simple. Easy peasy, latke squeezy.

We'll do Christmas at my house, where Noa will be scoring me. I imagine her walking around tapping a pencil thoughtfully against her lips as she docks us points for Santa waffles. I can't imagine whimsy is her thing. Then we'll traipse over to her house for Hanuk-kah. I'm *not* going easy on her. One mushy latke and it's all over for her. I'll dock my own people points under the Food category if it means beating Noa Hotchner.

"We need a grand prize," Noa says, frowning at the rubric. We erased Rabbi Josh's question and replaced it with this: "Sorry, Rabbi, but this is what Chanukah means to me."

"Winning is the prize," I retort.

Her mouth flattens into the thinnest line. "Fine. See you in, what, five days?"

"You're on," I say, rocking the chair back again. I give her my cockiest grin. "See you December twenty-fifth."

Like I said, mistakes *were* made.

Christmas is always on the twenty-fifth of December. You

probably know that even if you don't celebrate the holiday, because the entire Western world operates under Christian hegemony. That's just a fact, not a statement about Christianity, don't get it twisted. Hanukkah always starts on the twenty-fifth of Kislev in the Hebrew calendar.

Please don't ask me to explain the Hebrew calendar. I'm not made for that. I rarely use this as an excuse, but I'm a Reform Jew. It's a lunar calendar. I google when our holidays are, just like you should.

Because of said lunar calendar, sometimes Hanukkah overlaps with Christmas. It's possible the sun is also involved, but who can be sure? Not me.

The point being, when you have one Jewish parent and one Christian parent, and they decide to raise you in one religious tradition but honor the traditions of the other parent, this is the greatest mash-up of all time. Christmas in the morning, Hanukkah at night—it's like an entire day of eating and gifts and reading in your pajamas. It's literally the greatest day ever, and it only comes every few years.

So it's important, imperative even, when it comes to make the most of it.

I wait until we're stuck in the middle of the really long line of cars trying to exit the synagogue parking lot before I break the news about the competition to Mom.

"So," I begin, aware that my tone is suspicious from the start. "Can I have a friend over on Christmas morning?"

"In the *morning?*" Mom repeats. She's not a morning person. "Like, how early? Why can't it be the afternoon?"

"Because this friend's never experienced Christmas before, and she really, really wants to." I add a little whine to my voice just to seal the deal.

Mom shoots me a look. "Jordan."

"Yes?"

"Who is it?" Mom drums her thumbs on the steering wheel.

For a second, I consider lying. "Um, Noa Hotchner?"

"*Noa Hotchner?*" Mom repeats, almost lurching into the car ahead of us. "Have you *lost your mind*? You *hate* Noa."

Hate is such a strong word. It's not wrong . . . it's just, you know, not the right word.

"I don't hate Noa," I explain carefully. "She's just my mortal archenemy and lifelong nemesis."

"Your mortal archenemy, and you want her over for Christmas morning," Mom says in disbelief.

"Yes. We're arguing, and I'm going to win, but it involves her coming over for Christmas."

"Oh, well," Mom says sardonically, "if it involves *winning*."

I have never once texted with Noa Hotchner, because we have never had a reason to text. We've been on group texts together, obviously, but I've never directly replied to her, and she's never directly replied to me. So it's weird on Christmas Eve when I get a text from her, and it's just her.

THE WORST: are we still on for tomorrow

It takes me a second to remember who was labeled *The Worst* in my phone. Then I grin. I step away from my family and all my extended family celebrating in the living room into the quiet of the hall, where I can text her back. They're loud in there, and boisterous, and it's full of inside family jokes and stories. But tomorrow, it'll just be us. And Noa.

> **ME:** Yes, obviously. Please do not arrive before 8:30. My mom needs at least two cups of coffee before she can interact with the public.

> **THE WORST:** Do I need to bring anything?

My thumbs hover over the screen. Technically, no. But I did get Noa a present. So maybe that's weird.

> **ME:** I mean, it's a little late to be asking that. Everything's closed.

> **THE WORST:** Good point.

> **ME:** I think just yourself.

I almost add *and an open mind*, but Noa can't bring things she doesn't have, so why bother asking.

> **ME:** Did I warn you about my family?

> **THE WORST:** No? Uh, what should I know about them?

> **ME:** I have two older brothers, Eli and Ethan.

> **THE WORST:** Yes, I remember them.

ME: Okay. Don't hold them against me. They're not part of this contest.

THE WORST: I can agree to that amendment to the ground rules. Family not included.

ME: Good.

ME: Thanks.

THE WORST: See you in the morning.

I'm pretty sure my new goal is to make Noa Hotchner say *Merry Christmas* tomorrow. Just once. And mean it.

On Christmas morning, I'm giddy like a little kid again.

"I swear to God, if you don't relax," Mom grumbles as I dash between the kitchen, where I'm starting the Santa waffle maker, and the front window to see if she's pulled up.

She has not, and it's already eight thirty-one. I was going to text her, but Mom insisted that I call her so she wouldn't be texting and driving, and I am absolutely not calling Noa Hotchner on the actual phone.

Dad comes back in the side door with Josie, our ridiculous Lab, who bounds in with her muddy paws, leaping on all of us as Mom and Eli shout, protecting their cups of coffee, my other older brother, Ethan, does absolutely nothing to help, and I try to catch Josie before she reaches the living room. Wrapping paper is a delicacy in her culture, and we discovered this the hard way last year.

"Sam!" Mom bellows.

Dad shouts from the back hallway, "Guess who I found hiding around the corner?"

His voice is full of delight. Too much delight.

Oh *no.*

Dad's beaming as he marches into the kitchen, a hand on the shoulder of Noa Hotchner, who looks about as horrified as I feel right now. She's hunched her shoulders up and her auburn hair is pulled into a tight ponytail. She's wearing a dark green sweater dress and knit tights and boots, and she looks like she wants to melt into the floor.

"I saw her car idling by the bushes and I thought she'd broken down," Dad explained.

Noa meets my eyes, and for the first time since I've known her, she looks apologetic. "I'm sorry. You said not before eight thirty and I arrived early and I thought it'd be weird if I was just sitting out front of your house, so I was at the corner . . ."

"This ruins everything," I tell her, and I'm only half joking. "You were supposed to come in the front! That's how you can experience the whole thing!"

"The whole thing?" Noa repeats.

"*Christmas,*" I say, rolling my eyes.

I almost grab her hand out of instinct and I catch myself just in time, shoving my hands into my own pockets. Ethan catches the motion, glances at Noa and then back at me, a grin spreading across his face.

I lead her to the front hallway. "This is where we're starting with the aesthetic."

Noa pulls out her phone and holds it up. "I put our scoring rubric on Google Sheets and shared it with you."

Why is she like this? Who does this? This is maniacal. I love it.

The competition begins.

The best part of a Christmas aesthetic isn't vomiting Christmas in every direction. That's what people get wrong with their decor. There's an art to it.

It's the front hall railings wrapped in red-and-white-striped ribbon, garnished with golden bows, and the candles in the front windows, and the nutcracker family painted to look like each of us family members. It's my mom's favorite Christmas music playlist that goes from "Feliz Navidad" to a compilation of "Jingle Bells" in twenty languages.

"These," I say, pointing to a set of miniature reindeer pulling a miniature sled with a Santa sack full of miniature presents on top of a bookcase, "were made by my uncle."

"That's neat," Noa says.

I shake my head. "No, no, it's not just neat. Look."

I pull out the Santa sack and start to tug free all the little miniature presents. Boxes open and inside are tiny, extra-mini teddy bears. Bags open and inside are books, with text and covers of classics, and tiny, itsy-bitsy miniature knitted hats and mittens and scarves.

Noa marvels over them, and I try not to watch her too closely. But it's hard not to. Wonder and curiosity spill across her face as she unwraps all the miniature presents. She blinks in surprise when she pulls the tiny copy of *Twilight* out of the bag and holds it up to me, the classic cover of the hands and the apple pinched between her fingers. She'd painted her nails with tiny little candles. Her hands are a menorah. I want to quibble over the lack of a shamash, but I don't.

She carefully slides the *Twilight* book back into the tissue-papered bag. "This is cute. I'll concede the point."

"This is just the front hall," I say, helping rebox the other gifts and fit them into the Santa sack again. "Not even the tree."

Our tree has the quirkiest ornaments possible—ballerina pigs, Snoopy flying a plane, Santa in a tugboat, kissing frogs with Santa hats on, Santa's elves mooning you through the window of Santa's workshop—and a lot of ornaments we made in school when my brothers and I were kids. Paper plates with a lot of glue and glitter and a bad photo of us squinting in the sun, wearing shirts that say "CAMP AHAVA" and "HESCHEL JCC DAY CAMP 2014" because that's what we wore to school that day. There's even an ornament of Popsicle sticks dipped in glitter and glued together to make a Star of David.

Noa inspects all the ornaments and instantly finds one of those cheesy school ones of me. She turns it to face me, grinning. "I remember when you looked like this."

I cross my arms. "It was a phase."

"Yeah, of cutting your own bangs," she cackles. She looks at me closely. "Do you *still* cut your own bangs?"

My hands go immediately to my hair and I try to smooth it down. "No, my hair's just wacky this morning."

She hums a bit, and it's hard to tell if that's in agreement or observation. Mariah Carey starts to croon in the background, and I wish I were in the kitchen where I could grab Mom's phone and hit *next*.

"Noa!" Dad calls from the kitchen. "How many waffles?"

She looks at me, panicked, and I hold up two fingers. Two is a good amount of Santa waffles. Not too much. Not too little. You get to enjoy the Santa effect without getting sick of it. She calls back, "Two!"

"Syrup?"

"No, thanks!"

"Weird," I comment.

She laughs a little. "I hate when things get soggy."

I've probably eaten two thousand meals with Noa Hotchner over our lives between school and synagogue, and I never knew this about her.

"We're coming in!" calls Mom, like she needs to warn us, or like she's interrupting something. And judging by her facial expression when she rounds the corner, I think she expected to be interrupting something. She looks relieved as she carries her plate of waffles and coffee to the couch.

Ethan's close behind her, no waffles, just coffee. Eli's the opposite. All waffles. No coffee.

"So, Noa," Mom begins.

Noa's head jerks up, her eyes wide. Dad hands her a plate of waffles, which she takes without even looking.

"How's the competition?" Mom asks. "Are we winning?"

"Oh," Noa says with relief.

"What did you *think* she was going to ask you?" I want to know.

Noa ignores me. "I mean, you're getting high scores for Decor. I loved the little miniature presents. The ornaments are great. I admit that the tree is a good look. The Food—extra points for thematic shapes? And your commitment to the music is admirable."

"I'm sure we're getting docked points for Story," I explain to Mom. "It's not historically accurate."

"It's *not*," Noa says hotly, flushing.

I love being right.

Dad says to Mom, "I was not aware this was a competition."

"Everything's a competition," Ethan, Eli, Mom, and I say all together.

Noa points to us with her fork, chewing on a bite of Santa waffle. "That was good. You should take that show on the road."

As soon as we're mostly done eating our waffles, we dive into stockings and presents, and while it's a little awkward because Noa's sitting closest to the tree so she's helping hand out presents and most of them aren't for her, she gets into the act of dramatically reading off the labels. The labels have gotten more ridiculous as we've gotten older and as we no longer believe in Santa.

"To Eli, from your future physical therapist," she reads, handing it off to my brother, who is over the moon to unwrap one of those mats with all the sharp plastic pointy bits that are supposed to be like lying on a bed of nails. To each their own.

"To Susan from Josie," Noa says, handing off a present to my mom. "Josie's handwriting looks a lot like Santa's handwriting."

"Josie is an exceptionally thoughtful dog," Mom tells Noa with a wink. It's insoles for Mom's shoes, probably because she walks Josie more than the rest of us.

Noa picks up the next present and blinks. "To Noa, from Jordan." She looks at me. "I didn't realize presents were a part of this competition."

I really wish my family would stop staring at me like they are right now. "I thought it'd be weird if there was *nothing* for you."

I'd thought about this present a lot, and I'm a little proud that I didn't have to text anyone else in our class for ideas.

She opens it slowly and everyone leans forward to see what I got her. She pulls out the piece of warm-colored wood and sits it on her lap, looking at it.

"It's a cookbook holder thing," I explain quickly when she doesn't immediately say anything. "Because you've been baking so much lately, so I figured maybe—"

"This is perfect," she interrupts me. She looks up and smiles at me, and it's so genuine that I sit back on my heels like I'm the one who was hit in the face this time. I'm not entirely sure how I'm supposed to push her buttons ever again, if that's how she looks when she's actually happy. She grips the cookbook holder with both hands. "Drives me nuts when the page flips. This is absolutely perfect. Thanks, Jor."

She looks down at it and I make the mistake of glancing around the room. Ethan grins at me and mouths, "Jor," with a wink. I want to chuck a cookbook at his head to wipe the smirk off his face. I avoid the weird look Mom's giving me and reach for the next present, eager to move this show along and definitely eager to look anywhere but at Noa's face.

The rest of the present portion of the day moves quickly, and after that, we move on to cooking Christmas dinner and reading in the living room. Dad starts a fire in the fireplace and Noa wordlessly adds a point to the Decor column, and she glowers at me when she does it, which makes me laugh. The corner of her mouth tilts up and she sits at the end of the couch opposite me, her bare feet tucked beneath her and one of my mom's cookbooks on her lap. I didn't even know people *read* cookbooks, but Noa Hotchner apparently does, as absorbed in that book as I am in the next installment of my favorite weird lesbian necromancers in space series.

After dinner, when we're about to head over to Noa's house, my mom *hugs* Noa. "You're welcome here anytime, Noa."

At least Noa looks as surprised as I am. "Thanks so much, Mrs. Lutz. It was great to meet you and Mr. Lutz. Thanks for having me."

"And we're not just saying that for a good score!" my dad calls over Mom's shoulder unnecessarily. "But please leave us notes so we can improve for next year!"

"Dads," I grumble, sliding into Noa's passenger seat.

She buckles her seat belt and takes a deep breath before starting the car. "You know, if we gave points for family, I think it would have raised your score a bit."

I snort. "Okay, that scoring rubric might need a revision, and secondly, you can't improve a perfect score."

She rolls her eyes as she pulls out onto the highway. "It's not a perfect score."

"I feel like the Story part of the scoring rubric is unfair," I argue. "Everyone knows the story of Hanukkah. And we're *biased* to the story of Hanukkah."

"Not everyone knows it!" Noa says in protest. She slides into the turn lane at the first light on the highway and puts on her blinker.

"You live in this development?" I ask in surprise. "Have you always lived here? How come we didn't ride the bus together?"

"We moved here after eighth grade. And no, I don't ride the bus. Because you punched me in the face in third grade," Noa says. "And my mom felt it was safer if she drove me after that."

I'm quiet for a minute as Noa pulls up to her house, a plain old suburban cookie-cutter home that is a dime a dozen out here. I didn't remember that we'd once ridden the same bus together. I do remember punching her in the face.

"I'm sorry," I say quietly.

She parks in her driveway. "It's fine."

"It's not fine," I begin.

"Jordan, I was an asshole to you," she snaps, cutting me off. "I was a bully. I *hate* myself when I think about the things I said to you."

We sit quietly in the car, not looking at each other, just looking at the garage doors, listening to the hum of her car. The thing is, when I think of Noa, I don't think of her as a bully. *Bully* wouldn't even make a top ten list of words I'd put with Noa. A *snob*. *Elitist*. *Prissy*. One of those popular girls who makes everyone else feel like outsiders? Yes. But not a bully.

I take a deep breath. "I think it'd be unreasonable to expect kids eight years ago to understand gender spectrum, and also, I didn't even understand it. Either way, it doesn't matter, because I shouldn't have hit you. And I'm sorry if me hitting you made you afraid to ride the bus with me. I didn't know." She sniffs and I twist to face her, horror blooming in my chest. "Ooooh, no, no, no, please don't cry. Oh, I'm really bad with crying."

"I'm not crying!" Noa yells, very clearly crying.

She wipes her face on her sleeve.

My heart's pounding. But I sit there quietly, watching her stubbornly stare straight ahead and ignore my gaze. She takes a few deep breaths and then shakes her hands, exhaling hard.

"Okay," she says, and her voice is clear and strong again, like she never cried. "None of that happened. You can't let that sway your score."

"How would that *possibly* sway my score?" I demand.

"I don't know! Maybe you'd deduct points for emotional weakness!" she says, turning off the car.

"Oh yeah, because under the criteria for Decor it says *emotional strength*," I tease, a little harder than necessary because I think she needs that from me right now. This push and pull of our arguments and banter. Something normal. Something predictable.

She glares at me over the roof of the car as we get out. "And no pity points either!"

"I'll add it to the notes for needs improvement next year," I retort. I love being right.

She slams her car door shut.

I think I'm in love.

Oh my God, I'm in love.

With *Noa Hotchner*. This is such a bad idea. *This* is a mistake.

She's at her front door before I realize I'm still standing next to the open car door. She turns, staring at me. "Jordan?"

I shut the car door and take the steps up to her front door two at a time, half wanting to avoid questions about why I was just standing there staring slack-jawed into space, and half wanting to get inside and get this done with, immediately. And there's still a part of me that wants to rewind to a few seconds ago so I know where I went wrong, or maybe I should rewind to last week when I suggested this stupid competition so we'd never get here.

Noa's saying something as I step inside her home, but I don't hear anything she's saying. She touches my elbow and I jump away from her. Her brow furrows in confusion and then I see it, the way she carefully hides her hurt.

"You good?" she asks quietly. "I'm sorry. Maybe I shouldn't have said anything about—"

"I'm good," I say quickly. I take a dramatic sniff, eager to change the subject. "Potatoes."

"Fried potatoes," she argues, again, falling right back into our rhythm. "Delicious."

I pull out my phone and make a dramatic show of leaving notes in the scoring document. "Frying . . . dirt . . ."

She snorts, and clearly by habit, she pulls the ponytail holder out of her hair as she walks ahead of me into the kitchen. Her hair unfurls like a red flag down her shoulders, and I follow helplessly.

The kitchen's packed with people, and I didn't expect that. I stop in the doorway, and all the cool thoughts in my head, all my parent-pleasing-make-this-better-with-Mrs.-Hotchner skills just fly right out of my head, leaving an echoey space. It's easy enough to tell who her parents are—they're both tall like Noa, more limbs than torso, and awkward in the same kind of way, as they bump into each other twice behind the island trying to get to the stove and the sink. I imagine they do this every day. Then there's a family at the island, the parents trying to have a conversation with Mr. and Mrs. Hotchner while three little boys try to drive toy cars up and down their parents' arms and necks and heads. The parents ignore this so completely that I know this too happens every day.

"I'm home!" Noa announces when our presence in the doorway doesn't change the loud clamor of the kitchen.

"Noa!" her mom says with a smile, like she's just come home from a long break and she wasn't just gone for the day. She hugs her daughter. "How was Christmas?"

Noa pulls out her phone and consults the score sheet. "Honestly, not bad. I gave it a 4.5 on Decor, a 2.5 on Music, a 3 on Food, and a 1 on Story."

"Wow, harsh critic," I say behind her.

Noa shoots me a look that's equal parts annoyance and pleased.

I have no idea what to do with that. I probably would have before my revelation out at the car, but right now I am way, way out of my depth.

"Everyone, this is Jordan Lutz. Jordan, you've probably seen my parents around, Helen and David. And these are our family friends from Boston. Sheila, Aaron, and then these are their kids—Asher, Nate, and Jeremy."

"I have a red car!" screams one of the children.

"So cool!" enthuses Noa, who as far as I have ever seen could not care less about cars, regardless of their color.

"You're the kid who's doing the competition with Noa," says Sheila, shaking my hand.

"They're probably already scoring us," Noa says as she opens the fridge. "Jordan, you want anything?"

I want to tell her, *I'm giving you a ten out of ten. Five stars.*

But I also want to win. And I want to take this seriously.

I force myself to look away from her and meet the adults' suspicious but smiling faces. Her parents haven't even offered to shake my hand, which is how I know *they* haven't forgotten I broke their daughter's nose in third grade. Still, I want to make a good impression. Her dad's wearing an apron that says "THE GREAT LATKE WARS OF 2016," which automatically endears him to me.

"Hi, thanks so much for having me over," I say cheerfully. "Anything I can help with?"

"Latkes are almost done. We're ready for candle lighting, latkes, sufganiyot, dreidel . . . anything we're missing?" Mrs. Hotchner looks to her husband and to Sheila and Aaron.

One of the boys holds out a car to me. "Do you like cars?"

"Love them," I confirm.

"And yet you don't have your driver's license," Noa says, shutting the fridge. She holds a container of applesauce and a container of sour cream. She raises her eyebrow suggestively and I know exactly what she means.

"Sour cream," I say immediately.

Her face falls. "Oh no."

My entire *heart* bottoms out. "Oh *no*."

In the saddest, most dramatic voice, she says, "The Great Latke Wars have begun."

I pull out my phone. "Deducting a point in the Food section."

"Wow," says Mr. Hotchner. "You're letting her bad topping choices dictate the score of my latkes? These are world famous, I'll have you know."

I point at him. "Team Sour Cream?"

"You know it," he says in the most peak dad way. We knock elbows, since he's got a pan of hot oil in one hand and a spatula in another.

"Betrayal," Noa stage-whispers to her mother.

Helen shakes her head. "Don't worry, sweetheart, we outnumber them."

"Oh man, that'd be terrifying, if Hanukkah was not literally the story of an outnumbered army overcoming a much larger army!" I joked.

Noa rolls her eyes. "You cannot *seriously* be comparing yourself to the Maccabees."

I lean on the island, gesturing to the little kids. They immediately stop playing with the cars, because if there's anything little kids love more than cars, it's being part of secret sharing. I whisper, "You like sour cream more than applesauce, right? Because it's the *cooler* topping?"

The boys look like they're going to disagree with me, but I give them a little prompt, nodding my head a bit. And they catch on. They grin. "Yes, sour cream!"

I look over at Noa, grinning. "New recruits!"

"Cheating," she informs me, but just before she turns away to bring the sour cream and applesauce to the table, I can see another one of those genuine smiles on her face.

It's unfortunate that this started over my opinion of squishy potatoes as a signature meal for a holiday, because Mr. Hotchner's latkes are above and beyond the best latkes I've ever had.

"These are upsettingly good," I tell him.

"This is why we come over here. The latkes," Aaron tells me.

I get it. I really do. Understatement. They taste totally different from the latkes we make at home. Crispier, and yet somehow full of flavor. They don't just taste like very hot oil.

Mr. Hotchner grins. "It's a secret Hotchner recipe. Straight from Galicia."

Mrs. Hotchner sighs. "It's from *my* side of the family, which makes it a Kagan recipe."

Mr. Hotchner shrugs. "Right. Anyways, the secret is chicken fat. That's what gives it the flavor. The other part that keeps it from getting too mushy—"

I glance at Noa. "Right. The soggy part. Wouldn't want things to get mushy."

"—is potato chips mixed with the crackers or matzo meal or breadcrumbs, whatever you use."

I reach for the sour cream on the table. "So the answer to making better fried potatoes is a potato that's been fried to a crisp?"

"Bingo!" cries Mr. Hotchner.

"So have you changed your opinion of potatoes?" Noa asks, putting a disgusting amount of applesauce onto her latke.

"It's not that I don't like potatoes," I protest. "It's just that I think we could have done better, you know?"

"They're symbolic," argues Noa.

I point at the potato. "You think that they had potatoes in Judea?"

She crosses her arms. "The oil is symbolic, and you know this."

"Are they always like this?" Sheila asks Mrs. Hotchner.

"I honestly have no idea," Mrs. Hotchner says in return. "I didn't even know they were friends until a few days ago when Noa said Jordan was coming over tonight."

"It's a competition," we say at the same time.

I return to the question at hand. "I do, and I still don't get why potatoes. We could have done a lot of other things with oil than potatoes. Do Sephardic and Mizrahi Jews do latkes? I doubt it."

"So your issues with Chanukah food is largely Ashkenazi food," Noa guesses.

"Just potatoes," I protest. "They get all soggy and mushy."

"You just haven't had *good* latkes," Noa says firmly, leaving no more room for argument.

The table's small for this many people, but it feels cozy. Their menorah sits in the middle, the reflection glinting off the windows facing the street, an elegant bird made of a brass-colored metal, its feathers from its wings holding up the candles with the shamash at its head.

I think people think because I love the aesthetic of Christmas that I don't like Hanukkah, but I do. And there's something really specific about lighting a menorah and putting it in a window that I love. It's equal parts brave and spiteful, and I know it's supposed to be publicizing the miracle, but it also feels like throwing a middle finger up to everyone who's ever tried to kill us, to every anti-Semite, and to an entire world that feels hell-bent, more days than not, on pushing Judaism back into the shadows.

As soon as the little kids are done with the latkes and their blood sugar's been stabilized, Mr. Hotchner grabs the matches and hands them to Noa.

Noa strikes a match and lights the shamash and begins to sing, and I join in with her and her parents and Sheila and David, praising God for bringing the light of Hanukkah into our lives and into the world. The little kids stop fighting and sit quietly, watching in awe as the candlelight flickers. Noa picks up the shamash with gentle, careful fingers and lights the five candles, since tonight's the fifth night, and then tilts the shamash so the flame from the first candle melts the wax of the bottom of the shamash and holds it in its spot.

I've heard Noa chant and sing before, and I've always thought she had a pretty voice, but it carries here in her own home. Or maybe I'm noticing it more. Or maybe she's letting herself be louder, prettier, here than she does at synagogue. They move from the prayer into "Maoz Tzur," "Rock of Ages," and I follow along, even though we don't do this one at home. We switch into English at this point, and it never occurred to me until now that maybe my family's tradition of mostly singing and chanting in English at our Jewish holidays is so that my mom can participate.

After "Maoz Tzur," Noa moves the menorah into the windowsill, and the candlelight dances in the reflection. At home, through the trees and across the highway, I know that Mom, Dad, Ethan, and Eli are all finishing up their Hanukkah celebration and putting their menorahs in the windowsill, too. At home, we each have our own menorah and so the whole front of the house is just candlelight. That, and a Christmas tree. Visible from the road. We must really confuse the neighbors.

It's this beautiful moment, and all these feelings inside of me are making me deeply uncomfortable, so I pull out my phone. "It's time to score Hanukkah."

Noa rolls her eyes at me, but again, there's a little smile at the corner of her mouth.

"Extra points for the music," I pretend to muse. "Extra, *extra* points for not doing the Adam Sandler song."

"A classic," David protests.

"My brother Eli would happily sing it with you," I inform him. "But I think I'll have to walk into the sea the next time I hear it."

Noa grins. "Noted."

I groan. "Ugh. Classic mistake. Never arm your enemy."

Team Applesauce faces off against Team Sour Cream for a rousing game of dreidel that only ends when one of the Team Sour Cream's latest recruits falls asleep under the table despite all the shouts and attempts at cheating by shaking the table or pounding on it.

"I guess it *is* long past bedtime," Sheila says as her husband drags their son out from under the table and slings him unceremoniously over his shoulder.

Noa glances at me. "Yeah, we should probably wrap these scores up."

I really, *really* don't want to score this.

I don't even know if I want to win anymore.

What were we fighting about? Potatoes? Aesthetics?

All I know is that when we score this, the competition is over.

And this weird magical day is over. And I'm never going to get this again. Noa Hotchner with her feet tucked under her on my couch. Noa Hotchner's dad elbow-high-fiving me. Noa handing out presents with my family under our Christmas tree. Listening to Noa sing "Maoz Tzur."

It's not like I could challenge her to a rematch.

Wait, I could challenge her to a rematch. We'd have to do this again. I could wait a year, right?

"Jordan?" Noa asks, puzzled. Everyone else is standing, I realize, and Sheila's getting coats on the boys at the door. I'm still sitting.

"Right, right," I say quickly.

At the door, Mrs. Hotchner hugs me, which is weird, and says, "Next time bring your parents!"

I almost ask her if she has inside information. Will there be a next time?

But I don't. I just smile at her and then shake Mr. Hotchner's hand.

In the car, Noa shoots me a look as she reverses out of the driveway. "You're being quiet."

"Sometimes I'm quiet," I say, instinctively making everything an argument.

She takes the bait. "I've literally known you since you were still in diapers and you've never ever been quiet."

I scowl, looking out the window. "Pretty sure you were in diapers, too."

"Nope," Noa says cheerfully. "I was potty-trained early."

"A toilet-training protégée," I make myself joke. "Should have guessed."

"My parents *were* really proud, thank you," she says, but it sounds forced. When she pulls out onto the road again, we're both quiet. We don't say anything as she sits in the left-turn lane, blinker on, waiting for the light. And we don't say anything when she pulls up in front of my house. I expect her to idle, but she puts the car in park and turns it off.

"You can just drop me off," I tell her.

"Um, okay, first, you need to do your scores and we need to compare. And secondly, I left my present inside."

I want to think she did that deliberately, but I am just too sad that this day is over. This weird Chrismukkah competition is over, too.

I show her my rubric.

HANUKKAH
Decor: 2/5
Music: 5/5
Food: 3/5
Story: 4/5
TOTAL: 14/20

She gasps. "You deducted a point from the story?!"

"Okay, the story we *tell* is fun—small army of scrappy nobodies goes up against big invading force oppressing their religion and successfully fights them off, restoring the Temple, finding just a tiny bit of oil left for the Eternal Light and it miraculously lasts eight days—but the real story is that a lot of those scrappy nobodies were hardcore, hard-line Jews who believed assimilation was capitulation, and uh, my family's pretty assimilated, so it's kind of always there in the back of my mind when we talk about this story. It's hard to give that a perfect score," I argue.

I take a deep breath, gripping my phone so my hands don't shake. No one likes to talk about that part, but sometimes the way we do things in my assimilated, interfaith family makes me feel like such an outsider in Jewish spaces. Maybe that part of the story doesn't bother Noa and others in our class, but it bothers me.

"I mean, it's hard to hold people from thousands of years ago to modern standards, but I see your point and it's a fair one," she says, squinting at my screen. "Wow, high points for music."

I shrug as nonchalantly as I can. I'm not telling her I gave her that score for her singing. "Now your scoring."

CHRISTMAS
Decor: 4.5/5
Music: 3/5
Food: 3/5
Story: 1/5
TOTAL: 11.5/20

"Sooooo," she says suggestively, waggling her eyebrows.

I let my head thunk back against the seat. "Hanukkah wins."

She lets out a straight-up villainous cackle, clapping her hands together. "I win!"

I fight a smile. "Rude. I can't believe you scored the Santa waffles so low."

"A three out of five is satisfactory!" she protests.

"I demand a recount," I joke.

"We could rematch," she says. "Next year."

I look sideways at her, not daring to move my head. "Yeah?"

"We'd need new rules. We can't swap, obviously, because we

don't do Christmas, but I think we should each bring something to the other's holiday."

That's what I wanted, right? A rematch. A whole year. I wonder what we're going to do for the next twelve months. Pretend everything's normal? Go back to sniping at each other in religious school and ignoring each other at regular school? Holding grudges from elementary school against each other?

My chest aches at the thought of it. But I just say, "Yeah, that sounds like a plan!" as enthusiastically as I can muster.

We walk up my front path quietly until we get to the door, and then I can't stand it anymore.

"You should do Hanukkah with my family," I blurt out.

She hasn't put her hair back up, I realize, so when she looks sideways at me, part of her expression is obscured. "Yeah?"

"There are still three more nights," I add. "So like . . . you could come over tomorrow night, if you wanted."

She bites her lower lip. "I'm busy tomorrow night."

I swallow hard, looking away. "Right, right, yeah, okay, no problem. I didn't—"

She grabs my arm. "Jordan, wait. I'm just busy tomorrow night. I could come over the next night? Thursday? It'll be the seventh night."

There's a tiny part of me that wants to jab back at her, keep up the banter, argue about anything. I want to say, *I can* count, *you know*, or something snarky, but I don't. I grin at her, at the fact that she grabbed my arm and still hasn't let go. "Yeah?"

Her whole body relaxes with relief. "Yeah. That'd be fun. If you don't mind."

"No, that'd be great," I say, and then I can't stop babbling. "I know this started out because I was being a dick, but I really did have a weird amount of fun and I'm glad you came over this morning and I think your parents are really cool and I love your dad's apron and when you sang 'Maoz Tzur'—"

"I forgot your Hanukkah present," she says, interrupting me.

"Oh, that's fine," I say with a shrug.

"No, I mean, I have it, I just—" She shakes her head, cutting herself off. She's *blushing*.

She points up. I look up. There's nothing there but the light above our doorway that's full of dead bugs. We really gotta clean that out.

I look back at her, confused. She shrugs and says helplessly, "Imaginary mistletoe?"

I know what's about to happen about a split second before it does, which means I'm grinning when she dips her head and kisses me, and our teeth touch, which makes me laugh, and I *almost* fall over, but she grabs the front of my shirt, and that's when I'm kissing her back.

Later, long after I'm in bed with Josie asleep at my feet, probably dreaming of wrapping paper, I get a text. I roll over and pick up my phone.

THE WORST: I forgot to get my present from your house.

ME: We were busy. It's understandable.

THE WORST: Don't let me forget when I come over on Thursday.

ME: It's possible we'll be busy again. You might have to come over a third time to get it.

THE WORST: Third time's the charm! Merry Christmas. Happy Chanukah. Good night, loser.

It definitely doesn't feel like I lost the competition. I change her name from *The Worst* to *Noa*, debate adding a blushing smiley-face emoji to her name, and decide that's too cheesy and perhaps tempting fate.

I'm definitely going to win next year, though. Mark my words.

KWANZAA—DECEMBER 26 TO JANUARY 1

Habari Gani

BY KOSOKO JACKSON

Dear Mom,

Habari gani?

It feels weird to say that, to basically say, What's up, since you're not here, and you loved Kwanzaa so much. How you used to wake me up every one of the days with that expression, all excited and welcoming.

I remember how annoying it was. Now, I'd give anything to tell you, "What's in the news?"

But since I can't tell you, this will have to do.

It's been a while since I've talked to you. It's been hard to know what to say since you died. My therapist suggested that the best way forward is through. I'm not gonna be able to process my guilt if I don't address it. And if I don't address it, it will eat me whole from the inside out.

It's been about a year since you passed, and if I'm being honest, it's been a fast one. Most people think that when someone they care for dies, everything moves in slow motion. That's what TV tells us. But the truth is, there's just so much happening. Between the funeral, graduating from high school, and dealing with Dad, there's no real time to sit, think, and process, because if I do, everything falls apart.

You used to joke that Dad couldn't fend for himself, and that you were the one who kept everything together. But you were right, Mom. I don't blame him for falling apart, like a shoddily built Jenga tower. Like most people who knew you said, I take after you—always been self-sufficient, always been able to handle myself.

But according to Mr. Hawke, my therapist with the Coke-bottle glasses and the too-warm and -friendly smile, this isn't something I can just handle. So he came up with an idea. Kwanzaa was always your favorite holiday. While Dad and the rest of the family believed in the more traditional holidays, such as Christmas, your eyes lit up the most when we celebrated "Black Christmas."

And considering this is the first Kwanzaa without you, my therapist thought it would be a good idea to write a letter—not just any letter, mind you, but one that relates the seven principles to how my life has been, not only as a way to remember you but also to kind of show you how things have been since you left.

Since you died.

"Write it, read it out loud, and burn it," Mr. Hawke said. "Send it off into the wind."

I'm not really sure I believe in this mumbo-jumbo bullshit, but if I'm being honest, I'm not sure what else to do. I wasn't lying when I said that everything was moving faster than I thought it would after you died. What I'm finding out is everything is moving so quickly because it's impossible to anchor myself to anything.

I feel like I'm flailing, Mom—like there's a storm spinning me around, and my nails are clawing against the smooth surface of my life, trying desperately to hold on to something. Maybe this letter will help me move on. Maybe it won't do anything.

But I have nothing to lose but a few hours and some printer ink, I guess. So here we go.

Wish me luck.

Dear Mom,

Dad used to tell me you didn't want to move into Cedar Grove Estates.

He told me this when we were driving home from the funeral, just Dad and me in the car and an awkward silence between us that I didn't think was possible to fill. There was traffic on the highway—according to the soft sounds of the radio, a fifteen-car pileup. All I could think about were how many souls would be joining you in heaven that day. Some of them we probably knew. And that meant you wouldn't be alone.

There was some comfort in that, despite how morbid it was. I never told anyone about that thought, not even my therapist.

But while we were driving, inching forward maybe two miles an hour, Dad thumped his fingertips against the fake leather of the steering wheel and spoke out of nowhere.

"I'm thinking about us moving."

It seemed so random to me in the moment. I was a sophomore, and you had told me once that you and Dad had picked this neighborhood specifically for the school district, and I told him that.

"That's true," he replied. "But it feels weird being here without your mom. There's so much wrapped up in this place, so many memories. I can see her, feel her, everywhere."

One would argue, I thought, that would be a reason to stay. That's when he told me how much you hated it here.

"And besides, you know she never loved this place. She said there were too many white people." He chuckled. "When we drove through the maze-like streets of the cul-de-sac, she counted how many Black people were in the streets and judged the cars to decide if she thought a Black family lived there. She wasn't pleased. That's part of the reason why she made sure you went to church, a Black church, every Sunday. Why we visit her family during holidays, every holiday. Make sure you stay connected. I'm thinking maybe she was right, we should be around family."

I'm not sure if I agree with any of that. Honestly, moving kind of made it seem like Dad wanted to run from everything.

But to our surprise, when we got home, all those white people were waiting outside. At least more than a dozen. Most of them I knew because they lived next door or two or three houses over. But a couple had come from deeper inside the subdivision. Having heard about your passing, they decided to give their condolences.

Many of them offered casseroles and drinks, and some even provided food gift cards. But there were also those who offered services: to shovel the walkway if we needed it or drive me to school or help around the house—anything to just make things a little easier.

It reminded me of the first day of Kwanzaa: umoja, or "unity." How the community came together to help Dad and me. Pillars to keep us standing when we threatened to stumble.

If you guessed it, Mom, we still live here. Not only that, but Dad and I try to do monthly dinners with some of the neighbors. Dad became closer friends with Mr. Roberts, the widower across the street. They watch football together every weekend. I've even taught the Connor twins three houses down how to play piano. They suck at it, but it's nice to have a community. You'd be proud of Dad for stepping outside his comfort zone. For trying to build some sort of connection with people since you've been gone.

Even if none of them know how to cook anything good, we're working on that. Slowly but surely. Dad never mentioned moving again.

Dear Mom,

Kujichagulia. A word I could never say when I was younger. Dad always likes to remind me how I used to get lost in the syllables. Somewhere around the second or third, I would give up, my brow furrowing, and just stop like I hit a brick wall. It's funny to think how things that used to be so complicated, so big, so impossible to overcome, a few years later can be the simplest things in the world.

Speaking of things hard to overcome: You'll be happy to know that I came out to Dad. It was about three months after you passed. We were at the mall, shopping for a gift for Aunt Amy for her fiftieth birthday. It would be the first family event that we went to since you died. Dad had been holed up in the house, for good reason, and no one really pushed him to go out. I'm sorry to say I didn't either. Between school, navigating junior year, and trying to hold myself together, I just couldn't seem to find time to do the same for him.

But we still left the house, getting a gift about a week before. While we were taking a break in the food court, a group of girls from school walked by. You'd remember them. One of them was Olivia, the girl who used to be my best friend in elementary school. You remember her. Dark coils of hair? You used to always compliment her on them. How natural her hair was. Always praised her stepmother for making sure to learn how to take care of Black hair.

She's a cheerleader now, and I think this was the first time in the past couple of years I actually saw her up close.

It's funny how finding yourself in high school sometimes means leaving yourself behind.

"I wanted to say I'm sorry for your loss," Olivia said, hanging back a bit while her friends went to get a table. "Your mom was great. I still remember those small cucumber cakes she would make."

See? You hear that, Mom? The legacy you left behind extends outside our *family. When Olivia left, Dad asked me the question that I knew he was going to ask eventually.*

"She's cute."

Yes, I know that's not technically a question. But we all know the subtext there. You always did a good job of being the buffer between that impending conversation and Dad.

"She is," I said. I don't know why I blurted out the rest. But I did. "Her brother is cuter."

I remember watching Dad pause while chewing his Chipotle burrito. I don't know what I expected, but the way he just said "I'll take your word for it" wasn't the worst-possible thing I could imagine.

We didn't talk about it again. I don't think he's ever really asked me about my love life since then. But he didn't fly off the handle either. And I'm proud of myself for being brave enough to do that. I could have waited, till I went to college, till I graduated from college . . . the goalpost could have kept moving. But, and this is bittersweet, but something your death taught me? We don't have forever on this earth, Mom. And living unauthentically, especially around the people you love? Doesn't make sense. If the people who love you can't love you for who you are, then they aren't people you should keep in your life. And I respect myself enough to live my life openly, honestly, and truthfully.

Kujichagulia, or "self-determination"—to define ourselves, to be ourselves, and to respect ourselves. And I did just that.

Dear Mom,

Life is too short for us to live in shame, Mom. You taught me that. I just wish you were here to see it.

The one thing I was always thankful for was the fact you never made me get a job during school. You said it yourself: My job is to get good grades.

"A nine-to-five job will be waiting for you when you graduate, but

your focus right now needs to be on getting those good grades so you can get that."

I didn't appreciate it when you were alive. Of course, it was great to only have to worry about my grades. But when my classmates had spending money because they worked and could do whatever, I remember you and Dad always holding my allowance over me like I was ten years old.

I remember saying some hurtful things to you both that time I wanted to go to that concert with my friends, and you reminded me that I had already gotten an advance on my allowance—twice—and you weren't going to do it again.

I wish I could take back those words.

Going from a double-income household to a single one hasn't been easy for Dad. The things and the savings you left us in the will helped cover some stuff. We've been able to keep afloat.

Dad doesn't talk to me much about money. I think he thinks it's protecting me or something. But it's not like I don't know. I see the mail; I get it when I come home from school. I see the light on in the living room at three a.m. and hear Dad on the phone with bill collectors.

I'm not sure whether I'm thankful for him trying to hide it from me or whether I think he's doing such a shit job he should probably just come out and say it to my face.

Sorry. I shouldn't have cursed.

But you know Dad. He won't ask for help, not directly. Which is why when Aunt Amy came to visit during the summer, I was the one who told her.

I'm still not sure if I did the right thing. Dad, when he found out, wouldn't talk to me for the whole weekend. He wouldn't even tell me what I did wrong. But I know. I know Dad came from a home that was always on the knife's edge of being homeless. I know Dad watched his father ruin his mother, him, and his sister, driving them almost to homelessness multiple times. I know he promised he would never put that burden on his kid.

But the thing Dad doesn't understand is that we rise and we sink together. That's what you said in your note to us, right? To rely on each other.

"Ujima," you ended the note with—"To build and maintain our community together and make our community's problems our problems and to solve them together."

Sometimes, even adults need reminding of the simplest of things.

Dear Mom,

I thought about you a couple of days ago.

I mean, let's be honest, I think about you all the time, period. I think about you when I get up in the morning and how you used to make that creamed chipped turkey for me every Friday before school. I think about how after each school day, I'd tell you what I learned, and somehow we'd always get into an argument about a fact that one of my teachers said. I used to say you always thought you knew best, with your multiple degrees, and your love for Scrabble, and all those nerdy things. I used to be embarrassed when you would correct other people in public, or do the same to Dad and me when we were discussing something, like you couldn't wait to correct us until we got home.

But, joke's on me, isn't it? You never really cared if you were right or wrong, did you? You just wanted to teach me how to stand up for myself. How to argue, how to defend what I believed in.

I thought about you more than usual today. I was remembering back about four months after you died, when I was out shopping with some friends, trying to be a normal high school kid. Mr. Hawke said it would be good for me to get out of the house more. He even suggested, in a roundabout way, I try to get Dad out of the house too.

"I know you and your father feel closer to your mother there," Mr. Hawke said during the end of one of our sessions. "And I'm not telling you to abandon her, or forget her, or anything like that. But, it is important you don't get lost in those memories. *You find a way, even a small way, to step outside and experience the world. I imagine your mother would want that, for both of you."*

I didn't tell Dad what Mr. Hawke said. He wouldn't understand; you know how Dad closes in on himself when the smallest amount of emotion threatens to show itself. But I did try. I even told him I needed to go shopping for supplies one Saturday, for a project for Monday. A total lie, but it got us out of the house—despite all the grumbling that came from him.

I couldn't get him to come in, though.

"I'll wait in the car."

And, I get it. The only place open for what I needed was the outlet mall. You know, the one that opened about a year before you died. The one that had that store you always wanted to go to.

The one you never got to go to. That Black-owned store with all the different items, ranging from clothing to that kinara in the window you always wanted to buy to replace the one we usually use for Kwanzaa.

"I know Kwanzaa isn't technically an African holiday," you said. "It's African American, but it makes me feel closer to our people. Even if it doesn't make any sense."

Dad still talks about how you wanted to go to Africa, Ghana specifically. I remember when you were watching that TV show where celebrities went back to their countries of biological origin and how you thought that would be a good thing for us to do—for us to take DNA tests and figure out where you and Dad were all from and make a trip out of it.

"We can do it for your graduation," you said excitedly. I don't think I've ever seen you so excited.

I'm torn if I still want to do the test now. On the one hand, knowing your history is important. So many Black people don't know where they came from, and there's a part of me that feels like doing it is completing something we started.

But, and I'm not sure if this makes sense, but something about it feels . . . finite? Like as long as I don't do it there's always something lingering on the

276

bottom of the checklist. And if I never complete that checklist, you're still here with me. Nagging me to finish it. Reminding me. It doesn't make any sense to most people, but to me it does.

Anyway. Ghana.

I kind of think it was fate that my friends wanted to go into a shoe store that I had no desire to follow them in. So I took some time wandering around the mall, and at the very end of it, like the end of the universe, there was that African clothing store you always wanted to go into. And being here, without Dad, and you being gone? I dunno, it felt like fate to go in.

And Mom? You were right. It felt like home—not only because everything in there was beautiful but also because the woman running the store looked like you, if you were three inches taller and had darker skin, but still you.

I spent all my money in that store. I didn't really want to buy the things there; I don't know what I'm going to use a headdress for or a Ghanaian musical instrument that I don't know how to pronounce or play. But you always told us it's our job to support our community. Because if we don't, who will? This is why I'm working there once a week now, helping out with the books and the storefront—you know, getting out of the house and helping the owner as much as she's helping me.

It made me think of ujamaa, or "cooperative economics." To build and maintain our own stores, shops, and other businesses and to profit from them together.

It made me think of you.

P.S.: I bought the kinara.

Dear Mom,

The most important thing in most high school juniors' lives is preparing for college.

Everyone knows that, even Dad, someone who didn't go to college, unlike you. He's done his best to prepare me, pulling himself out of his depressive hole to support me in any way he could. But that was always your job. You were the one who understood the importance of an education. You were the one who was adamant about me going to an HBCU, like you did.

You were the one who was supposed to take me on a college tour across the country, even though we both know you really wanted me to go to Howard. But, Stanford, Duke, Emory, and University of Texas were all on the list. Some of which because I wanted to go, others because some of our family members went, and Emory because of the scholarship they dangled in front of us.

This moment, this defining moment that would change the trajectory of the rest of my life, was supposed to be shared with you. And you're not here.

My guidance counselor, Mr. Waynes, has tried his best. I never realized how awkward men could be when it came to emotions around other people, even when it was their job to know how to navigate situations like this.

"Anything you need, I'm here for you," he said. And he just kept repeating that like it would make things better.

I always wanted to tell him that if he wanted to help me, there were two things he could do. One, he could figure out how to go back in time or how to master necromancy. And two, if he really wanted to help me, he could stop saying this every single time we had a meeting and focus on how to make me more eligible for Howard.

Now I know what you're thinking; we never talked about Howard. And we didn't talk about it because whenever you brought it up, I would shoot it down. I think it was because I didn't want to follow in your footsteps, despite how stupid that sounds. I wanted to forge my own path to figure out who I am apart from you.

People always said, in the metaphorical ways, we were similar—in the way we approached problems, in the things that tweaked our nerves, and even the facial expressions we made when annoyed.

And that annoyed me.

But now, with you gone, I wish people would say it more. I wish they would remind me how much of you is in me because that means a part of you lives on.

I'm not sure what my purpose in life is going to be, but for now, going to Howard, being close to you, and even maybe living in the same dorm as you, makes sense. It makes me feel like that's the right path for me. Or at least maybe walking the same hallways as you will help me find my purpose.

My nia, or "to make our collective vocation the building and developing of our community to restore our people to their traditional greatness." Nia was always your favorite day of Kwanzaa.

It's becoming mine too.

Dear Mom,

You were always the gift giver in the family, the creative one who came up with the ideas of how to manifest somebody's dreams without them having to tell you what they were. It was a talent that Dad and I never got.

You used to tease us that it was because we were guys and that men just don't have the same intuition about someone's needs as a woman does. I didn't believe you; I thought this was just something you were saying to get a rise out of Dad and me. But I think you were right.

Dad was never a gift giver, and that didn't change when you died. My birthday is in April, as you know, and Dad forgot about it. It wasn't until the next day when I came downstairs that I saw him hastily trying to wrap a present. You should have seen the look on his face.

I think I should have been more upset. I'm not sure, but with everything going on I don't blame him. Every day was a little easier; that much is true.

But every day that you're not here is also a reminder about how empty our lives are, Mom.

And how much I miss you.

How much we miss you.

So when Dad's birthday came up in August, I knew I had to do something special. It wasn't in the same caliber of what you would have done, but I made sure to make all the same dishes that you used to make for him. One day, while Dad was working outside in the yard and I was cleaning the house, I found a box of your things that he had haphazardly put away.

I think that's part of the reason Dad had me cleaning the inside of the house and him the outside. I don't think he could process seeing those memories laid out in front of him. The idea of having to put them into storage made it feel like you were gone, and you weren't coming back.

But one of those things was a cookbook. So I took it while he was at work—Dad now works a double shift to help make ends meet, by the way—and made his favorite foods: fried catfish, green beans, pecan pie, you name it.

Was it as good as yours? Of course not. But it was something, and to see the look on his face, to see how exhaustion and stress rolled off his back like he was shedding skin, was worth it.

I miss a lot about you, Mom. But I miss your *kuumba*—your "creativity"— the most.

But, hey, maybe I got more from you than I thought. Who knows, maybe I even found my college major.

At least something good came out of this, right? Can I say that? Is that uncouth?

Don't tell Dad.

Dear Mom,

The last day of Kwanzaa was always bittersweet.

I used to love it. I'm not ashamed to admit the idea of moving on from this holiday . . . the culture, the singing, the presents—all of it—didn't elate me.

No one else I know celebrates Kwanzaa. No Black families at our school, and the white people I rub shoulders with have no idea what it is.

So it always felt like it was just another reason for me to be an outlier. Another thing that made us different and weird. I was ashamed.

And I'm pretty sure you knew that. You pushed me just enough to set the building block so that when the time was right, when I was old enough, I realized that there was nothing to be ashamed of about who I am—not about being a family who celebrates Kwanzaa, not about being a kid who has a father who doesn't have a college education, and not about being gay or not knowing what I want to do with my life.

You knew all these things about me and knew what hurdles I would face before I even knew what the hurdle was.

You were always my guiding light. And I miss you so fucking much, Mom.

But on the last day of Kwanzaa, which is fitting that it's imani—"faith"— I have faith that everything will be okay. I'll find my way, and Dad and I will put one foot forward and keep on trucking.

We'll never forget you, of course. But we'll be all right. Not because we have to be but because we can. We are the descendants of kings and queens, Mom. You always used to remind us of that. Our people survived so much. And we'll keep surviving. We'll keep thriving.

Even if you aren't with us, physically, I mean.

So, Mom, when you used to come into my room every day and ask me, "Habari gani?" "What is the news?" I hope when I burn this letter, my therapist is right, and it reaches you. I hope you're up there, reading all the things you've missed and have faith—have imani—that Dad and I will be all right.

Because we will. You made sure of that.

I love you.

About the Authors

Dahlia Adler (editor) is an editor by day, a freelance writer by night, and an author and anthologist at every spare moment in between. She's the founder of LGBTQReads.com; her novels include the Kids' Indie Next picks *Cool for the Summer*, *Home Field Advantage*, and *Going Bicoastal*, a Sydney Taylor Honor Book; and she is the editor of the anthologies *His Hideous Heart*, *That Way Madness Lies*, *At Midnight*, and, with Jennifer Iacopelli, *Out of Our League*. Dahlia lives in New York with her family and a wall of overflowing bookcases.

Candace Buford has always been drawn to stories with strong and complex people of color. She graduated from Duke University with a degree in German literature and holds a law degree from Penn State Law, as well as a business degree from Duke University's Fuqua School of Business. She is the author of the critically acclaimed novels *Kneel* and *Good as Gold*. Follow her on Instagram and X @CandaceBuford.

A. R. Capetta and **Cory McCarthy** are art monsters. They co-authored the bestselling *Once & Future*, a finalist for the New England Book Award and Best of 2019 by *Kirkus Reviews*, the *Boston Globe*, Tor, and Book Riot. A. R. Capetta is the author of fifteen books, including the Lambda Award winner *The Heartbreak Bakery*. Cory McCarthy's *Man o' War* won a Stonewall Honor, and he wrote and illustrated "Museum of Misery" in the Michael L. Printz Award winner *The Collectors*. The couple coauthored a *Much Ado* retelling in *That Way Madness Lies: 15 of Shakespeare's Most Notable Works Reimagined*. They live on ley lines.

Preeti Chhibber is an acclaimed author living in Atlanta, Georgia. She has written for Syfy, Book Riot, Polygon, and *Elle*, among others. Across prose, comics, and podcasts, she's written for characters such as Spider-Man, the X-Men, the Riddler, and so many more. Her debut YA rom-com, *Payal Mehta's Romance Revenge Plot*, came out in 2024. When she's not writing, she spends her time reading a ridiculous amount of YA, jumping into a brand-new fandom, or food-traveling her way through different countries. She's also the cohost of the *Desi Geek Girls* and the *Women of Marvel* podcasts, where she geeks out on the regular. You can learn more about Preeti and her work at preetichhibber.com.

Natasha Díaz is a born and raised New Yorker, currently residing in Brooklyn with her two daughters and extremely tall husband. Natasha's first novel, *Color Me In*, was published in 2019. *Color Me In* was a 2020 YALSA Best Fiction selection, a finalist for the Jewish Book Award, and winner of the Latino Book Award for Best YA Fiction Book, as well as the Azia Award for Best Mixed Race Fiction.

Natasha's writing has been featured in anthologies and novels told in stories, including *Wild Tongues Can't Be Tamed*, *The Grimoire of Grave Fates*, *House Party*, *Black Girl Power*, and *For the Rest of Us*. As a screenwriter, Natasha has developed television projects with FX and Disney networks.

Kelly Loy Gilbert is the author of *Picture Us in the Light*, a Stonewall Honor Book and *Los Angeles Times* Book Prize finalist; *Conviction*, a Morris Award finalist; and, most recently, *Everyone Wants to Know*. She lives in the San Francisco Bay Area.

Kosoko Jackson is a Lambda Award–winning author of the *USA Today* bestseller *The Forest Demands Its Due*. When not writing, he's trying to watch one hundred movies a year, working on his MBA homework, or juggling teaching responsibilities. He lives in New Jersey with his golden retriever, Artemis.

Aditi Khorana is the author of critically acclaimed and award-winning young adult novels, including *Mirror in the Sky* and *The Library of Fates*. Both are Junior Library Guild Selections and have appeared on many best book lists. Her debut novel is the subject of a TEDx talk, "Harnessing the Power of the Unknown." She teaches writing for young people at Antioch University's MFA program and also gives talks and teaches classes on the creative capacity of language to shape our world. She is currently adapting her debut novel for TV. In a former life, she worked as a producer at CNN, PBS, and ABC News and as an entertainment marketing consultant for Hollywood studios, including Fox, SONY, and Paramount. Her work has been featured on NPR, the *Los Angeles Review of Books*, NBC News,

BuzzFeed, Entertainment Weekly, Bustle, *Seventeen*, and HuffPo. She currently lives and works in Los Angeles.

Katherine Locke lives and writes in Philadelphia, Pennsylvania, with their feline overlords and their addiction to chai lattes. They are the author of *The Girl with the Red Balloon*, a 2018 Sydney Taylor Honor Book and 2018 Carolyn W. Field Honor Book, as well as *The Spy with the Red Balloon* and *This Rebel Heart*. They are the coeditor and contributor to *This Is Our Rainbow: 16 Stories of Her, Him, Them, and Us*, which had three starred reviews and made the *Kirkus Reviews* Best Middle Grade of 2021 list, as well as *It's a Whole Spiel: Love, Latkes, and Other Jewish Stories*. They also contributed to *Unbroken: 13 Stories Starring Disabled Teens* and *Out Now: Queer We Go Again!* They are also the author of the picture books *Bedtime for Superheroes*, *What Are Your Words? A Book About Pronouns*, and *Being Friends with Dragons*. They can be found online at katherinelockebooks.com and @bibliogato on Threads and Instagram.

Abdi Nazemian is the author of *Only This Beautiful Moment*— winner of the 2024 Stonewall Award and 2024 Lambda Literary Award—and *Like a Love Story*, a Stonewall Honor Book and one of *Time* magazine's 100 Best YA Books of All Time. He is also the author of the young adult novels *Exquisite Things*, *Desert Echoes*, *The Chandler Legacies*, and *The Authentics*. His novel *The Walk-In Closet* won the Lambda Literary Award for LGBT Debut Fiction. His screenwriting credits include the films *The Artist's Wife*, *The Quiet*, and *Menendez: Blood Brothers* and the television series *Ordinary Joe* and *The Village*. He has been an executive producer and associate producer on numerous films, including *Call Me by Your Name*, *Little Woods*, and *The House of*

Tomorrow. He lives in Los Angeles with his husband, their two children, and their dog, Disco. Find him online at abdinazemian.com.

Laura Pohl is the *New York Times* bestselling author of *The Grimrose Girls.* Her debut novel, *The Last 8,* won the International Latino Book Award. She likes writing messages in caps lock, never using autocorrect, and obsessing about *Star Wars.* When not taking pictures of her dog, she can be found curled up with a fantasy or science-fiction book or replaying *Dragon Age.* She has played Cupid more times than she'd like and prefers to see love in the movies. A Brazilian at heart and soul, she makes her home in São Paulo.

Sonora Reyes is the bestselling and award-winning author of *The Lesbiana's Guide to Catholic School* and *The Luis Ortega Survival Club.* Born and raised in Arizona, they write fiction celebrating queer and Mexican stories in a variety of genres, across ages. Outside of writing, Sonora loves breaking their body and vocal cords by playing with their baby niblings and dancing/singing karaoke at the same time.

Karuna Riazi is the author of the acclaimed *A Bit of Earth* as well as the duology *The Gauntlet* and *The Battle.* She holds a BA in English literature from Hofstra University and an MFA in writing for children and young adults from Hamline University. She is an online diversity advocate and an educator, and her work has been featured in Entertainment Weekly, Shondaland, and Teen Vogue, among others. A born and raised New Yorker, Karuna Riazi lives on Long Island.

Acknowledgments

This collection lived in my heart for so many years, it's still surreal to see it become a real book you can hold in your hands. I will never have enough thanks for my fabulous agent, Patricia Nelson, for finding it a great home, and for my editor, Karen Chaplin, at Quill Tree Books for *being* that home. Many thanks also to the Quill Tree team, including associate editor Allison Weintraub, senior production editor Erika West, copyeditor Sona Vogel, and to designer Jenna Stempel-Lobell and illustrator Meryl Rowin for the gorgeous and festive cover of my dreams.

Of course, an anthology is only as good as its contributors, and I'm so lucky that this one is full of the best—endless thanks to you all for the fantastic stories within. Thank you to Lindsay Chubak for her affirming beta read of my story, and to all the friends and family I've had the privilege to celebrate with over the years. (Most special thanks to my parents for having seventeen girls over for Simchat Torah my senior year of high school. I'm still sorry about that.) I love you all.